Never Let You Down

Never Let You Down

Mariah Wallace

Dedication

This book is for my husband. To the only one who truly knows how daunting this journey can be. Thank you for your endless support. I love you.

Table of Contents

CHAPTER 1   1
Liz

CHAPTER 2   10
Liz

CHAPTER 3   20
Liz

CHAPTER 4   30
Liz

CHAPTER 5   39
Liz

CHAPTER 6   49
Greyson

CHAPTER 7   57
Liz

CHAPTER 8   66
Liz

CHAPTER 9   75
Greyson

CHAPTER 10   84
Liz

CHAPTER 11   91
Liz

CHAPTER 12   101
Greyson

CHAPTER 13   111
Greyson

CHAPTER 14   122
Liz

CHAPTER 15   132
Liz

CHAPTER 16   143
Liz

CHAPTER 17   154
Liz

CHAPTER 18   165

Greyson

CHAPTER 19   **174**
Liz

CHAPTER 20   **184**
Greyson

CHAPTER 21   **195**
Liz

CHAPTER 22   **204**
Greyson

CHAPTER 23   **214**
Liz

CHAPTER 24   **224**
Greyson

CHAPTER 25   **233**
Liz

CHAPTER 26   **244**
Greyson

CHAPTER 27   **255**
Liz

CHAPTER 28   265
Liz

CHAPTER 29   273
Greyson

CHAPTER 30   285
Liz

CHAPTER 31   294
Greyson

CHAPTER 32   302
Liz

EPILOGUE   312

Chapter 1

Liz

Junior Year - Fall Semester

Tall.
Dark.
Handsome.
My kryptonite.
I throw my drink back, emptying my cup, and then hand it to my best friend, Maylee.

I say, "Wish me luck", as I strut over to him.

I want to introduce myself if nothing else. But I hope he gives me more than that.

About halfway to my target, I hear Maylee shout, "Get 'em, girl!"

I live for these parties.

My parents were strict with me growing up, so I didn't get to do as much as a typical teenager. I wouldn't say I rebelled once I got to college, but I let loose.

I'm still letting loose.

A lot.

These frat parties get wild: banging music, dancing, beer pong, spin the bottle, couples locking themselves in whatever empty room they can find. Though, that's not a behavior I condone. It doesn't matter though, because not one of those reasons is why I came tonight.

I came for the guy I'm currently walking toward.

Dylan Sinclair.

As I get closer, I'm able to make out his drool worthy features more clearly. Although, I can already describe every single one.

Dylan Sinclair is every girl's fantasy.

He has a head full of luscious, dark hair. It's just long enough to fall into his eyes and curl up at the nape of his neck.

His eyes are chocolate brown. But under the fluorescent lights in this frat house, they look hazel.

He has a chiseled jaw. A nose that fits his face perfectly. And lips that would make any girl jealous. They are the perfect shade of pink and full—extremely kissable.

I let myself appreciate the rest of Dylan's gorgeous body from head to toe.

His shoulders are broad. His arms fill out the fitted T-shirt he's wearing. And I'm pretty sure he has at least six chiseled abs hiding under it. Maybe more.

I let my eyes travel to his legs. It's obvious he isn't one of those guys who skips leg day. His quads fill out the dark washed jeans he's wearing exquisitely. In fact, he makes them look like the best pants known to man. Who knew jeans had so much potential?

While I'm slightly disappointed that I can't enjoy the view of his backside at the moment, I bet it's no less drool worthy than the rest of him. He clearly knows his way around a gym. With that thought, I take a minute to cool myself down. As I fan my face, I find myself thankful for the shot of tequila I took before strutting into the same room as Dylan. It was the confidence boost I didn't know I needed.

When I make it into the kitchen, he's leaning against the island casually with his ankles crossed and a red solo cup in his hand. I offer him my best flirtatious smile and then plop myself right up onto the counter, directly across from him. I cross my legs to feign nonchalance, hoping he doesn't notice how nervous I really am.

I can't believe I talked myself into this. But I'm a woman who knows how to go after what she wants. Or in this case, who she wants.

Before I speak, I straighten my spine and square my shoulders. I may not feel confident, but I will make sure I look confident.

"Hey."

Hey?

You would think after rehearsing this conversation in my head, I would have come up with something better to say. But nope. I'm internally cringing at myself while considering making a dash for it. As I'm planning my escape route, Dylan takes a step closer to me. I pretend not to notice.

"Hey. You're Liz, right?"

His voice is smooth. And at the sound of my name coming out of his mouth, I peek up at him.

I must look thoroughly confused. Every girl on this campus knows who he is, so I'm trying to figure out how he knows who *I* am.

He must be able to read my expression, because he lets out a chuckle while raising his hands in mock surrender. "Don't worry, I haven't been stalking you or anything."

I tilt my head to the side and furrow my brow, hoping he'll see the question in my eyes. He takes a few seconds to study my face. I feel the heat from his gaze down to my bones.

He gives me a smile big enough for me to see his teeth. Of course, they are the straightest, whitest teeth I've ever seen. I keep myself from admiring them for too long.

"I have some Pre-Med classes with Ethan. I've seen you with him and his girlfriend around campus. I guess you could say I got curious."

This information surprises me. It also has me feeling almost as confident as I look.

I lean forward and set my hands next to my legs on the counter.

Dylan is studying me with an expression I can't quite read. Now that I'm a few inches closer to him, I catch a whiff of his scent. It's wholly masculine. He smells like cedarwood with a hint of peppermint. Like he belongs in one of those cheesy Hallmark Christmas movies. In a flannel. With an ax in his hand. Come to think of it... I'd enjoy the sight of that.

I give him a smirk. "May I ask what exactly made you so curious about me?"

Right after the question is out of my mouth, he takes another step toward me, seeming to enjoy this conversation as much as I am.

He gives me a smirk to mirror my own. I lock it away, somehow knowing he most definitely does not hand them out freely.

"I won't lie and say I didn't notice your beauty first because I did. You're gorgeous. But what has me so curious about you is the vivacious energy you give off. I notice it every time I catch you during a conversation. I even noticed it when you threw back that tequila earlier."

He punctuates his sentence with a wink.

Meanwhile, his words steal the air right from my lungs.

No one has ever said anything like that to me before.

I'm at a loss for words. Something that doesn't happen often. If at all.

Looking down at the floor, I compose myself. I'm both flattered and slightly embarrassed. If he saw me throw back my tequila, then that means he's had his eyes on me tonight. I hope he didn't notice me ogling him, too.

When I find the courage to look back up at him, he's standing only inches from me. At my whopping height of five feet and four inches (thank you very much), I'm still not eye level with him. He must be almost six feet tall.

Taking one small step toward me, he places his hands right above my kneecaps. I hadn't even realized I uncrossed my legs. What I do notice is how gentle his touch is. It's the reason for my goosebumps. They're everywhere.

He offers me another smirk. "What's wrong Liz? Cat got your tongue?"

I laugh. "No. But you're the first person to cause me to be at a loss for words. Which yours were very flattering."

"I'll take that as a compliment."

I throw another smirk his way. "You most definitely should."

He removes his hands from my legs, and I miss his touch instantly. Without taking his eyes off me, he slowly walks backward until he's leaning on the kitchen island once again. I know he has more to say, so I wait for him to speak.

"Were my words flattering enough for you to consider a date with me?"

I act as though I'm contemplating what to say when—in reality—my response is already on the tip of my tongue. This conversation is worth dragging out if I can. Besides, I want to see if he's willing to play along.

"Hm, that depends. Were your words only used to score a date with me, or did you mean them?"

He laughs. "You really are something. And both. Would you have considered a date without my flattering you first?"

He's most definitely a charmer. By the smug look on his face, I'm positive he knows it, too.

I won't feed his ego. No matter how bad I may want to.

Crossing my arms over my chest, I shrug my shoulders. "I guess we'll never know now, will we?" I mimic him by punctuating my question with a wink.

He smiles and shakes his head. "You're killin' me, Smalls."

I recognize the movie reference immediately. Who wouldn't? It's one of the best sports comedies ever. He could have started with that, and I probably would have told him yes to the date right away. I consider telling him yes just for the reference alone, but this playful banter is way too much fun.

"Is 'The Sandlot' a favorite movie of yours?"

"It is. I'm glad you know it too. I was worried there for a second."

"Of course, I know it. Legends never die."

"You just keep getting better and better."

I smile flirtatiously as I flip my long, red curls behind my shoulders. "So, I've been told."

Dylan smiles at me as he shakes his head. "So, what do you say, Liz? Can I take you out?"

I stay silent for a beat as I picture myself going out on a date with the stud standing in front of me.

It's no secret he's the most attractive man I've ever laid eyes on.

Even if it doesn't work out, to say I got a chance to go out with a guy who has the whole female population pining after him is enough of a reason to agree to a date with him. However, I know I want more from him than a single date. I wonder if he wants that from me.

Other than the guy I dated freshman year, I don't really have much experience where dating is concerned. Sure, I've been out with a few guys here and there, but it was never with the intention of a serious relationship. If anything, I used those dates to prepare myself for the real thing.

I think I want the real thing with Dylan.

No.

I *know* I want the real thing with Dylan.

He seems genuinely interested in me, too.

I silently laugh at myself for even thinking through all of this. I knew my answer long before he asked. Dragging this out is my way of making sure I don't seem desperate. Well, that, and it's fun.

"Yes, you can take me out." Even though I have more to say, I wait for Dylan's reaction. As his lips tilt up into a smile, I carry on. "On one condition."

Amused, he crosses his arms over his chest. "And what's that?"

I smirk. "I get a second date."

"Is this to benefit me or you?"

"I guess you'll have to wait and find out."

He throws his head back and laughs. I can't help but notice the way his Adam's apple bobs as he does.

I mentally give myself a pat on the back for going after what I want.

You would think after growing up as sheltered as I did, I'd be afraid to face things head on. Satisfied with the outcome of this brief encounter, I smile to myself.

It's obvious Dylan is just as satisfied as I am. Before I have time to process what's happening, he strides over to where I'm sitting on the counter and places his hands on either side of me. He leans in close enough for me to feel his breath on my ear. The sensation is enough to make me dizzy.

He whispers, "You're going to be trouble and I can't wait."

Oh, he's good.

When I pull back to get a glimpse of his face, we're only centimeters apart. If I were to lean in just a little more, our lips would meet in what I'm sure would be the most electrifying kiss of my life. Just the thought of his lips against mine causes a rush of heat to form in my belly.

Too quickly, he removes his hands from beside me and takes a step back.

As I study the heat in his gaze, I can't seem to form any coherent thoughts. It wouldn't surprise me if his thoughts mirrored my own. I'm willing to bet they do.

A few seconds of silence pass before I hop down from the counter. "Text me." I throw a sly smile Dylan's way as I exit the kitchen.

He laughs, shaking his head as he does.

I probably should have given him my number before leaving him alone, but it's too much fun knowing he'll have to ask Ethan for it. I'm sure he's up for the challenge, which only proves going after him was worth it.

As I return to where I left my best friend, all I can seem to think about is how much I feel like my life is about to change.

Dylan may think I'll be trouble, but I have no doubt he'll be just as much trouble, too.

Maybe even more.

Chapter 2

Liz

Present Day

"Stephanie, can you please hold my calls while I meet with my one o'clock client today?"

My receptionist stops doodling to look at me, smiling as she does. "Of course, Ms. Carter."

As many times as I've told her to call me by my first name, she insists on keeping things professional—at least in the office.

Stephanie and I have gotten close since I started at Cee Newt Law as a family lawyer about six months ago. I'm thankful for how quickly she became someone I can rely on both in and out of the office. She fits in well with my friends, and they love her just as much as I do.

She keeps my schedule orderly and fields my calls all day long. Outside of the office, she is both a listening ear and a shoulder to cry on. Not that talking and crying is all I do, but my life can feel like a soap opera sometimes.

Okay, I may be dramatic.

Truthfully, I'm happy.

I've accomplished everything I set out to do after college graduation. My job is fulfilling, my friends are amazing, and my love life is lacking—that's how I prefer it. I couldn't ask for more. But sometimes I feel like something is missing. And I can't figure out why.

Somehow, I bring myself back to the present. Back to Stephanie.

Playfully, I roll my eyes at her. "Steph, I told you to call me Liz. There is no need for formalities unless a client is present."

She spins in her chair, facing me head on. "I know, but it feels too weird. Maybe one day. Please don't make me remind you about the last guy I worked for. I could never slip up."

I concede. "Fine." Lingering in the doorway, I try to remember what else I need from her. I'm not normally forgetful, but this week has been a beast. Thankfully, my last meeting ended early, so I have a few extra minutes on my hands. Now if only I could remember why I came out here.

As if she can read my thoughts, she asks, "Anything else?"

Then it comes to me. "Actually, yes! Can you let my one o'clock in as soon as he gets here? I'll take him early."

I don't normally do that—take my clients earlier than expected. But the extra few minutes allowed me to prepare in advance. And maybe... just maybe I'll get ahead of schedule.

She nods. "Sure thing."

"Thank you!"

After closing the door to my office, I sit down in front of my desk, preparing for my next few appointments.

While being a family lawyer can be extremely difficult, I truly love my job and take pride in the work I do. I handle a variety of cases. Each one is vastly different. It keeps work from feeling mundane, which is a major step-up from my other job. I'm so glad I kissed my HR days goodbye. All the hard work paid off.

It's still paying off.

As I'm going through some paperwork for my next appointment, my cell phone rings. I silently reprimand myself for forgetting to turn it off. Most days, I stay way too busy to take personal calls. When I see who it is, I answer right away.

"MayMay! What's up?"

Maylee has been my best friend for as long as I can remember. We met when we were six years old. We were inseparable. Much like we are now. She got married a few months ago, so I don't see her as often as I used to. But I'm thrilled for her. She deserves every second of marital bliss. Plus, her husband, Walker, is a major catch. She lucked out.

"Hey! Sorry to bother you at work. I wanted to catch you before you make plans. Do you have a second?"

I laugh. She knows me too well. It's rare for me not to have plans on a Friday. I haven't thought about what to do tonight with how busy this week has been. Hopefully, though, I'll be able to get out of here early. Fingers crossed.

"You know I'll always make time for you."

"You're the best. I wanted to see if you're up for a night out. Walker and I were thinking it would be fun to go check out some live music tonight. Stephanie is more than welcome to join us, too."

I do a little happy dance in my office chair. It's been a while since I've gotten to enjoy some live music.

"You know I'll be there. What time?"

"Yay! Eight. I can't wait to see you."

"Same! I'll see you tonight. Love you."

"Love you, too."

* * *

By the time I wrap up my day, it's nearing seven. So much for getting out of the office early. I sent Steph home a few hours ago, hoping I'd be right behind her.

I rush home to change and then make my way downtown. I'm so ready for a night out.

When I walk into the venue, I spot our group of friends immediately.

I practically squeal at the sight of my best friend. She's sitting in a big, circular booth with her husband, Walker. On the other side of her is a good friend of ours from the HR office we both used to work at, Kate. On Walker's other side sits his best friend, Greyson. Across from them are Walker's sister and her husband, Sarah and Matt, Steph, and two other paramedics that Walker works with, Sam and Charlie. It's been way too long since all of us have been free to hang out on the same night. It's good to see everyone.

I sashay over to the table as Maylee practically climbs over everyone to get to me.

As soon as I'm close enough, she leaps into my arms. "Liz!"

I laugh as I accept her embrace. "How much have you had to drink? It's only been two weeks since we last saw each other."

She takes a step back and playfully punches my shoulder. "Oh, stop. We went from living together to working together to separate lives. I miss you!"

"I know. I miss you, too." Peering over her shoulder, I eye the booth again. "Is there enough room for me over there?"

As Maylee opens her mouth to speak, another voice reaches my ears first. Even though I can't see him, I know exactly who it is. The timbre of his voice is unmistakable.

"I'll make room for you, Liz, or you can come sit—" I step around Maylee and hold up my hand to stop Greyson from finishing his sentence. I have no desire to know where he was going with it.

It doesn't matter how tall, dark, and handsome he is. And I don't care how badly he wants to take me home. Which he makes abundantly clear every time we hang out. He refuses to give up, even though I've turned him down every single time for *years*.

I don't do one-night-stands. I also don't do relationships either. Not that relationships are his thing. Until recently, I've watched him take home a different woman every weekend. It's absurd. Behavior I have no respect for.

"Don't you dare finish that sentence. I'm happy to pull up a chair or squeeze in next to Steph." I punctuate my sentence with a smirk.

Greyson, along with the rest of the table, laughs. Everyone is very aware of how I feel about him.

I take a seat as I greet everyone else. My eyes find Kate and Sam. I haven't asked her about what's going on between the two of them. Not that there is anything going on. But they seem closer than normal. It's apparent they've formed some sort of friendship.

I'm pulled from my observation when Walker asks, "How's work been, Liz?"

"It's been great. Definitely busy, but I love it."

Kate chimes in. "I'm so jealous of you and Maylee for getting out of HR."

"Yeah. I don't miss it. You should look for another job. You have a business degree, don't you?"

"I do. I'm just not sure what I want to do with it."

Sam speaks up. "I'm sure you'll figure it out."

His words are encouraging and cause Kate to blush. Hm. Interesting.

Steph nudges my shoulder. "How was the rest of the day?"

I turn toward her. "It was fine. I reviewed some of my cases to prepare for next week." While looking at my friends, I speak a little louder so all of them can hear me. "No more work talk, friends. Let's have some fun tonight."

Greyson lifts his pint glass full of beer. "I'll toast to that."

The rest of us follow suit, toasting to one another.

A few minutes later, the band plays. Ready to get this party started, I hop up from the booth, heading to the dance floor.

The men decide to join us a couple of songs in.

The dance floor is overflowing with people, but I'm having too much fun to care. Although, with a little more to drink, I won't notice the crowd at all. I slip away to order another cocktail from the bar.

As I'm sipping on my drink at one of the bar stools, Kate takes a seat next to me, alone.

I nod my head toward the dance floor where Sam is. "Hey. What are you doing over here? I figured you'd stick with Sam the whole night."

She rests her chin in her hands. "What's the point? It's not like he even knows I have a thing for him." Her eyes widen in shock. "Shoot. Did I just say that out loud?"

"You didn't have to. It's kind of obvious."

She makes a noise of frustration and then reaches over to take a sip of my drink. "If it's that obvious, then how come he hasn't figured it out?"

I roll my eyes. "Because men are oblivious. You know, you could just tell him how you feel."

"Not happening."

I take my drink back from Kate and then cross my arms, placing them on the bar. "Why not?"

She sighs. "Last time I confessed my feelings for a guy, it blew up in my face. Plus, I have way too much going on in my life. I doubt he would want anything to do with my drama."

I'm taken aback by Kate's confession. She sounds off. Though, I know this is not the time, or place, to ask for more details.

Instead, I give her some encouragement. "Well, I think Sam would be crazy if he didn't reciprocate your feelings. Honestly, I bet he's just too afraid to admit it. You're a total catch, Kate."

"Thanks."

"Are you sure this is just about Sam?"

"I don't know how to answer that."

"Okay. Well, I'm here if you need anything."

She doesn't respond, so I finish my drink and then pull her toward the dance floor. "Come on. Let's go have some fun. We'll worry about life later." Winking, I add, "And the guy."

The night passes in a blur.

It's just after midnight, and I'm more than a few drinks in. As I'm dancing to the beat of the music, large hands grip my waist firmly from behind. Assuming it's Greyson, I try to pull away from the unwelcome touch.

I do my best to escape his hold, but he only pulls me closer. A chill races down my spine as I realize there is no way it's Greyson behind me. I may not be his biggest fan, but I know he would never lay a hand on me against my will.

It isn't uncommon for this to happen when I'm out. Usually, I'm given a chance to decline. This is a completely different situation. My mind races with thoughts on the best way to handle this situation.

Finding my resolve, I reach for the unfamiliar hands with a death grip on my waist. There's sure to be some purple marks left behind as evidence.

As I spin to face the stranger, I trip over myself. I hadn't realized how much alcohol I consumed until this moment. I should have stopped the minute I felt tipsy.

Panicking, I look around to see if I can spot one of my friends, but it's a useless effort. There are way too many people on the dance floor.

I'm too unsteady on my feet to fight off the man attempting to dance with me. Judging by the way he won't let up, he's very aware of my half-inebriated state of mind right now. My only comfort is knowing we're in a public place. Where anyone can see us.

Hoping he'll finally take a hint, I try pulling myself from his hold, but he yanks me until my back is against his chest. It knocks the air from my lungs.

I wince. "Let. Me. Go."

His breath is hot in my ear as he leans in to say, "What's wrong? You don't wanna dance? Too bad."

I close my eyes and take a deep breath, willing myself to remain calm. It doesn't help that I can feel his arousal straining against my lower back.

"I don't want to dance. Let me go. Now." Using all my strength, I yank myself from his grip.

"You're a feisty little thing, are—"

His words get cut off by what sounds like a fist connecting with his jaw. I whirl around to find Greyson face to face with my perpetrator.

"She asked you to let her go, so I suggest you back off." The gruffness in his voice surprises me.

The man gives Greyson a shove. Meanwhile, I'm too stunned to move.

Thankfully, Walker and Matt step in to diffuse the situation before it gets out of hand. Unfortunately, we have the attention of a few too many people. And it isn't long before a security guard comes over to find out what happened. I let the guys handle it.

Out of my peripheral vision, I see Maylee making her way over to me. When I hear her voice, I relax. I'm sure the change in my stance is obvious.

"Liz, are you okay? Oh, my goodness. We were just at the table and the next thing we know Greyson is over here throwing punches."

"I'm fine. I just need to sit down and sober up."

Maylee carefully takes my hand and guides me to the booth.

Once I'm seated, I let the events of the night get the best of me. This is definitely not how I pictured my Friday night going. Men are the worst.

I sit at our table long enough for the club to empty.

It isn't long before my friends trickle out. I remain seated at the table, sipping on my glass of water.

"Are you sure you're okay? Walker and I can drive you home."

Greyson's standing close enough to hear Maylee and says, "I'll stay with her."

I see her eyes shift to me, asking for silent permission to leave me here with the one person I can't stand. I don't have enough energy to fight him on it. So, I nod.

She gives me a half smile. "Okay. I'll call you tomorrow."

As she and Walker exit the bar, Greyson slides into the booth across from me.

I lift my head to meet his gaze. "Thank you... for what you did." My words come out in a whisper.

"You're welcome." He nods toward the doors leading to the parking lot. "Come on. I'll walk you to your car."

When I stand up, I'm still a little unsteady on my feet, though it isn't from the alcohol.

Greyson catches me by the arm. His grip is firm, but gentle. "Woah, there. I got you."

We exit the bar.

I don't remember driving home.

Chapter 3

Liz

Present Day

Waking up to the sound of pounding is not ideal. What's even worse is realizing the pounding is coming from my head.

I bring my hands up to either side of my face and gently massage my temples, groaning out in pain and frustration.

I try to recall the events of last night, only I can't recall much. I'm sure it will all come back to me as soon as I get some caffeine into my system.

The thought of a warm cup of coffee is enough to force me out of bed. But not too quickly. Any sudden movement will only make the pounding in my head worse.

Afraid of the light that will surely stream in through my bedroom windows, I slowly open one eye at a time, wincing as they adjust to the light.

When both of my eyes are open and completely adjusted to the brightness, I realize my surroundings are very unfamiliar.

Where on earth am I?

I don't recognize this room.

I let my eyes wander, hoping I'll find something that will clue me in on whose room I spent the night in.

There's a charcoal dresser directly across from me with a few items strewn about. None of which looks familiar. To the right of the dresser is a closet door that is slightly ajar. There are a few clothes lying on the floor even though the hamper is close by.

Nothing jumps out at me.

I look at the desk to my left. Apart from a computer and a picture frame, there isn't much lying on top of it.

Then I see it.

A picture.

I scramble out of bed, still fully clothed (thank God), and pick up the picture frame.

It's a photo of Greyson and Walker with their arms over each other's shoulders. They look a little older than twenty in the photo.

Blame it on my exhaustion, but I take a moment to appreciate Greyson's attractiveness.

While he looks more boyish in the picture, he's just as handsome as he is now. Rugged even. He has the same deep brown eyes and dark hair. I appreciate how much more built he is now, though. Dare I say he's gorgeous? Not that I'd ever admit that to him. Or to anyone.

I set the picture down as the memories from last night come back to me in full force: the drinking, the dancing, the unwanted stranger forcing himself on me. Then there's Greyson coming to my rescue. While that's all I remember, it's enough.

I didn't put up a fight last night when Greyson offered to stay with me. But it's a new day. There's no reason he couldn't have driven me home. My house key is in my purse. I roll my eyes at the thought of having to deal with him this morning. Just what I need.

Especially after last night.

Not having a clue what time it is, I quietly open the door to Greyson's bedroom and make my way down the hall, through the living room and into the kitchen. I'm an early riser and I've learned that not everyone enjoys the early hours of the morning as much as I do.

This is the first time I've ever been in Greyson's house. And hopefully the last. He bought it recently. It's nice.

Honestly, it isn't what I envisioned. His living room is bright and open, and while there isn't much décor, it still feels like a homey space.

His kitchen is spacious. It's equipped with dark granite countertops, black cabinetry, and stainless-steel appliances. Honestly, it's the kitchen of my dreams. Too bad I have no desire to live in a house of my own. I can certainly afford one, but I love my little apartment.

The sound of my stomach grumbling pulls me from my thoughts and my perusal of Greyson's home.

I open the pantry in search of something to eat, but come to a halt when I see what's sitting at the coffee nook just on the other side of the pantry.

There's a bottle of water, two ibuprofen tablets, a full pot of coffee, and a note. Scribbled in boyish handwriting, it says, *I figured you could use this for the headache you surely have this morning. -G*

Scoffing, I roll my eyes and shove the note along with everything else aside. I refuse to give in to that man and his gestures. Letting him drive me home last night was a fluke. I'll make sure he knows that the next time I see him.

I walk the coffee to the sink and pour it down the drain. I'm so focused on emptying the contents of the coffee pot that I startle when I hear the garage door open and then close. Snapping my head up far too quickly, I find a shirtless Greyson walking toward me, clearly confused by what I'm doing. I can't help but notice the sweat glistening on his very muscular chest. If he were anyone else, I'd be a goner right now.

Instead of letting myself ogle every one of his muscles, I fix my eyes on the coffee draining down the sink. I turn on the water to wash it down, focusing on the way the color fades and then vanishes.

"Do you not like the coffee?"

I try my best not to let Greyson's gravelly post-workout voice send shivers down my spine.

I don't look up. "Do you not own a shirt?"

He chuckles. It's deep and rich.

I roll my eyes at the sound of it.

"I see you're feeling feisty this morning. How's your head?"

He strides into the kitchen and grabs a bottle of water from the fridge. His eyes wander to where he left the note for me this morning. I mentally reprimand myself for not getting rid of it, but maybe it's better that he sees I have no intention of accepting his niceties. He's only wasting his time.

"What exactly are you trying to accomplish here, Greyson?"

He holds his hands up in surrender. "I'm just making sure you're okay after last night."

Letting out an annoyed sigh, I narrow my eyes at him. "Is that why you brought me here instead of taking me home last night?"

He raises his eyebrows at me. "Is that a problem?"

"Yeah, it's a problem! You could have driven me home and then I could have avoided this back and forth." I gesture between the two of us for emphasis.

He just looks at me as he uncaps his water. As he brings it to his lips, he keeps his gaze on mine. I watch his Adam's apple bob as he practically guzzles half the bottle in one go.

After he twists the cap back on the bottle, his eyes meet mine, and I swear there's amusement in his expression.

I don't like it.

He shrugs. "I thought it would be easier to get you back to your car if you stayed here. It made little sense to drive you home when your car is still at the bar."

Okay.

So, maybe his reasoning makes sense, but that doesn't mean I have to like it.

"Uh-uh. No. *You,*"—I point my index finger at him—"don't get to do me anymore favors. Last night was a onetime thing. I'll call an Uber to take me to my car."

"Come on, Liz. Don't be ridiculous. I'll take you."

I narrow my eyes at him. "No."

He crosses his arms over his bare, sweaty chest. "Why not?"

"I don't know what your endgame is here, but I think you and I both know where I stand with you. Thank you for being my DD last night, but I can take care of myself."

"My endgame?" He uncrosses his arms and takes a few steps toward where I'm leaning against the sink.

The look in his eyes is intense. "I don't know what kind of guy you think I am, but I would never let one of my female friends get manhandled by some stranger in a bar and then drive home, all shaken up. Especially when that female is *you*."

His words surprise me, but I won't fall for them. I've been here before. I *know* Greyson. He's a flirt, and he knows it. He's had a lot of practice where flirting is concerned.

While I'm up for hanging out with him around our friends, this one-on-one situation will never happen again. It doesn't matter how attractive he is. He's tall, dark, handsome, and dangerous. I've warned *my* girl friends away from him.

I mumble, "I'm just one of many female *friends*." And then speak a little louder to say, "Like I said, I'll call an Uber to take me to my car."

He stays planted firmly where he's standing in front of me, shaking his head. "You're the most stubborn person I know."

Little does he know what he just said is my favorite compliment. I smirk. "Thank you."

Without waiting for a response, I walk out of the kitchen to track down my purse. Luckily, I find it on the coffee table in the living room.

I pull out my phone to see that it's dead. "You've got to be kidding me."

"Everything okay over there?"

I let out a frustrated sigh. "My phone must have died last night. Can I borrow a charger?"

"I've got a charger in my truck. Let me drive you to your car, Liz."

Because I have little of a choice, I say, "Fine."

This is the first, and last time, he will ever get what he wants from me.

That I can promise.

Once we're settled into Greyson's truck, he heads in the bar's direction where my car is. I'm hoping they didn't tow it. I don't really want to be stuck with the man next to me for longer than necessary. Plus, I'd love to take a hot bath. And I need to call Maylee too, considering I have several missed calls from her. She also deserves to be reprimanded for not pushing me harder to ride home with her and Walker last night.

Completely distracted by my phone, I'm surprised when we come to a stop.

That was fast.

When I look up, I realize we aren't at the bar.

We're at a café downtown.

But not any café.

We're at my favorite café.

"What are we doing here?"

"Getting you a cup of coffee."

I look at him in the driver's seat. He looks far too comfortable for my liking. Like us together is natural. "Why?"

"Because you didn't drink the coffee that I made you this morning."

"So?"

"So, I know you must be dying for some caffeine right now. I also know you would have stopped here on your way home, anyway. *So*, I'm saving you the trip."

I'm too dumbfounded to say anything. The lack of caffeine isn't helping either. I may be a morning person, but my brain doesn't function well without the stuff. That Greyson knows this about me says a lot. Actually, how does he know this about me?

As much as I want to argue with him, I can't. A vanilla latte with a shot of espresso and a dash of cinnamon is calling my name.

"What do you want? I'll go in and get it for you."

I don't want to give him any ideas, but his offer is too good to refuse. I'm still in last night's clothes and my wild red hair probably looks pretty untamed. Plus, he owes me for making me stay at his house last night instead of dropping me off at home.

"Sure. I'll take a vanilla latte with a shot of espresso and a dash of cinnamon."

He looks at me curiously, but says nothing.

Instead, he heads into the café to order my coffee.

I'm left wondering what exactly he's up to.

Thankfully, he returns quickly.

By the time we make it to my car, I feel much more energized, and the throbbing in my head has subsided. Not entirely, but enough.

Begrudgingly, I thank Greyson for the ride, hopping out before he can say anything in return.

As soon as I get into my car, I dial Maylee.

She answers on the first ring. "Liz! Finally! I've called you a dozen times. Where have you been?"

I clear my throat. "Well, you should know, considering you left me at the bar with him last night!"

"Wait, what? You're with Greyson?" She sounds surprised, probably because she knows how I feel about the dude.

"Not anymore. Why on earth did you not make me go home with you and Walker last night?"

She chuckles. "I asked, and you told me not to worry about it. He said he'd stay with you, and you gave me your 'I'm fine' look."

I sigh. "I was upset about what happened. You should have fought me on it."

"I know better than anyone not to argue with you. Anyway, how are you feeling? And please explain to me what happened last night after we left."

I sigh again. "Honestly, I don't know. Greyson drove me to his house, where I woke up this morning. He just dropped me off at my car and I'm headed home right now."

Silence greets me on the other end of the line.

"Maylee?"

"What aren't you telling me, Liz?"

"What do you mean?"

"I mean, you seem far more irritated than you should be. All he did was drive you to his house and then to your car. You can't possibly dislike him that much."

"No, I know. I'm just a little out of sorts today after last night."

Satisfied with my answer, she says, "Okay. Well, take a hot bath when you get home. You deserve it."

I chuckle. "Thanks. I plan on it."

We say our goodbyes and as I drive home; I think about what Maylee said on the phone.

If I'm being honest with myself, I am irritated.

I'm irritated because between Greyson's protectiveness last night and his thoughtfulness this morning, I don't know what to think. Those are two qualities of his that I've never witnessed before. And they're qualities that make him even more attractive.

It isn't just about the last twenty-four hours, though.

I've known Greyson for over three years.

I missed it.

Somehow, I missed that somewhere along the way he changed.

Now that I think about it, I realize he no longer has a revolving door of women coming and going.

Not that I care.

But I am glad.

Maybe now I'll be able to tolerate being around him more.

None of this means he still isn't trouble though, and where trouble is, I stay far, far away.

Chapter 4

Liz

Junior Year - Fall Semester

This week could not have moved any slower. The only thing that got me through it was texting Dylan every minute of every day.

I knew he would ask Ethan for my number. I just didn't expect him to ask for it first thing on Monday morning. Honestly, I'm flattered.

It's clear that he has every intention of treating me right this weekend.

That's right.

He asked me out.

Not once.

But twice.

We're going to dinner tonight and then to a drive-in movie tomorrow. He took my two date condition seriously and I'm not complaining.

I check my appearance in the mirror one more time. My long, red hair is hanging around my shoulders in loose waves. I did a smokey eye and paired it with a nude lipstick. The look is bold, but subtly so. I think I look perfect and I can only hope Dylan agrees.

My nerves are all over the place. I haven't ever felt this way before. And honestly? It's exhilarating.

I walk out of my room to join Maylee on the couch while waiting for Dylan to pick me up.

As soon as she sees me, she says, "You look gorgeous!"

I laugh as I do a little spin to show off the complete look. "Why, thank you."

I'm wearing black ripped jeans with a loosely fitted, fringed gray top. I picked out a pair of gray pumps to go with the outfit.

To top off the look, I accessorized it with a thick, black leather bracelet, and a black and charcoal stacked chain necklace with a bit of sparkle. It screams edgy and sophisticated. Much like me.

"Are you ready for your date?" Maylee asks as she raises her eyebrows.

"Are you kidding? More than ready."

She laughs. "I'm glad."

A knock at the door distracts me from our conversation.

She looks at me and smiles. "Don't have too much fun."

I smirk. "No promises."

The sound of her laughter follows me to the door as I open it before stepping out into the cool evening air.

Considering my nerves, I'm extra thankful for the fall weather. Hopefully, it helps to keep my perspiration at bay.

When I meet Dylan's gaze, my heart flutters in my chest.

He's gorgeous.

I mean, while I'm a sucker for dark features, he puts every other man on this campus to shame.

Before either of us says anything, he takes me in from head to toe. The heat in his eyes causes a warmth to envelope my entire body.

How is it possible for a simple look to have this kind of effect on me?

I break the silence first. "Hi."

He blows out a big breath of air. "Wow. You look..."—he shakes his head as if he's unable to find the right words—"... You are gorgeous."

"Thank you. You look great, too." I punctuate my compliment with a wink as I take him in.

He really looks great. Amazing. No less drool worthy than the last time I saw him. Although, this is the first time I've seen him dressed up. It's proof that he can make anything look good.

He's wearing dark washed jeans with a long-sleeved button-up shirt. The forest green color of his collared button up makes his brown eyes stand out. I peek at his maple dress shoes. Which are dressy, yet casual enough to pair nicely with his jeans. I like a man with some style.

He offers me his arm. "Are you ready?"

I grasp it without answering. His bicep makes my hand feel much smaller than it is.

As he guides me down the stairs of my apartment complex toward his car, I resist the urge I have to melt into him. It takes some serious self-control on my part. If I were alone right now, I'd be giving myself a pat on the back.

Like a gentleman, Dylan opens the passenger door of his Charger for me to slide into. I may have gawked a little at the sight of the beautiful vehicle. I'm not the least bit surprised he drives a sports car. The rev of the engine as he pulls out of the complex is music to my ears.

From the passenger seat, I lean against the door to face him. "Okay. I have to say it."

He smiles. And it. Is. Gorgeous. "What?"

"Your car is scoring you some major points right now."

He laughs. The sound of it is deep and hearty. It makes me giggle.

"You like it?"

"Like it? No, I love it. Seriously." As if to prove my point, I run my hands over the leather seat I'm currently occupying. Then I reach up and let my fingers run along the dashboard.

I catch him watching me with the same heat in his eyes from earlier. The tension in the air is palpable. Wanting to dissolve some of the said tension, I clear my throat.

"So, where are we eating?"

My question seems to snap him back to the present moment. "I thought we could check out Aria's." He dips his chin. "I mean, if that's okay with you."

I have to stop myself from letting my eyes bug out of my head. Aria's is a very upscale Chicago restaurant. I don't know how on earth a college junior can afford it.

I want to ask him if he's sure about taking me somewhere so nice, but think better of it. Something about the way he asked if it was okay with me makes me think he's nervous about what I might think of the restaurant. Like it's too much. He doesn't strike me as someone who lacks confidence in his decision making. I won't be the person to make him doubt himself.

Finding my resolve, I say, "That's more than okay with me."

He reaches for my hand across the console and interlaces his fingers with mine. He doesn't let it go until we arrive at the restaurant.

Once we're seated at our table for the evening, our waitress brings us both a glass of water and asks if we'd like anything else to drink.

I let Dylan take the lead. When he orders a glass of whiskey, I order a glass of red wine.

He keeps his attention on me from across the table. The heated look from earlier isn't as prevalent now, but it's still there. Just beneath the surface.

"Tell me about yourself, Liz."

Our waitress drops our drinks off and asks if we're ready to order. Both of us agree we need a few more minutes.

If there's one thing I don't like about first dates, it's the awkwardness. Our playful banter from the party last weekend is long gone. Instead, I'm expected to answer generic questions about myself. Which I find difficult to do. I blame it on my upbringing.

I deflect. "How about you tell me what exactly you want to know?"

He takes a sip of his whiskey. I find it oddly satisfying that he likes it neat. I can't stand when people mix the stuff with something like Coke.

"What are you in school for?"

Easy enough. "Pre-Law. I come from a long line of lawyers." Shrugging, I add, "I guess it's in my blood."

"That makes sense based on your negotiating skills I had the pleasure of witnessing last weekend." Winking, he adds, "It worked out well for me, though."

Knowing he's talking about the second date I coaxed him into, I laugh. "I'm glad you think so. What about you? I remember you mentioning Pre-Med classes. What's your plan after undergrad?"

"Medical School. I'd like to go somewhere on the East Coast, but who knows if it'll work out?"

I smile. "I'm sure it will. Is there any specific reason you pursued medicine?"

"My grandfather was a surgeon before he retired. I love listening to all his stories and learning about what he did day-to-day."

"Oh, wow. Do you want to follow in his footsteps?"

His brow furrows. "I'm not entirely sure. Enough about me. Tell me about your family."

I let out an unassumed laugh and then take a sip of my wine. "Honestly, there isn't much to tell. I'm an only child. My parents couldn't have another after me. It's probably a good thing. They run a tight ship. I wouldn't have wanted my younger siblings to deal with it. If I had any."

He shakes his head in understanding, and I appreciate him for not inquiring about my parents further.

They were kind, but strict. Too strict. It's why I opted to live on campus instead of at home with them. I wanted a normal college experience. There's no way they would ever allow me to "behave" the way I do now.

I put the thoughts of my parents to rest. "What about yours?"

"Luckily, my parents were chill. I grew up with four brothers."

I nearly choke on my water. That's a lot of boys under one roof.

"Your poor mother."

He laughs. "Yeah, she had her hands full."

Our conversation continues to flow throughout the rest of the dinner.

I'm pleasantly surprised by how charming and put together Dylan is. He'll make a brilliant doctor someday.

As we finish the last of the coffee cake we ordered for dessert, Dylan suggests taking a walk along the river walk. I love the idea, and there isn't a single part of me that's ready for this night to end.

Walking hand in hand with Dylan along the river is causing a whole onslaught of butterflies to flutter around in my stomach.

His large, calloused hand feels like it belongs in mine. Tingles spread up my arm as he gently traces circles on my hand with his thumb.

He's currently telling me a story about growing up in a house full of boys. He's second to the youngest.

Tears pool in my eyes from how hard I'm laughing. I attempt to rein it in so I'm able to speak.

I lean into his arm as I look at him. "You're gonna have to chill on the stories. First, you've got me laughing so hard that my stomach hurts. Second, you're making me wish I would have grown up with siblings."

He smiles down at me. "Your laugh is amazing, so I can't say I'm sorry for causing it, but I am sorry you missed out on having siblings."

I return his smile with one of my own. The sincerity in his voice means a lot. It means so much that I don't think before I speak my next words. "Yeah, it's why I want a big family someday. I was lucky enough to have an amazing best friend who is more like a sister, but I want my children to grow up surrounded by each other."

It's way too soon to be talking about what I want in the future, but it's not like I can take the words back now. Besides, it's better to get this kind of stuff out in the open to avoid breaking up later over a conversation that happens too late. Right?

As if Dylan can sense my doubt, he stops us in our tracks. "I do too... want a big family, I mean."

He runs his free hand through his hair after his admission. I know it's his way of hiding the vulnerability in his words. If anything, it makes me fall even harder for him.

I offer him a genuine smile. One of my larger-than-life smiles.

He looks down at me as he takes my other hand in his. I'm not sure how long we stand, staring at each other, before the air shifts between us.

It happens slowly.

His eyes dart to my mouth, and then back up to meet mine again.

Suddenly, we're standing even closer to each other.

Everything happens in slow motion.

He lifts his right hand to brush a stray curl behind my ear, letting his hand linger on my cheek.

There's no ignoring the heat in his eyes now.

He lowers his mouth to mine.

Slowly.

Reverently.

When our lips meet in a tender kiss, the spark of electricity between us is undeniable. A force to be reckoned with.

My lips part in a silent invitation. He takes it as he deepens the kiss.

Without hesitating, I kiss him back just as fiercely.

He tastes like peppermint with a hint of coffee cake from our dessert.

I pull him a little closer to me as I bring my arms around his neck, and suddenly our kiss turns more desperate.

Electric.

It's the most satisfying kiss I've ever experienced.

The best kiss.

One kiss.

That's all it takes for him to ruin me for all other men.

This kiss.

Right here.

It's everything.

Chapter 5

Liz

Present Day

Walking into the animal shelter on a Sunday afternoon feels a little strange. I'm usually here on Mondays and Wednesdays to volunteer if I can make it.

I love being a lawyer, but it consumes more time than my previous job. Consequently, I don't get to spend as much time here—my favorite place in the world. This is the only place I want to be, considering the weekend I've had.

Before heading toward the kennels, I step into the front office to greet Penny. She's sitting behind her desk doing something on her computer. There's a blonde woman I don't recognize leaning over her while pointing at the computer screen.

I come to a halt. "Oh, hi! Sorry to interrupt. I just wanted to make sure I stopped in to say hello before I get to work."

The smile that stretches across Penny's face lights up the entire office. Seeing it means the world to me.

Penny has been faithfully running this shelter for years. She kept it up even after losing her husband. While she's old enough to be my grandmother, she's more of a friend to me than anything else. Despite everything she's been through, her joy for life is contagious. I admire her.

"Hello, Liz! I'm surprised to see you here today."

I lean against the doorframe, letting out a sigh. "I know. This weekend has been rough. I'm hoping to end it on a positive note."

Penny frowns. "I'm sorry to hear that, dear."

"It's okay." I shrug. "Things happen. Is there anything specific you need today?"

"No, but while you're here, I want to introduce you to my granddaughter, Margaret. She'll be helping around here a lot more. My old age isn't doing me any favors, I'm afraid."

I step further into the office and stretch out my hand to shake Margaret's. "It's nice to meet you. Let me know if you ever need anything."

Kindly, she smiles at me, and when she does, I see the resemblance between her and her grandmother immediately.

While Penny has a full head of gray hair now, I know it was once a dirty blonde, much like her granddaughter's. They both share the same petite frame, ocean blue eyes, and kind smiles.

"Thanks. It's nice to meet you too."

I nod my head before walking out of the office and heading toward the kennels. It's beautiful outside today. I plan on taking full advantage of the sunny weather by taking some dogs out on the walking trails.

I grab two leashes from their designated hook, already knowing who I'm taking with me today.

I've fallen in love with a few too many dogs over the years. It's always hard when my favorites get adopted, but I'm thankful when they do. If any of them are here for too long, then they have to be euthanized. It breaks my heart. Luckily, it doesn't happen very often.

I find Milo, a German Shepard mix, in the very last row of kennels. He's chestnut and black with the most beautiful brown eyes. To say I've bonded with this dude would be a massive understatement. If I didn't live in an apartment, I probably would have adopted him by now.

"Hey, boy!" I greet him with as much enthusiasm as possible. Naturally, he trots right on up to me as I enter his space.

After I have Milo situated, I decide to bring Macy with us as well. She's a very hyper Lab mix. She and Milo get along well.

When I make it into the parking lot that leads to the main walking trail, there's a familiar gray truck that I'm certain belongs to Greyson. None of the paramedics are usually here on weekends, so I find it a little odd. Hopefully, I don't run into him.

After about half an hour of walking, I'm completely drenched in sweat. I wrap both leashes around my wrist to give my arms a bit of a break.

The only problem with my decision to do so is a stray cat comes trotting out of the brush. Before I know it, Macy takes off after it. Because she's practically attached to me, I'm forced to keep up with her. Or try, at least. So, I break into a sprint with Milo heeling at my side.

The pain in my wrist from being pulled along is almost unbearable. Using my left hand, I attempt to unwrap the leashes.

Now, I wouldn't call myself a klutz, but I am definitely no athlete. In my pursuit of Macy, and in trying to untangle myself, I lose my footing on the gravel trail, which doesn't bode well for me. I am, quite literally, being dragged. Hoping I'm close enough to the shelter, I call for help.

Before anyone hears me, Macy gives up in her pursuit of the feline. Not soon enough, though. When I stand up, I can barely move my wrist. Upon further inspection, it's tender to the touch and already bruising. Not to mention blood and gravel cover my legs.

Could this weekend get any worse?

When I look up from inspecting my injuries, an all too familiar figure is making his way toward me.

Great.

I guess this weekend *can* get worse.

"Liz? I thought I heard shouting." Greyson's eyes widen as he sees my legs. Before I can get a word in, he rushes over to me. "What happened? Are you okay?"

I'm not sure if it's from the pain, or from everything that has conspired this weekend, but tears threaten to spring free. I'm not a crier. So, the last thing I want to do is cry in front of the man standing before me. I do my best to keep the tears at bay.

Steeling myself, I say, "Do I really have to explain?"

He grabs the leashes from my hand. "No, but come with me. I want to check out your injuries. Your wrist looks pretty bad."

"Fine."

If he wasn't a paramedic, my answer would have been very different. At least that's what I'm telling myself.

Greyson gets Milo and Macy put up after he orders me to stay put in the bathroom. I debate making a break for it, but I actually want to make sure I don't need to go see a doctor for my injuries.

Who better to figure that out than the paramedic himself? Of course, he had to be here today. I roll my eyes at the thought.

After a few minutes, he comes strolling in with a first aid kit in hand.

I look at him questioningly. "Where did you get that?"

He sets it on the counter in the bathroom. While pulling out the supplies he needs, he says, "My truck."

"You keep a first aid kit in your truck?"

He ignores me.

Well, alright then.

Once he has everything he needs laid out, he stands in front of me where I'm seated on the counter.

He looks at me through his dark lashes. "This will probably sting. I just want to clean up your legs to make sure the cuts aren't too deep. Okay?"

All I can manage is a nod.

Gently.

More gently than I thought him capable of, he washes me off. It's another side of Greyson I've never witnessed. There's something oddly intimate about it. But he was right. It stings.

Too bad that isn't the real problem.

Not in the slightest.

The real problem is the way Greyson keeps touching my legs. I know he needs to touch my legs to get them cleaned up, but it's the way he's currently doing so.

He's touching me with so much tender care that I want to get as far away from him as possible.

I'm not a fan of the way his fingers delicately brush my skin as he washes my wounds—causing goosebumps to break out all over my body. Or of the way each calf tingles from where his palm holds my leg still. I'm especially not a fan of the tension that fills the air.

I'm not enjoying a single part of this.

I'm desperate for a distraction.

Scrambling, I ask the first thing that comes to mind. "Why are you here today? I thought you only volunteer on weekdays."

He doesn't look up from what he's doing when he answers.

"You're right. I do. Penny needed help with something."

"Oh." I'm not sure what I was expecting him to say, but it wasn't that.

I wonder if Penny asked him as a last resort or if he's her go to. Either way, it's sweet that he came. I'll give him that much. Although, I'd say that's generous.

"Your legs don't look too bad now that they're cleaned up. Can I see your wrist?"

Without waiting for my permission, he gently lifts my wrist to inspect it. I wince in pain when he does.

When he looks up at me to apologize for causing me discomfort, our faces are only inches apart. It's the first time I'm seeing his eyes up close. They're a deep brown. Gold flecks glimmer around his irises, making his eyes the most breathtaking brown I've ever seen. And now, at this exact moment in time, I really wish I wasn't a sucker for brown eyes.

I lean back to put some distance between us.

Greyson must pick up on my discomfort, because he clears his throat to apologize. "Sorry. I didn't mean to cause any pain. I don't think it's broken, though. It's probably just a sprain. Do you want me to wrap it for you?"

If he were anyone else, the answer would be yes. But I need to get out of this bathroom. I don't appreciate the way my body seems to respond whenever he's in my general vicinity. I don't know when that even started happening, but I'll do anything to stop it.

There are many reasons I will never let myself fall for Greyson.

Or anyone like him.

Or anyone at all.

"Nope. I'm good." I hop down from the counter without giving Greyson a chance to say anything. Then I gather my belongings before heading to the front of the shelter to make a break for it.

On my way up, Margaret comes out of Penny's office to say goodbye. Her eyes fix on something behind me. Or rather, someone.

"He sure is a looker, isn't he?"

I know who she's talking about, but I feign confusion. "Who?"

She nods her head in his direction. "That guy. Do you know him?"

I don't think before I speak. "Unfortunately."

She chuckles. "My bad. I didn't realize there was history there."

"What? No. No, no, no. There isn't. He's my best friend's husband's best friend. I've known him for a few years."

She gives me a suspicious look, but says nothing else about him.

"Well, I wanted to thank you for helping my grandmother out all the time. As soon as you walked out of the office, she started raving about you."

I smile. "Of course. She's wonderful. I'm glad she has you, too. I'll see you around."

"See ya." Margaret waves as I head out the door.

* * *

Maylee pulls me in for a hug as soon as she opens her front door, oblivious to the red wine bottle in my hand. Instead of releasing me from her grip, she shuffles us inside. The gesture makes me laugh.

"What's the hug for? You saw me two days ago."

I sent an 'SOS' text to her as soon as I left the shelter.

I'm all out of sorts.

As much as I want to blame it on the incident at the bar, or on the injuries I sustained today, I know neither of those reasons is accurate. I just refuse to admit what has me feeling crazy. Or rather, who.

"I'm just glad to see you in one piece. You had me worried yesterday, and your 'SOS' text earlier didn't help."

I give her a sheepish look. "Yeah, sorry about that. I didn't know what else to say. I probably should have just asked if I could come over."

She chuckles. "You say that like you wouldn't have just shown up without a warning."

I smirk. "You aren't wrong."

I follow Maylee into the kitchen, where she removes two wine glasses from a cabinet. I uncork the bottle and walk it over to the coffee table in the living room.

We sit in silence for a few minutes as we sip our wine. She has to know something is off. Usually, I'm never at a loss for words. I just don't exactly know how to explain what I'm feeling right now.

I don't even realize I'm staring off into space until my best friend's voice brings me back to the present. "Liz?"

"Hmm?"

She narrows her eyes at me. "What aren't you telling me?"

I hate that question.

I set my glass of wine on the table.

Then take a deep breath.

It's now or never.

With a scowl on my face, I cross my arms over my chest. "I'm irritated at your husband's best friend. *First,* he thinks it's okay to defend my honor. *Second,* he drives me to *his house* under the guise that I'm drunk. Which I wasn't. *Then,* he thinks it's okay to buy me a coffee from my favorite café. And *finally,* he tenderly attended to the injuries I received today when the dog I was walking chased a cat!"

Silence.

And then Maylee has the audacity to burst out laughing.

I throw my hands up in frustration. "This isn't funny!"

In between bouts of laughter, she finds her words. "It so is!" She gets herself under control. "You're attracted to him!"

I gasp. "I am not!"

She rolls her eyes. "Oh, come on. We both know that is one bald-faced lie. He's your type."

With a heavy sigh, I let myself fall back into the couch cushions.

She isn't wrong. Maybe I am attracted to Greyson. I mean, it's possible to be attracted to someone I despise, right? It doesn't mean I have to do anything about it.

I sit up tall, pulling my shoulders back. "Whether it's true, the two of us will never happen. You know my history, MayMay. And you know what kind of guy Greyson is. Even if I was willing to let go of my reservations with relationships, he's not someone I will ever consider dating. I refuse to be added to his extremely long list of women."

She sighs. "I know." Her words come out solemnly.

Luckily, she isn't one to push.

Instead, we switch gears, spending the rest of the night sharing details of our lives with each other.

My best friend's life looks nothing like I expected it to.

Honestly, mine doesn't either. And I'm not sure how I feel about it anymore.

Chapter 6

Greyson

Present Day

I can't get Liz out of my head. Her wild red curls and beautiful green eyes are all I see when I fall asleep at night. She's also the first thing I think about when I wake up every morning. Even on my days off, she's all I think about. Period. The end.

I'm in my garage lifting weights. I've been at it for an hour so far, and it isn't helping. Not that I'm surprised. I've known for a while I'm attracted to Liz. But my attraction to her has grown into something more. I'm not sure when it happened. Only that it did.

What went down at the shelter yesterday didn't help. If anything, it made things far worse for me.

When I was attending to her wounds, it took every ounce of self-control I'm equipped with not to close the distance between us and show her exactly what she does to me. I wasn't even touching her intimately. Who knew taking care of her injuries could be such a turn on?

The thing is, I know the contact affected her too. Every time I touched her, goosebumps formed on her skin. I'm sure that's why she looked so uncomfortable. She practically sprinted out of there when I asked if I could wrap her sprained wrist. Which I didn't think would be a big deal. I was sorely mistaken.

Since the very first day I met her, she has never paid me a lick of attention. At first, it didn't bother me. I would simply move on to the next girl. But I'll admit that after a while, I was bringing home random women just to distract myself from the pull I feel toward Liz. Eventually, it stopped working, so I stopped bringing women home altogether.

I've spent the last few months trying to get my life together.

I stopped getting drunk on my days off. Stopped sleeping around. And stopped being such a jerk. Looking back, I'm not proud of my decision making. But I have my reasons.

Coming from a broken home screwed me over. I blame my father for my commitment issues. He's a lying cheat who left my mom high and dry after having multiple affairs. I didn't want to do to a woman what my father did to my mom. So, I swore off relationships.

I was doing just fine until the day I met Liz Carter. It's absolute torture that she's the only woman on the planet who refuses to give me the time of day. I'm hoping to change that, though.

Pulling myself from my thoughts, I crank out my last set of bicep curls.

I need to take a quick shower and get ready for work.

* * *

I nod my head toward the guys as I walk into the station. "What's up, fellas?"

My best friend, Walker, greets me first. "Hey, man."

He and I have known each other since high school.

Sam follows with a fist bump. "Hey, bro."

"Matt isn't here?" I ask.

"Nah. Sarah worked both weekend shifts, so she's off today. He switched schedules with me to spend some time with her." Walker replies.

Matt is Walker's brother-in-law. He and Walker's sister, Sarah, got married about two years ago. She's currently pregnant with their first baby. I respect the man for adjusting his schedule to take care of his wife.

"How's she doing?"

"Her morning sickness is finally gone, so she's doing better."

"Nice. How are you feeling about becoming an uncle, man?"

Walker chuckles. "Pretty excited."

I nod my head at him as Charlie comes out of the break room. "Greyson, what's up?"

"Not much. Are you heading out?"

"Yeah."

"Alright. See you around, man."

Charlie throws up a peace sign as he makes his way out the door. I turn around and return my attention to Walker. He does a quick assessment of me. I know he can tell something is off.

"What's going on with you?"

I run my hand through my hair and look down at the floor, unsure how to answer his question. I used to be better about putting up a front. He knows me well enough to see right through me, though, so it's not like it would be worth it to hide whatever *is* going on with me. I never thought the day would come when a woman would frustrate me so much.

As if he can read my mind, he chuckles and says, "Man, she's really got you messed up."

"Thanks, man." I'm sure my sarcasm doesn't go unnoticed.

He just shakes his head as he laughs to himself. I appreciate him for not trying to have this conversation with me right now.

Walker is the only person who knows about all my drama. He's also the only person who knows how I feel about Liz. We've had plenty of conversations about her. It might be time to have another one. If only I knew how to set aside my pride and ask for some advice.

"Wanna grab a beer after work? You look like you could use one."

It's like he can read minds. Maybe that's what happens after settling down with the perfect woman.

I don't have time to give a response before we get called out.

While I hope whatever we're about to walk into isn't bad, I find myself thankful for the welcome distraction. I could use something to take my mind off the only woman who has ever taken up residence in my brain.

* * *

Walker clasps his hand over my shoulder. "Alright. What's got you so wired, my friend?"

I let out a frustrated breath, giving him the side eye.

He laughs before taking a drink out of his full bottle of beer.

We're at the same bar we hit up on Thursdays for karaoke since it's close to work. We had a couple of tough calls today, so neither one of us wanted to travel very far. Honestly, I would have preferred to go home after my twelve-hour shift, but Walker wouldn't have allowed it. Not before getting to the bottom of what's got me so "wired". As he so kindly put it.

He sets his beer back down on the bar, swiveling in his bar stool to face me. "Let me ask you this: are you gonna do anything about it?"

Feeling drained and defeated, I let out a long sigh. "I don't know what to do about it."

"You've had no problems going after a woman before."

The man has a point. But this situation is completely different. I wanted nothing long term with the women I've been with in the past. Every single one of them was a means to an end. I made sure each of them knew not to expect anything more from me. Unfortunately, that backfired because I'm positive Liz looks at me like I have no respect for women. The worst part is, I don't know how to change her mind.

"I know. But Liz is different. You know that. We wouldn't keep having conversations about her if she wasn't."

"Okay. What exactly do you want with her, man?"

"I want her. *Only* her." I emphasize the word 'only', hoping he picks up what I'm putting down.

Conversations like this are difficult for me. Walker doesn't truly understand. He isn't like me with women. For as long as I've known him, he never dated around. And now he's happily married to Liz's best friend, Maylee. Part of me envies him for it.

"For the long haul?"

I nod. "Yeah. I think so."

He narrows his eyes at me. "You think, or you know?"

"I'm pretty sure I would have given up by now if I wasn't interested in the long haul with her."

He dips his chin. "Fair enough."

53

"So, what do I do?"

He chuckles. "You make sure she knows you're interested in her for who she is. If I had to guess, she probably still thinks you only want her physically. Liz is stubborn. If you chase her, you need to make sure you know what you're getting yourself into."

"I know. Any suggestions?"

"Woo her. You know her well enough to know what she likes."

He's right.

I know Liz.

I know her better than she thinks I do.

I don't even think I realized how well I know her until recently. It's as if my brain has stored away every interaction or experience that I've shared with her.

Honestly, all I want to do is keep learning things about her. Experience things with her. She's the only woman I've ever had these thoughts about. If that doesn't speak volumes, then I don't know what does.

"Thanks, man."

"No problem. If you ever need anything where Liz is concerned, you can always talk to my wife. I'm sure she would be happy to help."

"I'll keep that in mind."

* * *

As soon as I get home from the bar, I take a quick shower before turning on a movie. I keep finding myself thinking about the conversation Walker and I had.

I'm going to do my best to make sure Liz knows I'm interested in her for more than just a one-night stand. I'll start with subtly and see how far that gets me. She won't appreciate or accept any grand gestures from me. At least not yet.

Remembering how sore her wrist was at the shelter yesterday, I send her a quick text to check in.

Me: Hey. How's your wrist feeling?

I try my best to focus on the movie instead of how anxious I feel as I wait for a response from her.

After about a minute, my phone vibrates.

Liz: Fine.

Honestly, I'm surprised she responded. And quickly, too.

Me: Are you sure? It didn't look fine yesterday.

Liz: Do you need something?

I laugh at her text.

This woman will not be easy to win over. But I'm up for the challenge.

I take it as a win that she's even replying to my text messages. She didn't have to. And I didn't expect her to either.

Me: I just want to make sure it isn't worse.

Liz: It isn't.

Me: Everything okay? You seem angry.

I know she's giving me short answers on purpose, but I enjoy getting under her skin. Plus, I'm genuinely curious about what she's up to right now.

Liz: I'm fine. Bye, Greyson.

Greyson: Let me know if you need anything. Night, Liz. ;)

Tossing my phone to the opposite end of my couch, I lean back in the recliner. I think I have an idea, but I don't know how thrilled Liz will be with me. I have to start somewhere, though.

Even though she said her wrist is fine, I know that isn't the case. The swelling and bruising are proof of that. That it was tender to the touch when I examined it yesterday is enough for me to know she's in pain, even if she won't admit that to me. I genuinely feel bad about what happened to her when she was walking Milo and Macy, but it's the perfect excuse to show her I care about her.

I pull on a shirt, grab my keys, and head to the store.

I've got some wooing to do.

Chapter 7

Liz

Present Day

"Good morning, Ms. Carter."

As much as I would prefer Steph to call me Liz, I'm not in the mood to correct her this morning.

Unfortunately, I have to greet her back since I'm known for being the most perky morning person on the planet.

It's a good thing I'm so good at faking it until I make it. One of my favorite qualities about myself is how well I'm able to mask my emotions. It pays off in so many ways. Especially in a courtroom.

I sing-song in response. "Good morning, Steph!"

She doesn't even bat an eyelash. Instead, she offers me a smile as I walk past her desk, reminding me I'm a seasoned pro. I know how to put my game face on.

As soon as I make it into my office, I gently kick the door shut with my foot.

I take a sip of my vanilla latte made just the way I like it—with an extra shot of espresso and a dash of cinnamon.

Only, I don't like this one because I didn't buy it.

Greyson did.

I'm not sure what's going on in that pretty little head of his.

When I opened the door to my apartment this morning, I discovered the vanilla latte, along with a few other items sitting in a basket on my welcome mat.

I would have known it was his doing even without the note, considering he's the only one who knows about my wrist.

What else did he leave at my front door, you ask?

Well.

He left a gel bead ice pack with a strap that fits around my wrist perfectly, a brace, a bottle of pain relievers, icy hot, and a warm cinnamon roll from my favorite café.

I stared at everything for a solid sixty seconds, trying to figure out how he knows I'm a total sucker for cinnamon. And I'm not talking about red, hot cinnamon. I'm talking about the cinnamon that's paired with sugar on cinnamon and sugar toast, or the cinnamon I whisk into my eggs when I make French toast, or the cinnamon that snickerdoodles are coated with.

Anyway, the gesture flustered me. I *never* get flustered. But that's beside the point. He has no right to be doing sweet, thoughtful things for me.

It's irritating.

I'm irritated.

Which is why, it's a good thing I have an enormous case I need to prepare for this week. It'll keep me focused on my most important priority: work.

I'll be putting in sixty to seventy hours this week. I can't afford any distractions.

Especially any tall, dark, and handsome distractions.

Nope.

There's only one downside that comes to mind when I think about how many hours I have to put into this case: I probably won't be able to go out with my friends this week. It happens from time to time. I can't say I mind though. I have nothing in my life that demands much of my time or attention. Which is fine by me.

A knock at my door startles me, interrupting my train of thought. "Come in!"

Steph pokes her head through the cracked door. "Hey, there. Do you need anything specific from me this morning?"

I seriously appreciate Stephanie so much. She keeps me sane when things drive me a little crazy. Plus, she's excellent with my scheduling. It's one less thing I have to worry about.

"I don't think so. If you could, though, can you please make sure I'm open after four the rest of the week? I need all the extra time I can get with the custody case coming up."

"Of course. Let me know if you need me to hang around the office a little later than normal."

I give her a pointed look. "Absolutely not."

She chuckles. "It was worth a try. Seriously though, I'm happy to do it if necessary."

"I know. Thanks, Steph."

Without dismissing Steph, I get up from my desk to pull some files I'll need today. I have a long day ahead of me full of client meetings, so I need to be as prepared as possible if I want to get out of here before nine o'clock tonight.

* * *

It's nearing the end of the day.

Steph pokes her head into my office to let me know she's heading out. With my head in my hands, she catches me at an inopportune time.

"Hey, I'm gonna head..." She lets her words trail off as I peek up at her. "Are you okay?"

I wave her off. "Yes, I'm fine. I just can't wait for things to calm down with Mr. Seymour's case."

There's sympathy in her gaze. "I'm sorry, Liz. Is there anything I can do?"

"Yes. Go home. Hopefully, I won't have to be here much longer." I offer her a weak smile, hoping it's enough.

"Alright. If you insist. But call me if you need anything."

"Thanks."

When I hear the elevator doors close behind Steph, I return to the papers littered in front of me. Custody cases are tough, but they mean the most to me.

Being someone who used to want a big family, I value the parent-child relationship. While I don't have kids of my own, and probably never will, I empathize with my clients in cases like Mr. Seymour's.

His wife left him years ago, promising to get sober, and thus started a chain of events that led him here. She found her way back to him nine months later with his child in her arms. He didn't even know she was ever pregnant.

Of course, he welcomed her home with open arms. I wish I could say they lived happily ever after, but he wouldn't be my client if that were true.

After returning with the baby, she refused to get the help she promised she would. Long story short, she left Mr. Seymour a few years later, abandoning her own child. A few months ago, she came back claiming she's finally clean. Mr. Seymour won't let her anywhere near their daughter, which backfired. His ex-wife is filing for sole custody.

It appears like she has, in fact, cleaned up her life, which makes this so much more difficult. These cases are never black and white. Obviously, there's a lot more to it. It's safe to say I have my work cut out for me. I desperately want to win this one.

A couple hours have passed when I hear the ding of the elevator. It's nearing eight o'clock, so I don't know who it could be. I'm not necessarily a paranoid person, but I'm glad I locked my office door after Stephanie left.

Not thirty seconds later, I hear the jingling keys before the lock flips on my door. Startled, I snap my head up to see the smiling faces of Steph and Kate staring back at me.

They whisper-yell, "surprise!", in unison.

I laugh. "What are you two doing here?"

I get up from my desk and walk over to them. That's when I notice the bag of food Kate's trying to keep hidden behind her back.

Steph laughs. "I tried to corral all our girlfriends, but Kate was the only one available tonight." She points at Kate with her thumb. "I knew you skipped lunch. And I had a hunch you more than likely have no plans for dinner, either."

As if on cue, my stomach grumbles. All three of us burst into laughter at the sound of it.

"You just made my night." Rubbing my belly, I add, "And my stomach's."

We all pull up a chair and settle around my desk. Kate pulls out Chinese takeout. I've never been more thankful for an interruption in my life.

When I reach for an egg roll, Steph's eyes narrow in on the wrist brace I'm wearing. I internally chastise myself for forgetting about it.

She looks at me, confused. "What happened to your wrist? I didn't notice that earlier."

I feign nonchalance. "Oh, I think it's sprained. It's been bothering me recently. I thought the brace would help."

Kate chimes in, pointing her fork at the brace. "What happened?"

I roll my eyes. "Let's just say, a dog walker, I am not." I let out a chuckle to hide my embarrassment.

I don't want to think about what happened at the shelter. It only reminds me of the infuriating man, who needs to learn how to take a hint. There's no way I'll allow myself to fall victim to his charms. And pursuing. Or wooing? I shove my wandering thoughts aside. Whatever he's up to, it will never, and I mean *never*, work.

"Hello, earth to Liz."

I quickly blink a few times to bring myself back to reality, realizing I didn't hear a thing either of my friends said in the last few minutes.

"I'm sorry, what?"

Steph chuckles. "Okay, I think you need to go straight to bed when you get home."

I mumble a quick, "Whatever", before returning to my kung pao chicken. I turn my attention to Kate, hoping to divert the conversation away from myself.

"So, Kate. Have any updates with that hunky paramedic of yours?" I punctuate my question with a smirk.

Steph's eyes widen. "What? Which one? Not that it matters. They're all gorgeous."

I roll my eyes.

Steph notices but says nothing. I know she'll question me about it later.

When I turn my attention back to Kate, her face is a shade of pink. She meets my eyes. "Thanks, Liz."

The sarcasm in her voice doesn't go unnoticed.

"Oh, come on. Steph won't say anything."

"No, I know. I'm not worried about that. There isn't anything to update you on. Sam and I are just friends."

I sigh. "Why don't you just tell him how you feel?"

Steph chimes in. "I'm with Liz. He'd be stupid not to reciprocate feelings."

"That's what I said."

Kate sets down her fork before taking a sip of her water. Warily, she sighs. "It's more complicated than that. I have too much going on in my personal life to worry about dating right now."

"I get that. Anything you need to talk about?"

She gives us a half-hearted smile. "Another time." She takes a bite of her food, and then asks, "How are you, by the way? We haven't really spoken since last weekend."

I know exactly what she's referring to. Honestly, I haven't thought about last weekend since I talked to Maylee about it the other day.

"Oh, I'm fine. It could have been much worse."

Kate nods.

Steph has a teasing glint in her eyes. I know exactly what she's thinking. "Speaking of hunky paramedics. That was something. Watching Greyson come to your rescue. Have you talked to him since?"

I roll my eyes as I scoff. "I'm not surprised he did."

Kate laughs. "I'm not either." She turns her attention to Steph. "Are you aware of Greyson pining after Liz for, oh, I don't know, four years now?"

I point my fork at her. "Now I don't feel bad for bringing up Sam."

My words draw a laugh from her.

Steph's jaw drops.

Until this point, I've kept her in the dark with Greyson drama. I'm sure she has some sort of idea, but nothing concrete. She also thinks I don't date because of my job.

Apart from Maylee, none of my friends know the real reason I've built impenetrable walls around my heart. I intend to keep it that way.

Steph's voice pulls me from my thoughts. "Okay, wait. Four years? Liz, how have you stayed away from that gorgeous man?"

I roll my eyes. "It's not that hard. Believe me."

After the words come out of my mouth, I know they're a lie. Kind of.

Steph's eyes practically bug out of her head. "Are you kidding? He's the best looking one." She looks at Kate guiltily. "No offense."

Kate laughs. "None taken."

Steph returns her attention to me. "What did that man ever do to you?"

I sigh. "He's only into one-night stands." I shrug. "That's not my style."

Kate speaks up. "I think you mean *was*. As in past tense. I haven't seen him leave an outing with a woman on his arm in a while."

She's right. I know she is. I've noticed the same thing. Though, I'll never admit it out loud.

"Honestly, that surprises me. From what I've seen, he's a catch. You should give him a chance."

I shake my head at my receptionist. "No way."

"Why not?"

"Can we not talk about this right now?"

"Fine. But I don't see the harm in giving him a chance."

I take a bite of my food instead of saying anything else. Luckily, Steph knows me well enough to drop it. She sees, daily, how demanding—and exhausting—this job is. Usually, I'm left feeling completely wrecked after my longest days. Today was one of those.

A small part of me knows she has a point. But there's a lot she doesn't know.

Even if Greyson's past didn't cause me concern, I'd still be on the fence because of *my* past.

It's a risk I'm not willing to take.

And I probably never will be.

Chapter 8

Liz

Junior Year - Fall Semester

"Let me take you on a trip."

I lift my head from where it's resting on Dylan's chest to meet his eyes.

We've been dating for a couple of months now, and it has been pure bliss. He's respectful, kind, funny, smart, and so many other things.

He takes such good care of me.

It's no surprise he wants to take me on a trip over winter break. Our relationship is moving at lightning speed. It's both exhilarating and terrifying. But every time I question it, he assures me I have nothing to worry about.

"Dylan, we should be worried about finals, not planning a trip. Besides, isn't that kind of serious? Are you sure you want to spend that much time with me so soon?"

I ask my last question with a hint of humor in my voice. If he wants to spend every waking moment with me, he isn't the only one. Being with him feels incredible.

As my head returns to where it was resting, I feel his chest move as he chuckles. He reaches up and starts running his fingers through my hair.

Then he kisses the crown of my head. "Of course I want to spend every waking second with you. You're the life of every party." I giggle. "I'm crazy about you, beautiful. Let's go away the weekend after finals. That way, you'll still be able to go spend the holidays with your family. They won't even have to know."

I sit up to face him, crossing my legs as I do. I hold his gaze, tilting my head. "You really have thought this through, haven't you?"

Let's just say my family doesn't know how serious Dylan and I are. And if my parents ever find out that I'm going away with him, I'll most definitely be in more trouble than I'd like to admit.

He smiles at me. "I have. So, what do you say?"

I give him my best eye roll. It's laced with attitude. "Fine. I'm in."

He's the only person who has ever broken through my stubborn exterior. I hated it at first, but now I kind of love it. It makes me feel lighter in a way.

The look of excitement on his face is undeniable. "Yeah?"

"Yes."

I lean over to kiss his cheek. As I pull away, he pulls me onto his lap.

He smirks. "Where do you think you're going?"

I laugh before he closes the small gap between us. He trails kisses from the bottom of my neck to the shell of my ear. I lean my head back to give him all the access he needs.

While I've enjoyed every aspect of our relationship, I've especially enjoyed the kissing. I can tell Dylan wants more from me, but I'm not ready for that. Besides, I always planned on waiting until marriage.

As Dylan kisses me, I try to keep myself as composed as possible, so I don't give him the wrong idea. It's obvious he's more experienced than I am.

When his lips finally meet mine, I take pleasure in how they feel against my own. Soft. Warm. Inviting.

I wrap my arms around his neck, pulling him as close to me as possible. He makes a noise of satisfaction from deep in his chest, and opens his mouth, inviting me in. I nip his bottom lip before giving him what he wants.

I relish in the way this feels. And in the way that he always tastes like peppermint.

The longer we kiss, the more frenzied it becomes. I've never had this kind of chemistry with anyone in my life. Every time our lips meet, the world around me evaporates. It's just him and me, and the electricity we produce together.

Carefully, Dylan picks me up without breaking our kiss. With my lips still fused to his, I shake with laughter. It doesn't deter him in the slightest.

We kiss until we break apart. When we do, we're both breathing erratically.

I look up at his face, enjoying the heat I see in his eyes. The way his hair is a mess from where I ran my fingers through it. The smile on his face that says more than words ever could.

"I like this look on you, too."

I chuckle. I don't know how he seems to always know what I'm thinking. "What look?"

"The look that says you've been thoroughly kissed."

I shove his shoulder playfully. "Anyway... where are you taking me? I don't believe we made it that far since you kissed me so thoroughly instead."

He winks. "You love it."

I smirk. "I do."

"I'm taking you to my family's lake house on Lake Michigan. I already talked to my parents. They're cool with us using it."

My eyes bug out of my head. "What? Are you serious?"

"Yeah. I think my mom's just excited that I finally have a girlfriend. She acted like a teenage girl when I told her about you."

I laugh. "Well, I can't wait."

"Good. Now where were we?"

* * *

"Knock, knock." I walk into my best friend's room, uninvited. She doesn't mind.

I make myself comfortable on her queen-sized bed. She looks up from her textbook, laughing.

"What?"

"Only you pretend to knock for no other reason than to make your presence known before coming into someone's room without permission."

I pick up a throw pillow and toss it at her. "Whatever. You know me. It's what I do."

She rolls her eyes. "You're right."

I toss my red locks over my shoulder as I say, "Of course I am."

We laugh in unison.

"So... what's up?"

I breathe in deeply and then blow out my breath on one big exhale. I don't know why I'm so nervous right now.

That's a lie.

I know why.

I've just been denying it.

Dylan and I leave for our trip tomorrow. This will be our first time spending the night together. I don't know what to expect or if Dylan expects anything from me. I don't think he does, but I want to make sure I'm ready. The only person I can talk to about this is my best friend.

I watch as Maylee stands up from her chair and sits across from me on her bed. "Talk to me." She reaches for my hand to give it a gentle squeeze.

It's her way of offering me encouragement while also letting me know she's here for me in whatever way I might need her to be.

To ease my nerves, I take another deep breath. I'm not used to feeling unsure of myself. Or letting others see my uncertainty.

I shrug. "I don't know what to expect this weekend with Dylan. Honestly, I'm nervous. Do you think we're moving too fast?"

She considers my words. I know her well enough to know she's putting a lot of thought into her answer before she lets me hear it.

"Do you think you two are moving too fast?"

"I don't know what to think. On the one hand, I think I could be in love with him."

"And on the other?"

Sighing, I shrug. "On the other hand, I have nothing to compare our relationship to. I haven't exactly dated anyone seriously before."

She nods. "I get that. I had nothing to compare my relationship with Ethan to either. But I knew I was in love with him early on. When we're young, I think it's only natural to fall in love quickly. I don't think you should let it make you nervous, though."

"When did you become so wise?"

She chuckles. "I don't know. Love does that to a person. But I can only say that because Ethan and I worked out. Neither of us has any doubts about our future together. Until you and Dylan have those conversations, I would be careful." She clears her throat. "And don't do anything I wouldn't do."

I practically shove her off the bed.

She catches herself.

Barely.

She laughs as I scowl at her. "What? I'm serious! Behave yourself."

"There's no reason to tell me that."

She rolls her eyes. "Liz, I know you. I know what you aren't saying. Personally, I think this weekend is a little fast, but I can't decide for you. Just be careful. Okay?"

"You know I will be." I get up from Maylee's bed and make my way to my room so I can finish packing, but her voice stops me in my tracks.

"Liz?"

I turn around. "Yeah?"

My best friend looks at me, concern clear in her gaze. "Don't let him put any pressure on you."

I nod. "I won't."

* * *

The Sinclair Family Lake House is amazing. Dylan failed to mention that it's the size of a mansion. Maybe I'm exaggerating a little, but seriously... It. Is. Huge.

As soon as we walk in, the first thing I notice are the floor to ceiling windows looking out at the backyard, where there's an amazing view of Lake Michigan.

The living room has high ceilings, and the most beautiful brick fireplace—painted white.

The kitchen is a dream come true. It's a beautifully remodeled kitchen with white cabinets, white and gray marble countertops, and stainless-steel accents and appliances.

There are about a dozen bedrooms. All of which are simply decorated with vibrant accent colors.

Carrying both of our bags, Dylan leads me to what will be our bedroom for the weekend. I can't ignore the butterflies in my stomach. Or the pit of anxiety. I told him I didn't want to stay in the same room, but he assured me everything would be fine. That he wouldn't do anything I didn't want to do. I still feel uneasy about it, but it is what it is. I didn't want to argue.

He places our bags in the giant walk-in closet before walking back over to me.

He grabs both of my hands and rests his forehead against mine. "So, what do you think?"

"This is amazing, Dylan. Thank you for thinking of this."

He tucks a stray strand of hair behind my ear. "Of course." He kisses me gently. "I have our whole day planned for tomorrow, but have nothing specific in mind tonight. Is there anything you want to see or do?"

I see the mischievous glint in Dylan's eyes. He knows I like to be in control. I love that he's letting me call the shots tonight.

I smirk. "Hot tub."

"Yes, ma'am."

It's safe to say I let the stress of finals get the best of me. This hot tub feels amazing.

I spent about half an hour sitting in front of the jets until I couldn't resist not being as close to my boyfriend as possible.

"Goodness, this feels amazing." I let my head fall back against Dylan's chest, practically melting into him. His chest rumbles against me as he laughs.

"I'm glad you're enjoying yourself. Can I get you anything?"

I stand up and turn around to hug his neck. When I pull away to meet his eyes, I'm immediately drawn in by the intensity in his gaze. The tension between the two of us has been off the charts tonight. But neither of us has made a move.

He grabs my waist, placing me on his lap.

He lowers his head until his lips find mine.

We kiss for several minutes until it's too much. I pull back and whisper, "Dyl-".

He cuts off my words by bringing his mouth to mine again in the most passionate kiss I've ever experienced.

Without breaking the kiss, he stands up and walks us inside.

With his muscular arms wrapped around me, I know I'm not going anywhere. I also have a death grip on his neck, so there's that, too.

When we make it to the bedroom, he sets me down on the bed. "You're perfect, Liz."

I can tell what's on his mind by the way he's looking at me.

And I know I need to be careful.

But I also know this is what I want.

I'm sure of it.

I think.

He kisses me gently before asking, "Have you ever—?"

I don't let him finish as I shake my head. "No."

He kisses me tenderly. "Hopefully, I'll be your only."

His words are the only reason I don't protest.

All I know for sure in this moment is that Dylan Sinclair is going to be my undoing.

I'm already coming undone.

Chapter 9

Greyson

Present Day

"Alright Penny, we're heading out. Do you need anything else?"

Today has been a long day, but there's nothing I wouldn't do for Penny. She has become like family to me. Especially since I've been helping her and her granddaughter out a lot more at the shelter.

The guys and I volunteer as much as we can. Penny's husband worked as a paramedic with us before he died, so I know it means a lot to her when we spend so much of our free time here.

Apart from Liz, no one knows the extent of time I spend here. It has become the outlet I never knew I needed. A second home. Something to keep my mind off my personal problems. A way to blow off steam. I need it.

As Walker, Charlie, and I are making our way out the door, Penny's voice stops me in my tracks. "Actually! Greyson, dear! Can you come in here? I just need you for a minute."

I nod my head in the exit's direction. "You guys go ahead. I'll meet you at the bar."

I walk into Penny's office to find her behind her desk, and Margaret tucked into a chair. The sight makes me feel a little uneasy. It looks like we're about to have some sort of formal meeting.

"Is everything alright?" The concern I feel is clear in my tone. I'm sure both women looking at me can see it written on my face, too.

Penny motions to the vacant chair next to Margaret. "Take a seat, dear."

I do as I'm told, waiting for Penny to cut to the chase.

"I have told no one what I'm about to tell you, but I need someone I trust to know."

She clears her throat. That's when I notice tears pooling in her eyes. She removes her glasses to wipe them dry.

When her face is free of tears, she looks me in the eye. "I'm retiring. I'm leaving the shelter to Margaret, but she'll need as much help as she can get around here. I have contractors coming out next month to expand the place. We're adding a training facility at Margaret's request. It's something I've always wanted to do, but when Burt passed, my priorities changed."

Before I think better of it, I blurt out the first thing that comes to mind. "Does Liz know?"

Silently, I reprimand myself. Why was that the first thing that came to mind?

Liz is going to be devastated that Penny's retiring. I feel like it's her who should be in this office right now. Not me. Though I'm glad Penny trusts me enough to share this news with me.

I clear my throat, feeling uncomfortable for letting that question slip. "You don't have to answer that. What I want to know is why are you telling *me*?"

As Penny opens her mouth to speak, Margaret chimes in. "I asked her to. You're a familiar face."

"She's right. I want you to look out for her. Help her as much as you can. Along with the rest of you boys."

Boys. Coming from Penny, it's a term of endearment. She treats us as if we're her flesh and blood.

I nod. "I think we can manage that."

Penny gives me a knowing look. "As far as Liz... she's my most loyal volunteer. I plan on telling her. But she hasn't been here much over the last couple of weeks. That new job of hers keeps her plenty busy. If you see her, let her know we miss her around here."

I smile nonchalantly, hoping my face isn't giving my feelings for Liz away. "I will. Thanks for telling me, Penny."

Standing from my chair, I watch as she makes her way over to me and pulls me into a warm embrace.

* * *

When I walk into the karaoke bar, I spot the guys immediately. They're seated at our regular round corner booth in the back.

The girls have yet to arrive. But I'm looking forward to the extra time with my friends. Our shifts at the station rarely coincide, making it hard to hang out as a group.

I get a round of "What's up?" and "Hey, man" from everyone as I approach the table.

I salute. "Glad to see everyone could make it."

Walker motions to a pitcher of beer and an empty pint glass. "Help yourself." He takes a sip of his own drink. "Is everything okay with Penny?"

"Yeah. She's fine. Just needed a favor."

After sliding into the booth, I make myself comfortable.

Once I'm seated, I nod my head at Matt. "How'd you convince Sarah to stay home for a few hours without you?"

He laughs. "I dropped her off at Walker's. Maylee's keeping her company."

Walker chimes in. "It's good for her. Besides, those girls are two peas in a pod when they're together. I'm sure she barely notices your absence."

Ever since Sarah got pregnant, she hasn't wanted Matt to leave her side. We give him a hard time about it, but it's all in good fun.

Charlie turns his attention to Walker. "You're next man."

Apart from Matt, Charlie is the only one of us who has been married before. He's got a few years on us. He and his ex-wife never had kids. I know he was relieved by that, considering how messy the divorce was. Or is. Maybe that's why his words to Walker come out as more of a warning than anything else. Little does he know how perfect Walker and Maylee are together. They'll have a baby soon. I'm sure of it.

Sam speaks up, too. "Nah. I'm willing to bet it won't happen soon. Being an uncle will keep him satisfied for a while." He directs his attention to me, looking at me like he's about to challenge me to something. "I bet Greyson over here will end up a married man before Walker becomes a dad."

"If Liz ever gives him the time of day."

The table erupts in laughter. I turn my attention to Charlie. "Thanks, man."

To my satisfaction, Matt has my back. "At least Greyson has options if he and Liz don't work out."

Charlie feigns offense. "Ouch." He pats Sam on the back. "At least I'm not alone. Right, man?" Sam raises his glass, downing the rest of his beer. "Cheers to that."

When he sets the glass down, I notice his eyes find someone across the bar. I know a desperate look when I see one.

Out of the corner of my eye, I see Kate walking over to our table. "I don't know, fellas. It looks like Charlie may be the last man standing."

Sam plays it cool. "Stop, man. She's gorgeous."

"You guys are the worst." We chuckle at Charlie's remark.

Kate approaches the table as our laughter dies down. "Hey guys, sorry I'm early. Hope I'm not interrupting anything." She looks between all of us suspiciously. "Am I interrupting anything?"

Sam waves a hand at her, feigning nonchalance. "Nah, you're good."

She raises an eyebrow in question. "You sure?"

"Yeah."

As she slides into the booth, she asks, "Are any of the girls here yet?"

Walker shakes his head, assuring her he'll reach out to Maylee, telling her to head over with Sarah. Kate can be shy around us without her friends.

Meanwhile, my mind wanders to Steph and Liz. Mostly Liz. I hope she can make it tonight.

About an hour after Maylee and Sarah arrive, Steph arrives too.

To my dismay, Liz is nowhere in sight. I ignore the disappointment I feel. It catches me off guard, considering it's not something I'm used to feeling.

Everything about Liz drives me crazy. Her wild crimson hair. Those emerald eyes. The way she lights up every room she walks into. And the feelings she ignites in me. Even her absence is driving me crazy. The dynamic is different when she isn't around. Not in a bad way. Just different.

"Hello. Earth to Greyson."

I snap out of my oblivion at the sound of Steph's voice. Maylee's chuckling next to her.

I smile sheepishly at the women across from me.

Maylee gives me a look of concern. "Are you okay, Greyson?"

I appreciate her genuine interest in my wellbeing. I certainly don't feel like I deserve it.

Let's just say I was a jerk to her when Walker started bringing her around more. I never did the whole dating thing, so I didn't understand why he spent so much time with her when they first met. I get it now. She's good for him and vice versa. I'm happy for them. A little envious if I'm being honest.

I clear my throat before taking a sip of my third beer. I need to slow down. But my mind has been some place else tonight.

"Yeah. Sorry. Is Liz coming tonight?"

Steph gives me a look I can't quite interpret. "No. She's preparing for an important case. I tried to get her to come, but she insisted she needs to be at the office all night."

"All night?"

"What's all night?" Walker asks before placing a kiss on his wife's temple. He must have heard us even though he was talking to his sister.

I drum my fingers on the table, getting everyone else's attention. "I think I'm gonna head out."

"What? Already, man?"

I make eye contact with Sam. "Yeah." I look at everyone else until my eyes land on Steph. "Has she had dinner yet?"

She scoffs. "No way. The court date is next week. She won't stop her preparation for anything."

She's right. Liz is stubborn. It's how I know she's a phenomenal lawyer. Her clients are lucky to be represented by her.

I look between my best friend and his wife. "I'm gonna take her dinner." Maylee offers me a knowing smile, so I direct my attention to her. "Any suggestions?"

"Pizza."

I nod.

"And Greyson."

"Yeah?"

"Prepare for a fight. The pizza should soften her up, though. She's a big fan of pepperoni and jalapeño."

"Go get your girl, man." I return Walker's fist bump as I get up from the table.

Steph is nice enough to follow me to the office to let me up with the condition that Liz doesn't find out she had anything to do with this.

She offers me a quick, "Good luck" after unlocking the door to the building.

I'm riding up to Liz's office in the elevator, pizza in tow, hoping I don't make a complete fool out of myself.

Liz is stubborn, but I have every intention of getting through to her.

Worst-case scenario: she'll put up a fight and make me leave.

Best-case scenario: I'll convince her to let me stay and get to eat with her. If I'm lucky, she may even have a conversation with me.

The elevator doors open, and I'm greeted by a slightly musty smell. The air must shut off at some point because there's definitely no airflow in here right now. I don't like the thought of Liz working here in this condition. Alone. It doesn't sit well with me.

She still doesn't notice I'm here as I approach her closed office door.

I pass Steph's desk on my right, and that's when I hear a fan whirring. Now I know why she didn't hear the high-pitched ding of the elevator.

When I make it to the door, I try the handle, but it's locked. I rap my knuckles on the door a couple times, holding my breath as I wait for her to open it.

As Liz opens the door, I hear her say, "Steph, I told you—" She stops mid-sentence when she sees it's me.

"Oh. I thought... never mind." She crosses her arms over her chest. "What are you doing here, Greyson?"

I release the breath I was holding in. There are a few ways I can play this. I go with my gut.

"Karaoke isn't the same without you." I hold up the pizza box. "I also heard about the case and figured you might need this."

I'm not positive, but I think I see Liz bite back a smile. Though, it probably has more to do with the pizza than me.

"If I didn't already know who goes to karaoke, that little line you used on me would have surprised me."

I chuckle. "So, then you know I'm being honest. It really isn't the same without you."

She pops out her hip. "So I've heard."

I raise my brow.

Liz rolls her eyes. "Steph."

I nod my head, waiting for her to invite me into her office to eat.

It's at this moment, I notice her disheveled appearance.

Don't get me wrong. She still looks as gorgeous as she always does, but it's obvious she has been running her fingers through her hair. Either out of stress or frustration. Maybe a mixture of the two.

Her pink blouse is untucked from her dress pants. There's a suit jacket abandoned on the back of her chair. And she has on a pair of house shoes. This lawyer thing suits her. It's the best combination of sweet and sassy.

Without intending to, I imagine what it would be like if she came home to me after work every day looking like this. What would it feel like if I got to run my fingers through her wavy crimson hair? Make her feel good.

I'd be sure to give her a proper massage first, enjoying every inch of bare skin under my fingers. She'd make a noise of appreciation at my handiwork. The thought has me holding back a groan. So I stop myself from imagining anything else before my own thoughts knock me on my butt. I don't need to give Liz a reason to wonder about what's wrong with me. She probably already does that when I'm not even around.

My eyes find hers. "Well, care to let me in so we can enjoy this pizza together?"

Chapter 10

Liz

Present Day

I can't believe I'm even considering letting Greyson walk into my office. But I'm tired. And hungry. Starving, actually.

His big brown eyes are pleading with me. And I've exceeded my limit for the night.

To top it all off, he looks insanely attractive in his dark-wash jeans and sky-blue T-shirt, which hugs his biceps perfectly. Plus, he brought pizza. What kind of girl would I be if I said no to pizza?

I compose myself, hoping it isn't obvious that I may have been ogling his muscles just a little.

I return my eyes to his face, secretly searching for the gold flecks surrounding his irises.

What am I doing?

I mentally chastise myself for getting distracted by this man. All I need to be concerned about is what kind of pizza he's currently holding.

Keeping my arms crossed, I square my shoulders and raise a brow. "What kind?"

Greyson stares at me as his face takes on a smug expression. Like he knows I'm not about to deny him entry into my office. "Pepperoni and jalapeño."

Of course.

Whichever one of my friends told him my favorite toppings is in some serious trouble.

The smug expression on his face isn't my favorite. It confirms what I already know: While Greyson may not be the man he used to be; he is still just as cocky. Arrogant even. If he thinks he can win me over, he needs to think again.

I step aside, making enough room for him to enter with the giant pizza box in his hands.

He confidently sets it on the small table in my office and then pulls out a few packets of peppers and parmesan cheese. He even brought paper plates and napkins. I'm impressed. He thought of everything.

Reluctantly, I join him at the table, digging right in. We eat in silence for a few minutes. Silence that I'm thankful for. Before getting a few bites into my stomach, I was way too hungry to hold any sort of conversation. Not that I want to.

My thoughts come a moment too soon because the sound of Greyson's deep voice drowns out the silence. "How's the case coming?"

I set down the slice of pizza I was about to take a bite of. "You really want to hear about the case?"

"Is it important to you?"

"Of course."

"Then, yes. I want to hear about it."

His answer surprises me. It means a lot that he cares enough to ask about this case.

"I can't disclose anything since everything I discuss with my clients is confidential. But what I can tell you is this case means a lot to me. It's the most difficult one I've had since starting this job."

He looks at me with a question in his eyes. I know what he's thinking.

"It's a custody case. Anytime children are involved, I feel a lot more pressure to win."

"Why do you feel so much more pressure?"

I shrug. "In this specific case, things can get complicated. I can prepare as much as possible, collect every piece of evidence, gather all the information to be used against the other party, but there's always a possibility it still won't be enough to ensure victory. I can only hope what I have is enough."

"And what's victory?"

"Full custody for my client."

"How do you know he or she deserves it?"

I take a moment to think. But not about his question.

I realize how much I'm enjoying this back and forth with him. No one, not even Steph, takes this much interest in what I do for a living. It may be Greyson I'm talking to, but I take this job seriously enough to be honest with him.

"It's hard to put into words. I have good relationships with all my clients, but there are a few who I just have these gut feelings about. Or instincts. I don't know. Call them what you want. Being a lawyer, it's only natural to want to win every case. With my clients... I *need* to win each case. Not for myself. For them. This is one of those cases I need to win."

I take a deep breath as I think of Mr. Seymour's daughter.

My heart aches. For her, mostly.

I want her to end up with the parent who's going to give her the best life. A life full of love, and a multitude of opportunities. I've done enough research to know who's more equipped to care for her. But going up against a biological mother who claims she has cleaned up her life is never easy.

"There's a lot on the line."

While I was speaking, Greyson leaned a little closer to me. I don't think he meant for it to happen, though. And I'm not sure how I missed it.

It's clear he's genuinely invested in everything I just shared. But there's something else in his expression as well. Something I can't quite place.

We sit in silence. It's deafening. Making me all too aware of the tension that fills the air. Tension that seems to find us whenever we're alone together.

Greyson clears his throat. I can tell he's searching for what to say. So, I give him time to find words, enjoying his lack thereof.

Finally, he says, "Wow, Liz. That's... I don't even know. You're legit. I know you can win."

I challenge him. "How could you possibly know that?"

He inches just a little closer to me. "Apart from all the preparation you've done, call it a gut feeling I have about you."

"Mhm."

He smirks. Then, slowly, it turns into a smile. And that's when I notice his dimples.

I didn't even know he had dimples.

Of course, just when I thought he couldn't get any more attractive, I find another part of him to like.

It's infuriating.

Ugh.

Time to go.

I need to get him out of my office so I can pack up.

As I'm about to open my mouth and kindly ask Greyson to leave, he speaks up. "I have one more question for you."

I raise an eyebrow. "Yeah? What's that?"

I hold my breath as he just about closes the distance between our faces. If I didn't already know his intentions, I would think he's about to kiss me. At least he's smart enough not to try anything.

"What are your gut feelings about me, Liz?"

Oh, goodness.

Is it hot in here?

How do I even answer that question?

I don't know how I feel about him.

Better yet, I don't *let* myself feel anything for him.

Or anyone.

Before he picks up on my train of thought, I steel myself. "I don't know that I have any gut feelings about you, Greyson."

It's the best answer I could come up with.

He takes it in stride.

A ghost of a smirk appears on his face. "Yet."

For the first time since we met, I think I might actually agree with him. The thought is terrifying. That's how I know it's time to end this exchange.

I reel myself back in, refusing to get caught up in a banter that feels way too familiar.

Quickly, I rise from my chair, hoping it isn't obvious how uncomfortable I feel.

"I should probably pack up and head home." I add a closed mouthed smile at the end of my sentence.

Greyson stands as well and starts clearing the table. "Thanks for letting me crash your night."

I don't look up from packing my belongings. "Yeah."

"Seriously Liz. Thank you. I had fun."

The sincerity in his tone surprises me.

When I think about it, I had fun too.

The ease of conversation with Greyson was exactly what I needed after burying myself in my work. He doesn't need to know that, though.

I meet his gaze. "Just don't make a habit of it, okay?"

"No promises."

I deliberately roll my eyes for him to see. He says nothing else as we leave my office and head our separate ways.

* * *

Today is the day.

This custody case has consumed my thoughts all day, every day, for months.

As I do a once-over of myself in the mirror, I take a deep breath. It does nothing to release the anxiety in my chest.

It's hard to describe everything I feel before walking into a courtroom. A lot goes on in my head, but none of it matters. I do what I do for my clients. And for their loved ones. They're what matters most.

The outcome of this case will affect multiple lives for years down the road. I try to keep my emotions out of it. But I can't lie to myself by believing I'm not most worried about Mr. Seymour's daughter. She has no say in where she ends up when this is all said and done. Which is why I will fight as hard as I can for the best outcome.

Quickly, I gather my things before making my trek to the courtroom.

As I'm about to reach my destination, my cell vibrates in my bag. I pull it out to turn it off, but not before I see Greyson's name on the screen.

I contemplate whether to read his message. Against my better judgment, I tap his name to open his text.

Greyson: Good luck today, Liz. ;)

I smile down at the words on my screen but decide not to reply.

Now is not the time to figure out my feelings for the most infuriating man I've ever met.

Instead, I turn off my phone, muttering, "here goes nothing", under my breath.

Chapter 11

Liz

Present Day

Walking into my office the morning after a seemingly enormous case is indescribable.

While there's still work to be done, I have the privilege of getting to shake off the stress, anxiety, and weight of it all.

It's hard to describe how incredibly exhausted I am mentally, emotionally, and physically.

But we did it.

We won.

Mr. Seymour has full custody of his daughter.

Every little detail mattered until the very end.

When the elevator doors open, I'm immediately greeted by an overly enthusiastic Steph.

I've barely stepped out of the elevator by the time she has me pulled into a hug. "I know I should probably act way more professional right now, but I'm so proud of you! You did it!" She pulls back, clears her throat, and reaches out to shake my hand. "Well done, Ms. Carter."

I laugh. "You are too much, Steph. And if it's any consolation, I prefer the hug over the stiff handshake."

She joins in my laughter. "So, I hope you don't mind, but I texted the girls to see if anyone is available to celebrate tonight. Matt and Walker both work so Sarah and Maylee were already planning on hanging out. Kate's free, too. What do you think?"

I offer her one of my signature smirks. "You know me. A night out is just what I need."

"Yay! I'll text our group chat to let everyone know."

I say, "Sounds good", before walking into my office.

What I see when I make it through the door stops me in my tracks.

The most beautiful floral arrangement I've ever seen sits on top of my desk.

The colors are vibrant: red, different shades of pink, and orange, all mixed, making a beautiful bouquet. There are roses, lilies, and daffodils, with baby's-breath mixed in sporadically.

"Steph!"

"Yeah?"

I turn around to look at her, pointing over my shoulder at the arrangement in my office.

She's grinning at me like the Cheshire Cat.

"Did you do this?"

She says nothing, instead keeping that ridiculous grin on her face.

I narrow my eyes on her. "Steph."

Without letting her grin diminish, she shakes her head 'no'.

I stay silent, hoping she picks up on the fact that I'm waiting for her to give me more information.

I watch her smile falter before she squeaks out, "Please, don't be mad at me!"

"What? Why would I..." I let my words trail off, realization hitting me. "Greyson."

"Yeah." She drags out the word. "He may have heard about the outcome of yesterday through the grapevine. And I may have helped him out with the flower delivery."

I nod. "I see."

I don't give her a chance to say anything else as I step back into my office, closing the door behind me. It isn't because I'm mad at her, even though she probably texted everyone the minute I shared the news with her, meaning she is the grapevine. So technically, it is her fault Greyson knows about the outcome of the case. I just can't believe he did this. It was so thoughtful and sweet. It means the world to me after he sat in this very office, listening to me talk about the case while we ate my favorite pizza together. Pizza that he bought. Delivered. And ate with me because he knew I hadn't eaten dinner.

Rubbing my temples, I let out a sigh as I stare up at the ceiling.

I know what all of this means coming from him.

He has made his feelings, and intentions, incredibly clear.

I just don't know what it means for *me*.

All I know is I have a lot to think about.

* * *

For the first time in weeks, I make it home in time to have a quick dinner before meeting the girls at one of our favorite spots on the river walk in Chicago.

I'm so thankful for a night out. It has been a while since I've been able to take part in a proper 'GNO'.

As I walk into the restaurant, I spot Kate at one of the high top tables near the bar.

Feeling on top of the world in my white crop top, high-waisted skinny jeans, and black pumps, I strut over to her. "Hey!"

She laughs as she throws her arms around my neck. "Congrats on a job well done. So proud of you."

"Thank you. I appreciate that."

I look over her shoulder, spotting Steph walking out of the restroom. "Hey girl, hey! Glad the party's finally here."

I wink. "You got that right."

The three of us put in our orders at the bar, and then get comfortable chatting away while we wait for Maylee and Sarah to arrive.

"Liz!" I practically jump into my best friend's embrace as soon as I hear her voice.

"MayMay! I've missed you."

She gives me a squeeze before letting me go. "I've missed you, too."

After I give Sarah a quick hug as well, all of us chat away about everything under the sun.

It feels good to catch up with everyone.

It isn't until I'm a few drinks in when I consider letting loose.

And I don't mean in a practical sense like dancing. *That* is a practical way to let loose.

Instead, I let loose in the most impractical way possible.

My mouth moves faster than my brain can tell it to stop. "Girls?"

I quickly throw the rest of my drink back, slamming it down on the table when I finish. The empty glass taunts me as I stare at it. Then the panic sets in. And when I look up from my glass, four sets of eyes are staring back at me. I immediately regret ever getting their attention, but I have to get this off my chest.

Speaking as quickly as humanly possible, I blurt out, "IthinkI'mattractedtoGreyson!"

I get, "What?" thrown my way by each of them.

I point my finger at no one in particular, waving it around. "No. Don't do that. I know you heard me. Don't make me say it again."

"I can confidently say none of us actually understood the gibberish that just came out of your mouth." Kate's remark has everyone, apart from myself, laughing.

Maylee agrees. "Yeah, Liz. Could you try saying that again? Maybe breathe in between words this time."

I narrow my eyes in her direction, knowing Maylee well enough to know she has a pretty good idea of what I said.

Desperate to avoid repeating myself, I shift my attention to Sarah. "Please tell me you understood what I said. And *please* share it with the group, so I don't have to say it again."

Sarah throws a look my way that I'm pretty sure she has only ever given her brother. "I don't know. I think you may need to say it again."

I let out an exasperated sigh. "Fine." I groan. "I. Think. I'm. Attracted. To. Your. Brother's. Best. Friend."

My eyes scan the faces of each of my friends.

Steph looks like the Cheshire Cat for the second time today.

Maylee's holding back her smile by biting her lip—her signature move.

Kate looks dumbfounded.

And Sarah looks like she's struggling to hold in her laughter. Or she needs to pee because of her pregnancy. But what do I know?

"Better?"

Steph's the first to say something. "I think we need to hear you say his name. For all we know, you could be talking about Sam." She winks at Kate.

Kate chimes in. "Or Charlie."

Maylee chuckles. "Liz, come on. Is it really that difficult for you to admit?"

I roll my eyes. "Out loud? Yes. It is."

My best friend looks at me with sincerity in her eyes. "In all seriousness, all of us have your back. Admitting it doesn't mean you have to do anything about it if you don't want to."

"Thanks."

Steph adds, "Yeah. You have our support. But I will say I'm totally shipping you and—" She stops herself before uttering his name, waiting for me to say it instead.

I sigh. "Greyson. I'm attracted to Greyson."

I watch as my friends all simultaneously shout, "Finally!"

It's followed by laughter.

Well, except from me.

Instead, I roll my eyes to hide my smile.

Apart from Steph, they've all witnessed Greyson's endless pursuit of me. I just didn't know all of them support it.

It used to get on my last nerve—all his efforts to get my attention. Now, I don't mind it so much. I might even enjoy it a little.

The sound of Steph's voice pulls me from my thoughts. "So, are you gonna do anything about it?"

I groan before resting my head in my hands.

After a few seconds, I look up at my friends. "I don't know. I haven't thought about it much. Honestly, though, probably not." Time for a subject change. Clapping my hands together, I say, "But enough boy talk. I need another drink before I hit the dance floor."

Thankfully, my effort to divert their attention is enough. We place an order for another round of drinks before dancing the rest of the night away.

It's the most fun I've had in a while.

* * *

Thoughts of Greyson have lingered all week. No matter what I do, I can't shake them.

His chivalry is getting the best of me—the very best of me.

He was so much easier to resist when he'd spend every weekend with a different woman. I knew I could never be with someone like that.

But now?

He's everything I could ever ask for in a man.

Not only is he the tall, dark, and handsome type that I prefer. But he's also kind. Caring. Thoughtful. Compassionate. The list goes on.

He has my walls—the walls I've worked so hard to build around my heart—crumbling one by one.

It's uncomfortable.

Yet here I am.

I thought long and hard about this decision. While it may be a little over the top, I need to talk to him in person. Which is why I'm currently on my way to his house.

The only reason I know how to get there is because of the other night. The other night when he oh so kindly took care of me after standing up for me at the bar.

I had Maylee double check his schedule with Walker, so I know he's home this weekend.

I pull into his driveway, feeling nervous. Honestly, I'm all out of sorts. So, I take a few minutes to find my composure while admiring his house.

It's a simple one-story, outfitted with gray brick, and white shuttered windows. He has good taste. I mean, he has a thing for me after all. I chuckle to myself at the thought, clearly feeling more confident than I did just moments ago.

I got this.

Walking up to the porch, I take a deep breath, and then ring the doorbell.

As I wait, I hear him approach, but when the door opens, it isn't Greyson.

Instead, I'm greeted by a beautiful blonde woman who looks to be about my age.

I do the best I can to hide my surprise.

She smiles. "Hi! Can I help you?"

Before responding, I take a moment to look her over.

She's about four inches taller than me, with toned muscles. Her skin is tan, unlike mine. And her smile is bright and cheery. The exact opposite of how I feel right now.

I square my shoulders and muster as much confidence as I can.

This woman will not intimidate me. Even though she more than likely spent the night with the man who I thought had changed.

What was I thinking?

I should have known.

Maybe a small part of me did. Maybe I just didn't want to admit it to myself. Or maybe Greyson was tired of waiting for me to come around. This just goes to show some people are incapable of change. Especially when they don't get what they want.

Whatever.

"Is Greyson here?"

"He's in the shower. Do you want to come in and wait?"

I'm taken aback by her offer.

Clearly this was a casual, no strings attached hookup. Or maybe she's just a friend. But if that were the case, she probably would have shown her face at some point.

"Nope." I pop the 'p' a little too aggressively. Not like I care, though.

With more speed than I knew I was capable of; I turn around and walk to my car.

The woman yells, telling me to wait. But I don't acknowledge her as I slam my door and peel out of the driveway.

I'm pretty sure this situation wouldn't have bothered me a week ago.

But now?

I'm angry, hurt, and confused.

A small part of me hopes I'm wrong. Greyson's track record doesn't do him any favors, though. So, I doubt that's the case. I guess he gave up, since I wasn't allowing him to make any progress with me.

As I'm driving home, my phone rings through the Bluetooth in my car.

I don't even bother to see who it is before ignoring the call.

Not thirty seconds later, it rings again.

This time, I check the caller ID to see Greyson's name flash across my screen. But I ignore the call once again, turn off my cell phone, and toss it into my purse.

He doesn't need to explain himself.

And honestly, I don't want to hear it.

Chapter 12

Greyson

Present Day

When I emerge from my bedroom, I find Brie sitting comfortably on my couch in the living room.

She sure loves to show up unannounced.

And answer my door, apparently.

"Who was at the door?"

She shrugs her shoulders. "I don't know. She was cute, though."

Cute? What the... that's weird.

"She?"

I don't know who could have possibly showed up at my house this morning. Having just moved in a few months ago, few people know where I live.

I rack my brain for who it could have been, quickly realizing that Maylee and Liz are the only female friends who have ever seen the place. It would be weird for either of them to show up here. Especially unannounced.

"What did she look like?"

Brie chuckles. I ignore it while patiently waiting for her to give me more information.

"She was short with red hair."

Shoot.

Liz.

"Did she say why she was here? Did you tell her who you were?"

"Okay. Wow." Brie holds her hands up in defense. "Chill. She asked if you were here. I told her you were in the shower and asked if she wanted to wait for you, but she left."

"Please tell me you told her who you were."

"I didn't get that far. She kind of left in a hurry."

I throw my head back in frustration, knowing exactly what Liz is thinking right now.

Pulling my phone out of my pocket, I frantically dial her number. It rings a few times before she puts me through to voicemail. I try once more, but sure enough, I get her voicemail again.

Knowing she's too stubborn—and probably too angry—to answer her phone, my only choice is to go after her.

There's no way I'll let a simple misunderstanding ruin all the progress I've made with her. Slow progress. But with her, progress is progress.

Without a second thought, I stride into the kitchen, hurriedly grabbing my wallet and keys.

Brie yells after me. "Greyson! Where are you going? We're supposed to meet your mom in an hour. You can't keep avoiding her!"

"Brie, I've told you a million times... I'm not avoiding my mom. I'm..." I let my words trail off, running a hand through my hair, not wanting to have the same argument we always do. "Look, I'll call her to let her know I can't make it."

She follows me to my truck.

I watch as she crosses her arms over her chest. Such an attitude.

Disappointed, she shakes her head. "Fine, but please go see her soon. I know she invited you to dinner tomorrow without the rest of us. She wants to talk about everything."

"I know. I gotta go. Lock up when you leave, alright?"

She gives me a tight-lipped smile, dipping her chin once in silent agreement.

As soon as I get in my truck, I head toward Liz's apartment. When I'm out of my neighborhood, I call my mom to make sure she knows I'm not standing her up purposefully.

"Hey, honey. It's about time I heard from you."

I ignore the guilty feeling in the pit of my stomach. "Hey, Mom. I know. I'm sorry. Look, I can't make brunch today. I, uh,"—I hesitate, not knowing how much I should share—"I have to take care of something important."

She sighs. And now I've got three disappointed women on my hands. One of which I'll be fixing things with today.

"I know you don't approve of my decision, but we need to talk about it. He wants to meet you, honey. He's nothing like your father."

I know she's right. But I don't have the mental capacity to think about anything other than Liz.

Instead, I decide to accept the dinner invitation. Even though it's the last thing I want to do.

"I'll be at dinner tomorrow, alright? I promise."

"Thank you, honey. I love you."

"I love you too, Mom."

* * *

When Liz opens the door to her apartment, the look on her face tells me everything I need to know.

She's livid.

"What are you doing here, Greyson?"

Ouch. Her defenses are up.

I haven't heard her talk to me like that in quite a while. And I don't like it. Not one bit.

This conversation is about to be uncomfortable.

I have to tell her who Brie is. And if I do that, then I'm going to have to give her the full story. It's not like I have another choice.

Liz is worth it, though.

"Can I come in? I need to talk to you."

She crosses her arms over her chest. A defense mechanism. I'm about to get an earful from her. "There's nothing to talk about."

"Yes. There is. I need to explain who answered my door this morning. And you need to explain what you were doing at my house." Smirking, I add, "I'm curious."

Liz rolls her eyes, and for a split second, it looks like she's going to shut the door in my face. But I'm surprised when, instead, she opens it wider, gesturing for me to come in.

I let out a deep sigh of relief. The wooing I've been doing has achieved more than I thought.

I take a seat on the chair next to her couch, giving her space.

Leaning forward, I place my elbows on my knees.

I take a deep breath as I prepare to fill Liz in on my family situation.

"I'm waiting."

Infuriating.

This woman is infuriating.

But again, she's worth it.

So, here goes nothing. "The blonde girl who answered my door isn't who you probably think she is."

Liz gives me a pointed look. "Is that so?"

"Yes, Liz." I meet her eyes, hoping she'll hear me out. Hoping that armor of hers cracks. Just the slightest. "I want to make it clear to you I have no intention of being with a woman unless that woman is you. I was hoping you had figured that out by now, but I'm willing to acknowledge my past doesn't do me any favors. Sorry about that, by the way. Truly, I am."

My confession doesn't seem to surprise her. If anything, she looks relieved. But because she's the most stubborn woman on earth, she doesn't admit that to me. What she doesn't realize is how good I am at reading her.

"Okay. Then who is she?"

I blow out a ragged breath. "She's my step-sister, Brie."

Her face transforms into an expression of shock, eyebrows nearly reaching her hairline. Her green eyes widen. And her mouth drops open to form an 'o'. She's adorable. I have to hold back the chuckle threatening to come out.

"You... you have a step-sister? I could have sworn you were an only child."

"I was." I run a hand through my hair.

If I want to get anywhere with Liz, I need to give her more details. Honestly, she's the only person I want to tell.

"I also have two step-brothers."

Her head falls forward in disbelief. "What? Since when?"

"My mom, she uh... she ran off and got remarried a few months ago. I didn't really know how to handle it, since she hadn't been dating the guy for very long. Which is why no one knows." I hesitate before dipping my chin. "Except you."

"Oh, my goodness, Greyson. I didn't even know your mom was single. I'm sorry. That's not the best way to find out you aren't an only child anymore."

Unable to help myself, I laugh at her remark. She couldn't be more right. I love the way she worded it. "Yeah. Tell me about it."

"What about your dad?"

My father.

He's a topic for another day.

I want to tell Liz everything about myself. But not before I get a little farther with her.

Instead of answering her question, I take the conversation in a completely different direction.

A direction I am way more interested in.

"I'd rather discuss the reason you showed up at my house this morning."

A look passes over her features that I can't quite place. I sit, patiently waiting for her to answer.

She squares her shoulders. It's something she does a lot. I see her composure and confidence every time she does it. But I can't always tell whether that's how she truly feels. Sure of herself.

"I went over there to thank you for the flowers last week."

I lean back in my chair. "You could have just texted me."

Without hesitating, she says, "I know, I know. I went over there to thank you. But there's also something I want to talk to you about."

A million thoughts cross my mind. My heart beats frantically in my chest.

It isn't like Liz to want to talk to me about anything. I'm always the one asking her questions. Or pushing her to let me in. I'm eager—and maybe anxious—to hear what it is she has to say. For her to show up at my house means it must be a pretty big deal.

She takes a deep breath. "What you said earlier about making your intentions clear... you have. It's become obvious how you feel about me."

I nod. "Okay."

"I came over to be honest with you about how I feel."

"How you feel. Got it. About what?"

"I'm confused."

Her words are like a punch to the gut. Confused. Not what I was hoping for. I say nothing, willing her to say more. To be more specific.

"Don't look so disappointed." Her words bring me back to the moment.

I hadn't realized I was avoiding making eye contact with her. When I finally meet her gaze, she's smirking.

"This is really hard for me to admit to you." She raises an eyebrow. "Don't make me regret it."

"I won't."

"I'm attracted to you, Greyson. But here's the thing... I'm not interested in a relationship. I'm willing to hang out here and there. To see where things go." She closes her eyes, and when she opens them again, she breathes out, "As friends." Then she adds, "I can't promise I'll ever be able to give you more than that."

Well.

That's confusing.

But I'm willing to do anything for the woman looking back at me right now.

If she wants to be friends, then I'll be the best friend she's ever had, while holding on to the hope that our mutual attraction for each other will grow into something more. It's all I have to hang onto at this point.

"Thanks for telling me. And I know it's difficult for you to do, but can you tell me if your feelings ever change?"

She smiles. It's full of warmth. A warmth that rivals her fiery personality. It's the first time I've ever gotten such a bright smile from her.

"I'm still trying to figure my feelings out. But yes. I can do that."

That's all I can ask for.

It'll have to be enough.

Not sure what's left to say, I stand up to leave.

Liz stops me, though. "Wait. I just told you I want to be your friend and now you're leaving?"

She gives me her signature smirk again, making me laugh.

"Do you want me to stay?"

She regards me thoughtfully. "Have you met your step-dad?"

I guess her question is my answer.

I sit back down, sighing as I relax into the chair. "No. I will tomorrow, though. I've been avoiding it. That's why Brie was over. She's convinced I'm angry with my mom. I don't have the heart to tell her it has more to do with her parental figure than mine."

Liz frowns. "I'm sorry. Is there anything I can do? I have a lot of knowledge where families are concerned." She winks, and it makes my heart soar.

Liz hasn't ever acted like this around me before.

I could definitely get used to it.

"I'll let you know if I need anything. I just need to get through dinner tomorrow."

She stands up from the couch and makes her way into the kitchen. I watch her walk away, enjoying the view.

The woman is gorgeous.

Every single part of her.

Every curve.

Her back is to me when she speaks again. "Would it help if you had some moral support?"

"What do you mean?"

She fills two glasses with water, handing me one when she gets back into the living room.

After she takes a sip, she makes herself comfortable on the couch. "I'll come with you. As your friend." She shrugs, like her offer is no big deal. Like we're old friends. "And as a thank you..." She lets her words trail off, looking at me nervously.

"As a thank you."

It wasn't a question, but she nods, anyway.

I smirk. "For the flowers?"

She laughs.

The sound is music to my ears.

"For the flowers."

Smiling like a lovesick fool, I keep my gaze fixed on her face. And for the first time since I met Liz Carter, I witness her blush.

It starts at the base of her neck and travels all the way up her face until her cheeks are a rosy pink. It's beautiful. Something I hope I get to witness again.

Repeatedly.

Because now that she's finally letting me in, I'll do whatever it takes to keep her close.

Because the beautiful woman staring back at me is worth fighting for.

And I plan on fighting hard for her.

Chapter 13

Greyson

Present Day

Hanging out at Liz's apartment yesterday was the highlight of my week.

After she agreed to be my moral support at dinner with my mom and her new husband, we fell into a comfortable conversation.

While I know Liz well, there's a lot more to her than I thought.

Her passion for life is inspiring. She makes me feel alive, and truthfully, I haven't felt that way in a long time.

I should have worked harder to build a friendship with her first, instead of treating her like she's disposable. I can't believe I resorted to treating women the way I did, because I was afraid that I'd end up like my father. The thought makes me grimace.

Honestly, I didn't think I'd ever be able to commit. That's why I never even tried. While I was always up front about my intentions with the many women I brought home, it doesn't make my blatant disrespect for any of them okay. I see that now.

The sound of the doorbell ringing pulls me from my thoughts. It must be Liz. I tried to convince her to let me pick her up for dinner tonight, but she said it would feel too much like a date. She wanted to meet me at my mom's house. But somehow, I convinced her to meet me at mine instead.

I'll take advantage of all the time she's willing to give me.

I'm greeted with her larger-than-life smile when I open the door.

Though I want to, I resist the urge to check her out. Knowing her, she would call me out on it. I'm willing to respect her friendship boundaries.

For now.

"Hey! Are you ready?"

I shut the door behind me. "Yeah. Let's get this over with."

As we make our way to my truck, she sighs. "Greyson, try to keep an open mind."

"Yeah, yeah."

She rolls her eyes, but says nothing.

We spend the drive over to my mom's house in companionable silence, apart from Liz singing along to the music playing through the speakers.

When we pull up to my childhood home, I turn my attention to Liz, letting the truck idle in front of the house.

"Thanks for doing this for me. I owe you."

"You definitely don't owe me anything, but you're welcome."

Without waiting for me, she gets out of the truck and heads to the front door. She throws a smirk over her shoulder. "You coming or what?"

The action draws a laugh from me as I jump out of my truck.

When I reach her side, she surprises me by grabbing my hand to squeeze it once. I appreciate the gesture for what it is. She knows how uncomfortable I'm feeling.

My mom answers the door with a bright smile on her face. "Greyson, honey! I've missed you."

I watch as her eyes take in the beautiful redhead standing next to me.

I may have failed to mention that I was bringing a friend.

I didn't want to risk my mom telling me it wasn't a good idea.

An expression passes over my mom's features that I can't quite place. I think nothing of it as I step through the threshold and give her a hug. "Hey, Mom. I've missed you, too."

I take a step back to introduce Liz. "This is Liz. A friend of mine."

Liz offers my mom an adoring smile as she takes a step forward to shake her hand. "Hi. It's nice to meet you."

My mom smiles at her kindly. "You, too." She gestures into the living room. "Come meet Phil."

I take in the man standing across from me and relax when I see he looks nothing like my father.

Hopefully, he isn't anything like him either.

Phil extends his hand. "Greyson. I've heard a lot about you. It's nice to meet you."

I return his handshake. "You as well, sir."

"You don't need to call me that. Phil is fine." He turns his attention to Liz. "And this must be your girlfriend."

Liz coughs to cover her laugh.

I clear my throat. "She's just a friend."

My mom pipes up. "Well, that's too bad. She's beautiful."

I should have seen this coming.

All my life, my mom has wanted me to find a nice girl to settle down with. I know it disappointed her when I eventually told her I didn't want to risk a failed marriage after witnessing what happened between her and my father.

The only person I'm willing to risk anything for is the woman handling this situation with her impressive composure and confidence. If it doesn't work out with her, then I don't want it to work out with anyone.

"Phil, I'm Liz. A friend of Greyson's. It's so nice to meet you."

"Nice to meet you." He looks up at both of us. "Let's eat, shall we?"

* * *

Dinner went over smoothly. My mom shared a little about her and Phil's relationship. It was weird for me to listen to, but I can tell she's happy. That's all that matters to me. She went through way too much with my father to spend the rest of her life alone.

There were a couple times when I felt uncomfortable listening to Phil share details about the timing of their marriage. But all it took was a gentle brush of Liz's fingers against my jean clad thigh to help me relax enough to get through it. She's something else.

After dinner, I'm sitting in the living room with Phil while my mom and Liz are cleaning up the kitchen.

I tried to convince them to join us, but they insisted on cleaning. They're more than likely talking up a storm in there. Which wouldn't surprise me.

Liz draws people to her. She did it over four years ago with me when I met her at the animal shelter. She does it with our friends whenever we're all together. And now she's doing it with my mother. No wonder she has so many clients as a new lawyer. She's the only person I would want to represent me.

The sound of Phil's voice brings me back to the present. "Greyson, I can't tell you how much I appreciate you being here."

Unsure of what to say next, I take a deep breath.

He must pick up on my discomfort because he speaks up again. "I apologize if this is weird for you, son. I don't know what I would do if my mother called me to tell me she ran off and married a stranger."

He hit the nail on the head.

I clear my throat as I sit up a little straighter, trying not to look uncomfortable. "I appreciate you saying that, Phil. All I want is for her to be happy. I can tell she is."

And that's the truth.

I haven't seen my mom smile so much in my entire life. Even before my father's first affair, she never seemed this happy.

"I hope she is."

"Can I ask you a question?"

Phil gives me a slight nod.

"Did she ever tell you about my father?"

His face takes on a somber expression. I can see the pain he feels for my mother in his facial expression. It means more to me than he'll ever know.

"She did. I experienced something similar in my first marriage, too. I think it's part of the reason we progressed so quickly."

I nod. "Why else?"

Phil leans in. "Let me tell you something, son." His eyes flick to the kitchen quickly before focusing on my face again. "One day you'll meet a woman who makes you want to be better, and you'll know she's it for you. I wish I would have known that at your age." He looks over his shoulder once more before leaning back in his seat. "Your mother makes me want to be a better man, and that's how I know she'll always be the one. I'm the best version of myself with her. I can't say the same about my previous marriage."

I consider his words.

As I do, realization dawns on me.

I understand what he's saying because I feel the same way about Liz. Involuntarily, my eyes wander to the kitchen, where she and my mom look to be deep in conversation.

Liz could ask me for anything, and I'd be down for it. All while working to be the best version of myself. For her. All for her.

When I return my attention to Phil, he has a knowing smile on his face. I don't acknowledge it. Instead, I attempt to feign nonchalance by scratching the back of my neck, causing him to chuckle.

"Friends, huh?"

"Hopefully not for long."

He reaches for me to clasp his hand on my shoulder. "Atta boy."

* * *

"Can I take you out for some ice cream?"

We left my mom's house ten minutes ago, and I'm hoping I can score some extra time with Liz this evening.

Looking over at her from the driver's seat, I can tell by the way she furrows her brow that she's thinking hard. Probably about the answer she wants to give versus the answer she thinks she should give. I know she wants to say yes. She's just too stubborn to admit it.

I don't give her time to turn me down. "Come on, please. As a thank you."

She nods her head. "As a thank you." Then she turns in her seat to face me. "Are we going to keep doing things for each other under the guise of a thank you?"

Her question makes me laugh. "If that's what it takes to spend time with you, then sure."

She sighs. "If I agree to ice cream, will you promise me this isn't a date? I already told you when—"

I cut her off. "First, I remember what you told me. Second, if I'm ever lucky enough to score a date with you, it will be much better than taking you for ice cream."

I smirk.

She gives me her signature eye roll before crossing her arms in defiance. Even though she admits defeat. "Fine."

When we pull into the parking lot of the ice cream parlor, her face lights up.

"Wow. I didn't know you loved ice cream so much."

She gifts me with another eye roll. "It isn't the ice cream, per se. This place has cinnamon ice cream. Have you ever had cinnamon ice cream? It's worth dying for."

I laugh. "You and your cinnamon."

After waiting in line, we eat our ice cream without saying much. Although, I wish Liz would say something. Anything would be better than what I'm currently getting from her.

Every few bites, she makes a sound of approval.

It's torture.

And I feel ridiculous for wishing I was the ice cream cone in her hand.

I should be thankful I even get to sit across from her right now, enjoying her company. It's a major step up from where I was with her just a few months ago.

She catches me staring at her. "What?"

"Nothing."

"You were staring."

"No, I wasn't."

"You totally were!"

I search for a reason to give her, hating that she caught me. "You have a little ice cream." I gesture to the corner of my mouth, feeling guilty for lying.

Unknowingly, she gets revenge by using her tongue to lick up the imaginary ice cream on the corner of her lips.

I hold back a groan.

Kill me now.

"Did I get it?"

I try my best to look casual. "Yep. All good."

As we're finishing up our ice cream, I go out on a limb by bringing up what I know is an unwelcome topic on Liz's end. But I'm curious.

"Can I ask you something?"

"Yes." I don't miss the way she draws out the word like she's skeptical of what exactly my question is.

"Will you ever let me take you on a date?"

Looking down at the table, she sighs. "I don't know."

"Can you tell me why?"

"I'd rather not get into details."

"Let me ask you this... is it me or dating in general?"

In my mind, the question I ask is valid, considering I haven't ever witnessed Liz in a relationship. I never understood why. Men practically fall at her feet when we're out with our friends. She has let a few of them dance with her or buy her a drink, but never anything more. There must be a reason for that. And the more time I spend with her, the more I want to know why. Even though I'm well aware that I probably haven't earned the right to know.

She sighs again. "Please drop it. I already told you I'm attracted to you. I'm willing to see where our friendship goes. Please don't push me on this." She stands up from the table, making her way to my truck.

I can't ignore the pang of guilt in my chest when I see the look on her face as she does.

I follow her, gently placing my hand on her arm when I catch up to her. "Who hurt you, Liz?"

She pulls out of my grasp, looking offended.

My question was genuine, but apparently it was the wrong thing to ask.

"Greyson, drop it."

I take a few steps back, giving her space. "Okay. I'm sorry."

She lets out a deep breath and rubs her forehead with her thumb and forefinger. "It's okay. Thanks for the ice cream. Apart from your pushiness, I had a good time."

While I'm surprised by her confession, I know it's an attempt to steel herself. She's extraordinary at it, but in this specific moment, I see past it. Her walls are strong, but they aren't impenetrable. I just hope she eventually lets me in.

* * *

After giving this a lot of thought, I'm currently on the way to my best friend's house. It isn't to see him, though. I'm on my way to see his wife, who is best friends with the woman I'm head over heels for.

When I questioned Liz last night, I wasn't expecting her to shut down dating completely. I want to find out what I can about why. While I don't expect Maylee to give me every detail, I'm hoping for something.

I care about Liz. I want to *take* care of Liz. In any way I can. Even if it'll only be as a friend. At first.

Reluctantly, I knock on the door to Walker's and Maylee's house.

Maylee opens the door. It's clear she's surprised to see me. "Hey, Greyson! Walker isn't here right now."

Placing my hands in the pockets of my jeans, I say, "I'm actually here to see you."

She gives me a warm smile. "Oh, okay. Well, come in."

When we make it into the living room, I look around.

It still looks the same as it did when I lived here. Except for the wedding photos lining the walls, and the feminine touches that Maylee has added since moving in.

I think about my house. How I wouldn't mind the same additions. But only if they're added by Liz.

Right.

The reason I'm here.

Maylee takes a seat on the couch.

I follow suit.

"Is everything okay?"

I think about how to answer her question, not sure what to say.

What comes out of my mouth is, "I asked Liz out on a date... kind of." I stumble over my words. "I mean, she knows I want to take her on a date."

"Mhm. And what does she think about that?"

"She hasn't told you?"

She chuckles. "I know where she stands. Among other things."

"Other things?"

Maylee tucks her legs underneath her, gazing at me thoughtfully. "Has she shared anything about her past with you?"

"No. I alluded to it last night. Which didn't work out so well for me. She told me to drop it and completely shut down. That's why I'm here, actually. I was hoping you could help me. I don't know what to do."

"Keep doing what you're doing. Give her time to come around. I know she will."

"Are you sure?"

"The only person she's ever let her guard down around since him is you, Greyson. That should tell you all you need to know. The rest is Liz's story to tell. Not mine."

I nod in understanding.

While she didn't give me any details, she told me enough.

Liz is hesitant to give me her future because she doesn't want to relive her past.

I won't blame her for that.

What I will do is whatever it takes to make sure she knows I'll never let her down the way she was before.

Chapter 14

Liz

Junior Year - Spring Semester

Listening to the hum of Dylan's ceiling fan could put me to sleep. So could the way he's drawing idle circles on the small of my back. He does this every time we finish studying.

Truthfully, the few months we've spent together have been some of the best of my life. Even though we've faced some hardship. Like after what happened on our trip together. I told Dylan I didn't want to get into the habit of taking things too far. Like I mentioned, I've always pictured myself waiting until the day I marry the man of my dreams. Though it's difficult to separate that man from Dylan. Because I'm pretty sure Dylan is that man.

His deep voice pulls me from my thoughts. "Do you wanna go to the party tonight?"

The party.

Right.

It's the last big one before spring break. The whole campus has been buzzing about it.

Since we started dating, we've steered clear of most. Dylan claims he prefers spending alone time with me instead of showing up at parties, hoping I'll be there, too. While I doubt that's the only reason that he ever showed up at raging frat parties, I appreciate the sentiment.

But I won't lie. I miss partaking in them. I spend most of my free time with my amazing boyfriend. It would be nice to see my friends. Even if we hardly take part in the party activities.

"I do." Excited, I sit up. "I really do! Maybe Ethan and Maylee can join us if that's alright with you?"

He kisses my forehead. "Of course, it's okay with me. Anything for you, baby."

"You're the best."

He smirks. "Oh, yeah?"

I smirk right back. "Yes. I'll prove it to you."

"I like the sound of that."

I place my hands on Dylan's chest to trail my fingers up and over his shoulders until they're around his neck. Then I kiss him senseless. It's not like I have anything better to do before the party, anyway.

* * *

Walking into the biggest party of the year on Dylan's arm feels like a dream.

Because he's easily the hottest guy on campus, I pulled out the big guns tonight.

My hair flows down my back in beach waves. My makeup is on point. I did a smokey eye with a Liz twist—glitter.

I'm wearing a fitted black dress that does wonders for my curves. And I paired it with my favorite pair of sparkly stilettos. I have to compensate for my short stature. Especially when standing next to my boyfriend, who looks like he could be a professional basketball player.

I feel confident and beautiful. It's quite the combination.

As we walk through the living area and into the kitchen in search of drinks, Dylan leans down to whisper in my ear. "You have the attention of every guy in this frat house, Liz. It's driving me crazy."

"Good thing I'm already yours then, right?" I wink.

He gives me a quick kiss on the lips. "Don't forget it."

The butterflies I've grown accustomed to flutter wildly in my stomach. I'm convinced I'll never get used to his charm. He knows how to lay it on thick.

"You know I won't."

"Good. Drink?"

"Yes, please."

"Us too, Dylan!" At the sound of Ethan's voice, I turn around, finding Maylee at his side.

"There you guys are. I guess we lost you on the way in."

Dylan hands us our drinks one by one. When I take my cup from him, he pulls me close, planting a kiss on my lips.

"You guys are ridiculously cute, but please save it for when we're not in a public place."

The guys laugh at Maylee's remark.

She shrugs her shoulders once before joining in their laughter.

All of us fall into casual conversation for a while.

I'm so thankful for my best friends and my boyfriend. I knew college was going to be amazing simply because I'm away from my overbearing parents. But I couldn't have predicted this. Everything feels right. As it should.

About an hour into the party, Dylan pulls me into a secluded corner. "Do you wanna get out of here? I wanna take you somewhere."

"Where?"

He smirks. "Don't worry about where. It isn't far. We can walk."

The look in his eyes tells me all I need to know. "I'm in."

* * *

When we reach our destination, I'm out of breath. "Dylan, this is crazy. You said it wasn't far."

He laughs. "It wasn't. I just failed to mention how many stairs were involved. But I promise it'll be worth it. It's just down this hallway."

After climbing an outrageous number of stairs, Dylan leads me to a rooftop balcony overlooking the city.

I can see the whole Chicago skyline. The lights look amazing against the dark night sky with the moon hanging in the background. It's breathtaking.

"Wow."

"It's amazing, isn't it?"

"Yeah. It is."

"Listen, I wanna talk to you about something."

Dylan sounds uncertain. Which is unusual. He's always so sure of himself.

I try to sound calm and collected to keep him from doubting himself even more. "What's up?"

He takes a deep breath as he looks out at the city. "I got into a pre-med internship program. It starts this summer."

"Dylan! That's amazing!" I reach up to hug him, but he catches my arms to lower them back down.

He takes my hands in his. "Before you get excited, you need to know it's in Boston. I won't be able to visit Chicago. The program is intense. But I need to do it because of what it can do for me when the time comes to apply for medical school."

My heart sinks with the news. I won't lie and say I hadn't thought about what our summer would look like. We both live in the city, so I thought we would have all the time in the world to spend together leading into senior year.

"Oh. That's still exciting, babe." I steel myself. "We can make it work."

"Are you sure?"

I give his hands a squeeze. "Of course."

He leans down and presses his lips against my own.

The kiss starts out gentle, and I know he's telling me how much he appreciates me. My support.

I wrap my arms around his neck, pulling myself against his chest. Then the kiss goes from gentle to electrifying. It's always like this with us.

When he pulls back, the look in his eyes is one I haven't ever seen before.

I think I know what it means, though.

He gently brushes some stray strands of hair behind my ear. "I love you, Liz."

The words steal the air right from my lungs.

He must notice because he adds, "I know it's fast, but I mean it. I love you."

I don't even have to think about whether I feel the same way. I've known for a while.

"I love you too, Dylan."

The smile he gives me could light up the entire world.

He wraps me up into his arms, and I bury my face against his chest, getting a whiff of his cedar and peppermint scent.

"What do you say about going on another trip with me?"

"For spring break?"

He smiles and nods.

"I'd love that."

"Where do you want to go?"

"Let's go to the beach."

"Sounds good, baby. I'll make it happen."

* * *

Spring break on the beach with Dylan has been nothing short of spectacular.

I'm dreading our return to school.

Thankfully, we have one more night together before heading back tomorrow afternoon. In honor of our last night, we're enjoying a candlelit dinner on the beach.

"Have you applied to any law schools yet?"

I've been dreading this conversation. Both of us have big plans for ourselves, and I'm not sure if our futures will end up aligning.

I've applied to a few schools in Boston because I know that's where Dylan will more than likely end up. He just isn't aware of that little tidbit of information yet.

Before looking up from my plate of food, I take a second to consider how much to tell him. "I have."

"Where at?"

With my fork, I scoot my unfinished meal around on the plate in front of me. "I've applied to some in California, and one in New York. I want to keep my options open. Hopefully, I'll have a few to choose from. I also applied to some schools in Boston."

"You did?" I can't quite read the look on his face, but he sounds surprised.

"Is that okay?"

He reaches for my hand across the table. "Of course, that's okay. I was planning on talking to you about this, anyway. I want you to come with me, Liz."

"To Boston?"

"Yes."

"This summer?"

He nods his head. "And after graduation."

I open my mouth to respond, but then close it again.

I can't believe he wants me to come with him. Figuring it would be my last one, I was planning on spending the summer in Chicago. But that was before we got so serious.

Now?

I'm willing to do anything for him. Just like I know he'd do anything for me.

"I need to figure out logistics, but I'd love to come with you. It'll give me a chance to get to know the city before law school. Maybe I can find myself an apartment. If I get in, I mean."

"You will. And don't worry about logistics. I already have an apartment lined up big enough for both of us, and I can help you move in before my schedule gets crazy."

"Are you sure that's a good idea?"

He lifts my hand to his lips, giving it a gentle kiss. "Positive. I love you, baby. I don't think there's any reason to delay our future together."

It may seem fast, but I couldn't agree more.

There's no one I want to be with more than the man sitting across from me.

Too bad forever can't start today.

* * *

Finals are always difficult to get through. I feel an immense amount of pressure to ace every single one. I need to keep my grades up if I want to get into a good law school program.

The only thing keeping me motivated to study is thinking about my future with Dylan.

I still can't believe he wants me to come to Boston with him this summer. I know he'll be busy, but it will give me an opportunity to focus on my internship as well.

That's right.

I'll be an intern at a very prestigious law office in Boston. Despite my doubts, everything is falling into place.

The sound of Maylee entering our apartment distracts me from the textbook in front of me.

Sure enough, I hear her footsteps nearing my bedroom before she knocks lightly.

"Come in."

"Hey, I wanted to check on you after this morning. Are you feeling okay?"

I cringe as I recall how I spent my morning.

Waking up and feeling nauseous isn't ideal. And eating breakfast did not help like I thought it would. My stomach couldn't tolerate the cinnamon toast I had eaten.

I shrug. "I feel fine. Just stressed."

Maylee nods her head as she steps further into my bedroom. "Has that happened before? You haven't been sick enough to throw up since we were kids."

I chuckle. "MayMay, I'm fine. I probably just ate something bad. Or it's stress related. There's a lot more riding on these finals than previous ones."

I focus on my study materials again, hoping she'll leave me be. I don't have time to worry about anything other than acing my finals.

"Was this morning the only time it happened?"

Dropping my pen, I groan while looking up at my overly concerned best friend. "Yes. Why are you asking?"

She drops her eyes to the floor. Letting out a deep breath, she returns her eyes to mine. "I love you like a sister, okay? So please don't take this question the wrong way."

I roll my eyes. "Spit it out."

"Did you and Dylan—"

I cut her off. "Don't be ridiculous."

"You didn't answer the question, Liz."

"Only a few times."

She's disappointed. That much I can tell.

"Liz—"

Unable to help myself, I cut her off again. "I don't need a lecture. I know I messed up."

Even though I snap at her, she stands her ground. "That's not why I came in here."

"Okay. Then why did you?"

"Have you gotten your period yet?"

"No." I'm feeling defensive, so I don't let her get a word out. "But you know as well as I do, my periods can be irregular. Especially when I'm stressed. Seriously. I'm not concerned."

She bites her lip. It's a sure sign there are a million things going on in her mind. I know she's carefully thinking through whatever it is she's about to say. "Okay. Fine. But if you get sick again, please promise me you'll take a test just to be on the safe side. Okay?"

"Fine. I will. Can I go back to studying now?"

Without another word, she walks out of my room, closing the door behind her.

My guilt settles in.

Honestly, I didn't mean to dismiss her like that, but I'm kind of bothered by the way she jumped straight to the worst-case scenario.

There's no way I'm pregnant.

Chapter 15

Liz

Senior Year - Summer

I'm pregnant.

I waited until after finals to take a test, wanting to stay focused on my grades. But I knew it was likely, considering I've been suffering from morning sickness for two weeks.

Just as I thought, I'm about eight weeks along.

I've never been more scared in my life.

Currently, I'm on my way back from the doctor, heading to Maylee's and my apartment, where I plan on calling Dylan to give him the news.

He's already in Boston.

His internship started as soon as finals were over. Mine doesn't start until the last week of May.

Truthfully, I don't know what I'm going to do about the internship.

I don't know what I'm going to do about anything.

My stomach is in knots as I walk up to my apartment, thinking about how Dylan will handle this conversation.

While he's always so supportive and loving, I'm not naïve enough to think that a baby won't put some strain on our relationship. I just hope he's as willing to make this work as I am.

Sitting on my bed, I dial his phone number. The anticipation just about kills me as I listen to my call ring out a few times before he answers.

"Hey, baby. I'm glad you called. I miss you."

I take a few deep breaths.

In.

Out.

In.

Out.

"You there?" The sound of his voice is the only thing keeping me afloat.

I clear my throat. "Yeah. Sorry, babe. I miss you, too. How's Boston?"

"It's amazing. I can't wait for you to be here. You should have come up when I did."

"I know. I had some things to take care of. Speaking of, there's something I need to talk to you about."

I've never struggled with my composure, but this moment is proving to be difficult. I can't deny the shakiness in my voice. Knowing Dylan, I'm sure he notices it, too.

"Is everything okay? You sound off."

Here goes nothing.

"Dylan..." I hesitate, unable to form the words.

"Baby, you're scaring me. Are you okay?"

I take one last deep breath before I let the words tumble out. "I'm pregnant."

Silence. It's what greets me on the other end of the phone.

I try to stay patient as I wait for him to say something.

"Babe?"

"I'm here."

"Did you hear me?"

"Yes, I heard you. Just processing." He sighs. "When did this happen?"

So far, he sounds fine. Maybe a little surprised, but he isn't freaking out like I thought he would be.

"I'm pretty sure it happened over spring break. I'm about eight weeks along."

"How?"

Even though he can't see me, I shrug. "I told you we shouldn't have—"

He cuts me off. "Did you tell anyone?"

I sigh. Of course, he doesn't want to have the same discussion we had after the first trip we took together.

Not wanting to argue, I answer his question. "Maylee knows, but she promised not to say anything."

He sighs again.

This time, it sounds weak. Defeated. He's frustrated. Or shocked. Both of which are understandable.

"Make sure no one else finds out about this yet. We can figure out what to do once you're here."

I close my eyes, hoping he isn't saying what I think he is. "What exactly do you mean by that?"

"Well, we're college seniors. We need to figure out how to handle a pregnancy while tackling everything else we have going on."

My shoulders relax. "So, you want to keep the baby?"

"Of course, I do. Do you?"

"I do. You know I've always wanted a big family."

"It's just happening a little sooner than I thought." He hesitates briefly. "Did you think I wouldn't want this?"

"Honestly, I didn't know what to think. All I know is, I didn't want you to feel like you have to give anything up. I know this internship is important to you. I know your entire future is important to you."

"Baby, *you* are important to me. We can figure this out. Besides, I'm not worried about the future. I'm worried about you right now. How are you feeling?"

It's a loaded question.

One I'm not sure I know how to answer.

On the one hand, I'm so relieved he's willing to make this work. But on the other, I'm terrified about where I go from here.

Thinking about leaving Chicago for the summer has me feeling unsettled. I want to be in the comfort of my home during this pregnancy. Plus, I need to figure out how to finish school and where to get a job. One of us is going to have to give something up. I don't want it to be him.

Finally, I settle on, "Honestly, I could be better."

"I'm sorry, baby. Why don't you fly up early so I can take care of you? All my free time will be yours."

I smile. But it falls when I realize I don't want to go to Boston. I need to be in a place where I'm familiar with my surroundings.

"I don't think it's a good idea for me to spend the summer in Boston."

"What are you saying?"

"I'm saying that I need to be close to home. Especially in the early stages. What if something happens? We'd be alone without support."

"What could happen?"

After experiencing what my mom went through after having me, I think it's only natural for me to be concerned.

She miscarried many times before giving up completely. We tried to get her to go see a doctor about what could be wrong. And my dad also tried to convince her to try IVF, but she was too afraid it wouldn't work. Her miscarriages broke her. In fact, they almost broke my parents. I watched my dad pour himself into my mom the way he does his cases. He never gave up on her. It was hard on their marriage, but somehow, they made it through. I know it's part of the reason they're so protective of me. I may not love it, but I understand it. I'm their rainbow baby.

I take a deep breath. "Babe, you know my mom's history. I need to be here just in case. Plus, I want you to focus on your internship. It's important for you. Now more than ever. Okay? It's just for the summer. It'll fly by. And I have Maylee and Ethan. They'll be here if I need anything."

"I'd feel better if you were here with me. That way, if something happens, I'm around."

"I know. And I get that. I really do. But I need to be comfortable. I promise to keep you updated on everything. Maybe you can come down for my next appointment?"

He sighs. "I don't like it, but I'm not about to fight with an aspiring lawyer. I've learned the hard way. You better call me every day. I'm going to miss you like crazy."

"Of course, I will. I miss you already."

"I love you, Liz. We're going to figure this out."

"I know. I love you, too."

* * *

The sound of Maylee's key clicking in the lock wakes me from where I'm sleeping on the couch.

"Hey, sorry. How are you feeling today?"

I rub my eyes to remove the sleep from them. "Tired."

Who knew how daunting the first trimester of pregnancy is? I feel run down all day. It's awful.

"I see that. Have you talked to Dylan today?"

I don't bother making eye contact with my best friend. "No."

I had some light bleeding this morning, so I made an appointment with my gynecologist for tomorrow.

I'm still only twelve weeks along. My emotions are already all over the place. I won't be able to handle it if Dylan worries more than he already is. The bleeding could be nothing.

"Have you told your parents yet?"

"What do you think?" I sigh. "They don't even know I have a boyfriend."

"You need to tell them."

"I'm going to bed." I don't give her a chance to say anything else before leaving the living room.

Now that I'm finally able to sleep, I look forward to getting into bed every night. It's the only time when my mind can rest, and I don't have to think about what has become of my life or what I'm going to do about everything.

While I'm excited about having a baby, there are still so many unknowns. I don't love feeling so unsettled. This wasn't what I planned for myself, but I'm not naïve enough to think life always works out the way we often want it to.

I can do this.

* * *

"Ow, ow, ow."

I wake up to extremely uncomfortable pain. As the pain worsens, I clench my stomach, rolling into the fetal position as I do.

It isn't until I tuck my legs together tightly that I feel something wet and sticky covering the inside of my thighs. Reluctantly, I reach down to touch the substance. I bring my fingers up to my face to make sure it isn't blood. When I see it is, I let out a quiet sob.

Memories of my mom's many miscarriages come flooding back in full force.

I hope this is nothing.

But my gut tells me something is very, very wrong.

* * *

I don't think I've spent so much time crying in my entire life.

After Maylee heard me sobbing in my room, she came to check on me. When she realized what was happening, she drove me straight to the hospital.

Upon arriving, I got a room right away, where the doctor confirmed what I already knew.

I miscarried.

As soon as we got back to our apartment, I told Maylee to give me some space.

I'm holed up in my room. Have been for hours now, going over everything I was told at the hospital.

Unfortunately, the miscarriage isn't over yet. It will take several days for everything to pass, possibly several weeks.

I had to schedule an appointment with my gynecologist to make sure everything looks okay. There's still a possibility I'll need a D&C, which I'd like to avoid.

I feel defeated, wondering if there's something I could have done to prevent this. Wondering what exactly I did wrong.

I also feel guilty for not being able to carry to full term.

I'm devastated. Hopeless. And unable to fathom going through this again.

I continue to wonder about what could have been.

While I didn't plan on getting pregnant, I was excited, slowly coming to terms with how different my life would be. But now it will be different for a completely different reason.

Nothing could relieve the ache in my heart.

I can't find words for what I feel.

The weight of it all is just too much.

A light knock at my bedroom door startles me.

"Liz, can I come in?"

"Sure."

"Is there anything you need?"

Sniffling, I shake my head at Maylee.

"Okay. Well, Dylan's here."

My head snaps up from where it's resting on my knees.

"What? I wasn't ready to talk to him yet."

She sighs. "I know. Ethan called him. Let him be here for you, Liz."

As soon as she exits my room, Dylan walks through the door.

I hadn't told him what had happened yet. I didn't want to distract him from his internship. Or make him come all the way here from Boston.

As soon as he's settled next to me on my bed, I fall into him. When I feel his arms envelop me, I let myself fall apart.

He kisses the crown of my head, letting his lips linger a little longer than normal.

"Sh. I'm here. I am so sorry, baby."

I'm not sure how long we spend, limbs tangled, mourning the loss of the life we created together. But I'm thankful for his presence. I needed him more than I realized.

I hope we can get through this. And come out stronger on the other side of the pain.

* * *

Senior Year - Fall

"I can't do this anymore, Liz."

All the oxygen in my body seems to evaporate as I stand staring at my boyfriend, wondering what he's talking about.

My heart beats erratically in my chest. "Can't do *what* anymore, Dylan?"

I'm terrified of his answer.

"This." He gestures between the two of us. "It's too much."

I let out the word, "What?" on an exhale, unable to believe what I'm hearing.

Things between the two of us have been difficult ever since we lost our unborn baby. Recovery hasn't been easy. Far from it. But as far as I knew, we've been fine. Coping as best we can, despite the challenges we've faced.

Classes started over two months ago. I've been doing the best I can. But there are just some wounds that time can't heal. Suffering through a miscarriage is one of them. For Dylan, I've tried to hold myself together. Not wanting him to feel like he has to carry the weight of this all on his own.

Tears pool in his eyes. "Being with you is too painful. How are we ever supposed to move past this? You won't even touch me."

"How can you even say that?" As soon as the question is out of my mouth, tears come out of nowhere. They cascade down my cheeks furiously. I've gotten good at crying. It's all I've been doing lately.

"Please don't make me explain what I mean."

Shaking my head, I look down at the floor beneath my feet. It takes every bit of self-control I have not to scream at him in anger. How could he be so selfish?

"You aren't the only one who's hurting. I am too. I hurt every single day. But how can you say being with me is too painful? I feel enough guilt as it is."

"Baby, I love you. You have nothing to feel guilty for. I just think it's best if we go our separate ways, start over. Maybe if we aren't around each other, things will be easier. I-"

I cut him off. I can't bear to hear any more of what he has to say.

"Leave."

"Liz, I–"

With tears still cascading down my face, I say, "Just go." His eyes follow my finger as I point to the door.

Dylan opens his mouth, but then closes it again.

I stand still, staring at the man I thought I loved, wishing I could undo everything that ever happened between us.

The pain is too much.

Right now, it's almost unbearable, but I keep my head held high.

Finally, without uttering another word, he walks out the front door.

And out of my life.

For good.

That's when I realize he was my entire world until he wasn't anymore.

Chapter 16

Liz

Present Day

Greyson: Oh, come on. You've already knocked me down as far as I can go, beautiful. ;)

Shaking my head, I smile down at my phone screen.

It has been weeks since I accompanied Greyson to his mom's house for dinner.

Since then, we've hung out a handful of times, and we text every chance we get. He flirts shamelessly with me, while also respecting my boundaries. The same friendship boundaries I'm so close to forgoing myself.

"Please, tell us what that smile is all about, Liz."

My head snaps up, but not before I school my features. It's becoming increasingly more challenging to hide whatever is going on between Greyson and me.

"I don't know what you're talking about, Steph."

"Oh, stop. We've all noticed it prior to today. Well, I have anyway. You've been more smiley at work, too. It's weird."

Maylee pokes her head out of the pantry. "She has a point. You seem more..." She lets her words trail off, searching for the right one. "Chipper."

I feign offense. "I'm always chipper!"

"Okay. Fine. You're always giddy. That, my friend, is new for you."

Steph chimes in. "You are. And we all know it's because of a certain devilishly handsome paramedic." She fans her face for emphasis. Which draws a laugh out of each of my friends.

I roll my eyes.

Still laughing, Kate pushes back from the table to get up. "As much as I'd love to stay and obsess over your love life, I have to go. It's getting a little late."

I furrow my brow. "It's only nine."

"I know, but I have a job interview first thing tomorrow morning."

"That's great, Kate!"

She gets a simultaneous, "Good luck!" from all of us as she heads out.

Maylee returns to the table with some more snacks to munch on. "Just admit defeat and give the man what he wants."

Steph waggles her eyebrows as she sing-songs. "You know you want to."

"You're both ridiculous. And insane."

Steph pops a pretzel into her mouth. "We're definitely not. The tension between the two of you when we're all out is palpable."

I narrow my eyes at my friends. As I'm about to give a snarky reply, the front door opens. I think nothing of it—figuring it's Walker—until Steph's eyes widen just a little. "Speak of the devil. I'm gonna head home. Have fun!"

She winks over her shoulder on the way out.

I whisper shout, "You stink!" Then I look over at Maylee. "You planned this."

She knew Walker and Greyson had plans tonight. There's no way she can deny it.

She doesn't bat an eyelash. Instead, she has the audacity to chuckle. "I did no such thing. But I gave my husband free rein."

I exhale dramatically.

"Oh stop. Let's have fun. It'll just be the four of us, so there's no pressure to hide anything."

I want to say something in response, but I don't. Because she has a point.

She and Walker are very aware of how Greyson and I feel about each other. Over the last few weeks, it has become clear that my attraction has grown into actual feelings. Which kind of terrifies me.

Scratch that.

It completely terrifies me.

The love I know is all-consuming.

It can heal, but it can also hurt. It happens when it's least expected.

I would know.

I won't survive again if it does. Which is why I'm still so on the fence about where to go with Greyson. He has done nothing but prove he's changed. But that doesn't mean he won't run at the first sign of hardship. It's not like he has any experience where relationships are concerned.

I'm also scared about whether he'll accept what I want. At least, knowing his history.

And honestly, I don't know if I can change the way Greyson has. To completely reject the life that I've been living in solitude.

I'm content. And more than willing to deal with the feeling that something is missing. Because I don't want to acknowledge that the missing piece could very well be a fulfilling relationship.

The sound of Greyson's booming voice pulls me from my thoughts. "Good evening, ladies. How are my two favorite women?"

The smile on his handsome face, paired with the playful wink he throws our way, does something to the dormant butterflies in my stomach.

Walker punches his shoulder. "Watch it, man. One of those women is my wife."

Maylee and I both laugh.

Smirking, I eye the tall, dark, and handsome man who has weaseled his way into my life, and possibly my heart, if I'm honest. "What exactly are *you* doing here?"

He sits down next to me, placing his arm on the back of my chair.

He leans in too close for comfort. "I missed my *friend.*"

The way he says the word 'friend', along with his proximity, causes goosebumps to form on my neck, before spreading over the rest of my body. He must notice because he winks at me. Which earns him a sassy eye roll. He takes it in stride, laughing it off.

I shift my focus to the two people I almost forgot are in the room with us. "So, what are we doing tonight?"

Maylee eyes her husband. He shrugs. "That's up to the two of you since we crashed your girls' night."

"We were just planning on snacking and talking the rest of the night."

I smirk. "How about we mix it up tonight?"

I'm not surprised when Greyson chimes in. I knew he would. "I like the sound of that."

"Of course you do. Anyway, I was thinking we could play a game or something."

"What do you have in mind?" Walker asks.

"I was thinking about charades. We can team up. Guys versus girls?"

"I'm in, but only if Liz agrees to be my partner."

Oh, he's good.

I should have known Greyson wouldn't play by anyone else's rules but his own. And because I've let him weasel his way past my defenses, I give in. "Fine."

* * *

I've never laughed so much in my life.

Charades is a ton of fun when playing with the right people.

It turns out the four of us are extremely competitive.

If I've learned anything about Greyson, it's that he knows how to let go and have a good time. And he has absolutely no shame with acting things out. I think he might be the most enjoyable person I've ever hung out with. He's certainly the most fun charades teammate I've ever had.

Dare I say he's the best charades partner I've ever had?

We're all tied up.

It's Greyson's turn.

If I guess correctly this time, we win.

Neither of us likes to lose.

We will not lose.

Are we taking this a little too seriously?

Maybe.

Definitely.

But that's what's making this so much fun.

After reading the piece of paper he draws from the bowl on the coffee table, he rises from the couch confidently.

I watch as he acts out whatever was on his piece of paper.

He raises a hand to his mouth as if he's holding an ice cream cone. But when he starts his performance, I realize he's impersonating a singer. It's a vague clue. But because I'm the karaoke queen, I'm confident in my abilities to guess this before our opponents.

Maylee shouts, "Taylor Swift!"

He shakes his head as he gives up on the microphone. Instead, he dances. Which he's terrible at. I think he's doing the moonwalk. Believe it or not, it's difficult to tell.

When he raises his arms to do the "Thriller" dance from the hit music video, I jump out of my seat, yelling, "Michael Jackson!"

I beat Walker by a millisecond.

Greyson shouts in victory.

I join him. "Hah!"

Walker shakes his head at us. "That was such an easy one to end with, and you're both insane."

Maylee laughs. "Imagine what it was like growing up with her."

I place my hands on my hips, popping one out as I do. "Oh please, you loved it." Then I flip my hair over my shoulder. "I'm the life of every party."

Greyson chuckles. "That you are." He turns his attention to Walker. "Mind if we get the fire pit going?"

"Great idea."

Sitting in front of the fire with three of my best friends is exactly what I didn't know I needed tonight.

We haven't spent time like this together since before Maylee and Walker got married.

The only difference is I can stand being around Greyson now. In fact, I enjoy being around him. His presence almost makes me forget about all the pain I once felt all those years ago when my entire world came crashing down around me.

Maylee and Walker went inside, claiming they'd be back, but that was over twenty minutes ago.

It's not lost on me what they're up to. Two grown adults playing matchmakers.

Greyson's sitting across from me, staring at what's left of the crackling fire. I've been stealing glances at him all night, enjoying the way the light from the fire dances across his features.

Tonight is the first time I've allowed myself to truly admire him. The bone structure in his face is exquisite. I didn't know how much I appreciate a good, strong jawline. Or perfect cheekbones. Occasionally, he purses his lips. The action is a major turn on. And it makes me wonder what's going on in that gorgeous head of his.

I don't know if it's the three glasses of wine, or my undeniable curiosity, that cause me to blurt exactly what's on my mind. "What are you thinking about right now?"

Greyson lifts his gaze, focusing intently on my face. His look is full of intensity.

"You."

I swallow. "What about me?"

He nods toward the house behind me. "Do you think they're coming back outside?"

While I'm thrown off by the change in subject, I gladly accept it. "I doubt it. It's obvious what they're up to."

"Yeah."

A few moments of silence pass between us.

"Can I ask you something, Liz?"

I take a deep breath, hoping he isn't about to start a conversation I'm still not ready to have.

I don't talk about my past.

Maylee knows all about it. But she knows not to bring it up. It's just too painful. If I don't talk about it with her, then there's no way I'll talk about it with anyone else.

Reluctantly, I nod my head. "Sure."

"Do you remember the conversation we had at your apartment? The one after you showed up at my house?"

I nod.

"Have you figured out your feelings?"

I know I have feelings for him.

Feelings I'm terrified of.

Feelings that are way too familiar.

I can't deny they've become feelings I want to explore. It would drive me crazy not to. And maybe that was Greyson's goal all along.

"I have."

He nods, giving me a few seconds to find my composure. I love how he knows me well enough to know how unsure of myself I am right now. Which is totally unlike me. But in my defense, I never thought I would be in this position again. Giving into feelings for someone. Especially someone who used to infuriate me so much.

I pull my shoulders back, sitting up a little straighter as I do.

As I open my mouth to say the words, the back door opens.

Walker looks between the two of us before clearing his throat. "Sorry to interrupt, but I think we're going to call it a night."

Maylee pokes her head over his shoulder, smiling like a lune.

I narrow my eyes in her direction. "We'll head out. Thanks for letting us hang out."

We say goodbye to our friends.

When we make it outside, Greyson follows me to my car.

I don't notice how close he is to me until I spin around to face him.

I'm eye level with his toned chest. The gray T-shirt he's wearing does nothing to hide the contours of his very defined muscles.

I take a quick step backward to find my composure and Greyson's face.

"Are you okay, Liz?"

"Mhm. Fine."

"What were you about to say?"

I blank. "What?"

"Outside. What were you going to say before Walker interrupted?"

Right.

Feelings.

I have feelings for the only man who has ever flustered me.

Here goes nothing.

"I—"

Greyson cuts me off. "This is hard for you to admit, isn't it?"

"Yes."

"Then don't. I don't want to force you to tell me how you feel if you aren't ready."

I appreciate his thoughtfulness so much, but he deserves to hear the words.

And I need to say them. "No, I need to say it. I have feelings for you. I can't believe I do, but I do."

With a wide smile on his face, he takes a step closer to me. I watch his eyes as they study my face. They move from my eyes to my flushed cheeks, down to my lips, and then back up to my eyes again.

My chest rises and falls a bit more dramatically as I wait for Greyson's next move.

He brushes a strand of hair behind my ear before leaning in.

I don't move. Afraid to break the all too familiar tension between us.

Just when I think his lips are about to meet mine, in what I'm sure will be the best kiss of my life, he moves his head to the right.

Bringing his mouth to the shell of my ear, he whispers, "It's about time."

Goosebumps erupt on my skin.

All.

Over.

They're accompanied by a shiver that races down my spine.

Taking a second to catch my breath, I mentally reprimand myself for letting him play me like that.

Not that I'm ready to be kissed by this man, anyway. Something tells me our first kiss is going to rock my world. The thought scares me, but I keep my features schooled. I won't let him see the effect he has on me.

At least not yet.

He steps back. "Now, can I finally take you on a proper date?"

I nod.

"Can I hear you say it?"

I nod again. But this time, I use my words, too. "Yes."

Relief washes over his face. "Finally."

Chapter 17

Liz

Present Day

Five years.

It has been over five years since I've been on a date.

I'm freaking out.

I don't feel like myself.

I'm flustered.

I'm nervous.

I'm terrified.

Clearly, I don't know how to handle this. The sad part is, as a twenty-seven-year-old woman, I should.

But I don't.

I almost texted Greyson to tell him I don't feel well. But I talked myself out of it because I refuse to be a coward. And I deserve the chance to fall in love with someone.

I need to give myself the chance.

I *want* to give myself the chance.

Instead of spending any more time psyching myself out, I get ready for my date.

I don't know what the plan is for tonight, so I haven't settled on an outfit just yet. Starting with my hair and makeup is preferable, anyway.

I style my long, red waves into loose curls, tying up half my hair into a ponytail. The other half rests comfortably over the front of my shoulders and down my back. My makeup is light and natural. I add just a little gold shimmer to my eye shadow, before topping off the look with a neutral lip color.

As far as what to wear, I go with a loosely fitted navy dress. It pairs perfectly with my favorite strappy nude heels. Adding some simple jewelry completes the look. I do a quick once over in the mirror, before getting my things together.

I'm still a ball of nerves, but at least I'm a composed ball of nerves.

Before I know it, there's a knock at my door.

I smooth out my dress, taking a few deep breaths as I do.

When I step outside, my nervous energy dissipates as I take in the incredibly handsome man standing on my doorstep.

Greyson's ridiculously good looks used to get on my last nerve, but now I have no problem letting myself revel in them.

I'm no longer a sucker for dark features.

Nope.

I'm a sucker for his dark features alone.

Everything from his messy dark hair to his deep brown eyes to his perfectly tanned, olive skin has my heart wanting to burst.

He's wearing slacks with a dusty blue button-down shirt. He rolled his sleeves up to his elbows, bringing attention to his muscular forearms. I let myself enjoy the view, while wondering what it would feel like to run my fingers along every inch of muscle he has.

He looks incredible.

I don't miss the look on his face as he eyes me from head to toe before handing me a bouquet of brightly colored flowers.

I smile at him for being intuitive enough not to go with a cliché choice.

Bringing them to my nose, I smile as I smell them. "Thank you. These are beautiful."

"You're welcome. *You* look beautiful."

"As do you."

Did I really just say that?

He chuckles. "Are you ready?"

"Yes. Where are we going?"

He gives me a look I can't quite read. "You'll see."

The drive is peaceful. Quiet. Usually, I don't enjoy silence. But with Greyson, I don't mind it.

I'm sure he can tell how nervous I am. I appreciate him for not bringing attention to it.

In what feels like no time, we reach our destination. I was too busy thinking about my nerves to realize where we are. And now, I'm thoroughly confused.

"Greyson, this is your house."

He laughs. "You're right. It is."

"What are we doing here?"

"Going on our date."

"Okay. I don't understand."

"Just trust me. Close your eyes."

"Fine." I roll my eyes before closing them.

He guides me to the front door, where I hear the jingle of his keys before the lock clicks.

When we walk inside, I'm greeted by a glorious smell coming from his kitchen. My stomach grumbles in anticipation, reminding me I haven't eaten today. I was too nervous.

"Ready?"

"What do you think?"

"So sassy."

"You love it."

"I do. Now open your eyes."

Without hesitating, I do what he says, and I'm blown away by what I see.

On the ground beneath my feet are red rose petals. As I let my eyes wander further, I see a path of them leading to the kitchen table, which is covered in a white tablecloth. Sitting on top of the table is a dimly lit candle and place settings for both of us.

I bring a hand to my mouth. "This..." I let my words trail off, not knowing what to say. This is incredibly sweet. I didn't know Greyson had this in him.

He looks at me sheepishly. "Do you like it?"

I walk along the path of rose petals until I'm standing across from him at the table.

"Like it? I love it. Why did you go to all this trouble? We could have gone out."

He moves around the table, stepping closer to me. "Because you're worth it. Because I could tell you've been nervous about this date since I asked you. I didn't want you to feel any pressure, so I thought we could hang out here instead. And because I know you, Liz. Contrary to what you might believe. I've spent the past four years learning who you are."

I look at the man I thought I knew.

While I haven't always agreed with the choices that he makes—or used to make—I see there's so much more to him than I thought.

"Thank you. This is amazing."

He pulls my chair out, gesturing for me to sit. "You're welcome."

He plates our food and then pours each of us a glass of Cabernet. I smile, knowing he truly has been learning everything about me, considering the Cabernet he poured is my favorite.

The food looks delicious.

He made us spaghetti with homemade meatballs. As we dig in, things between us feel comfortable, like we've done this a thousand times.

"I never found out what you and my mom talked about after dinner a while back."

I smirk. "You."

"Care to expand on that?"

Thinking about the conversation I had with his mom makes me smile. I think she knew it was only a matter of time before Greyson and I got together.

"She filled me in on a few details about you. She talked to me about your dad, too." Greyson's expression deflates. His smile turns into a frown. "Do you want to tell me about him?"

"What do you already know?"

I exhale. "What he did, and how it affected you. Can you tell me about it?"

I'm trying to get him to open up without being too pushy. It's important to me for him to talk to me about this. I only know his mom's side of things. I want to understand Greyson's side of things as well.

He sets down his fork and then takes a sip of his water. I give him the time he needs to find some composure. I can only imagine how difficult of a topic this is for him.

"When I was young, he was a great dad." He shrugs. "As far as I knew, anyway. But as I got older, I started noticing his withdrawal. So naturally, I relied on my mom a lot more. She isn't very good at hiding her emotions. Eventually, I knew something was off."

"How did you find out?"

"I got home from school one day, and he was gone. I found my mom in her room, crying. She told me everything. It wasn't the first time he cheated, but he was finally tired of breaking his promises, I guess."

My heart breaks listening to Greyson talk about his father. I let him tell me everything, knowing he probably doesn't talk about this with anyone.

When he's gotten through the worst of it, he looks at me longingly. "I had my reasons for making the choices I did. I was always honest with the women I was with. Not that it makes a difference."

I stop him before he continues. I understand what it feels like to make a mistake. To feel guilty for something that can't be changed. "Greyson, you don't need to explain."

"I want to."

Surprised, I nod.

"I didn't want to commit to someone because I didn't want to hurt a woman the way he hurt my mom. It took her years to smile again, Liz. I couldn't stand it. It killed me. What I didn't see was how much my own choices were impacting her, too. She caught on to the games I played. I remember the day she sat me down and asked me if I would ever settle down."

He shakes his head.

"Grey—"

Cutting me off, he says, "I told her no. But in the back of my mind, I was thinking of you." My breath hitches at his words. I'm sure he noticed, but he keeps talking. "I'm not telling you any of this to freak you out. I just want you to know how sorry I am for being a jerk and not always treating you with the respect you deserve."

From across the table, I grab his hand. "Thank you for telling me all of that. I know it probably wasn't easy."

"No. But you're the only person I've ever wanted to tell."

I smile.

With my hand still in his, he stands up. I give him a questioning look, but he just smiles while leading me to his backyard.

We step outside onto a covered patio. Upon looking around further, I see a hand-built fire pit. There are chairs, and s'mores supplies already waiting for us.

"You are just full of surprises."

He winks. "You know it."

"Who would've thought."

Greyson meets my eyes, repeating my sentiment back to me. "Yeah. Who would've thought."

There's something about the way he says it. But I don't let myself think too hard about it. Instead, I head toward the fire pit.

We make ourselves comfortable in front of the fire. The flames dance in front of us thanks to the cool Chicago breeze. And I think about how this night couldn't get any more perfect.

While I haven't been on many dates, this is by far my favorite one. Greyson thought of absolutely everything.

I'm wrapped in a blanket with a thermos of decaf coffee in one hand. He even bought cinnamon graham crackers for the s'mores.

Currently, I'm waiting for my marshmallow to turn a nice golden-brown. "You know what would look perfect back here?"

"What?"

"String lights. You could hang them on the roof of the patio, or maybe off the side. I think it would complete the vibe you've got going."

He looks around briefly, considering my idea. Visualizing it. "Yeah, that would be pretty cool."

"This is impressive. Did you do all of this yourself?"

"Yeah. I have a lot of free time on my hands when I'm not working. I'm hoping that changes, though."

The look he gives me makes his meaning clear.

"I guess we'll see."

There's heat in his gaze when he meets my eyes. "We'll see."

We return our attention to the now perfectly cooked marshmallows. Both of us work to get our s'mores made. It's a messy task, but we have fun doing it.

I bite into mine, letting out a satisfied noise. Greyson laughs.

With my mouth full of sweetness, I ask, "What?" It only makes him laugh harder. "What?"

He calms himself down. "You."

"What about me?"

He smiles. "You just make life more fun. I don't know anyone else who can make eating a s'more sound and look so cute."

Embarrassed, I take a sip of my coffee.

It doesn't help.

I sit and wonder how he does this to me?

Over the course of a few months, I've felt things I never did in my previous relationship.

Flustered.

Nervous.

Embarrassed.

Giddy.

It's an overwhelming realization. The power he has. To make me feel things I'm afraid to feel again. I'm not sure how to handle it. All I know is I want to give in to this man so badly. My thoughts are consuming me. Needing a minute to myself, I quickly retreat inside.

It doesn't take long for Greyson to find me in the kitchen attempting to collect myself as I pace back and forth. "Hey. Are you okay?"

With my back to him, I blow out a few breaths and shake out my hands. "Yeah. Yeah, I'm fine."

"Are you sure?"

"Yeah." My voice comes out softer than I intended it to.

"Will you look at me, Liz?"

Slowly, I turn around to find him standing only a couple of feet away.

He doesn't move.

I take a moment to study his face. The desire in his eyes. The longing.

I'm not sure when it happens, but the air around us changes. Shifts. The normal tension is there. But there's something different about it. It's a little overwhelming.

As if Greyson feels it too, he takes a slow step toward me. "Liz?"

He says my name like he's asking for my permission.

I'm well aware of what he wants. And when I say his name, it's my surrender. My inability to fight this attraction—these feelings— any longer. "Greyson."

Before I have time to blink again, he closes the distance between us.

His mouth comes down on mine in an all-consuming kiss.

The way he's holding my head between his hands at the base of my neck is driving me wild.

I kiss him back slowly at first, relishing the way his lips feel against my own.

As soon as I find my confidence, I smile against his lips. He nips at mine. And maybe it's the months of holding myself back. Or that the tension between us broke the moment our lips connected. But the move undoes me.

I kiss Greyson like I have kissed no one else before.

I give him the invitation I know he wants.

With one hand on my back and the other resting against my cheek, he pulls me closer. Greedily, I run my hands up his chest and around his neck.

I bite his lip, refusing to be the only one completely consumed by what's happening between us.

We kiss until Greyson pulls back to look at me.

When he does, there's so much adoration in his expression. I'd lose my balance if he wasn't holding me up.

Slowly. Tenderly, he places kisses down my neck.

When he makes it to my collarbone, I whisper, "Grey."

I expect him to keep placing tender kisses along my neck and chest to see how far I'll let him go.

Instead, he looks at me. When he whispers, "Lizzy girl" in my ear, the nickname causes an onslaught of butterflies to take flight in my stomach.

I love it.

No one has ever called me anything other than Liz.

And now, no one ever will.

Except him.

Whatever he sees on my face has him bringing his lips to mine once again.

This kiss is gentler, though. But just as passionate as the one before it.

I'm consumed by this kiss.

Consumed by him.

It should be captivating.

But it isn't.

I've felt nothing like this since the very last time I kissed Dylan Sinclair.

And while kissing Greyson is a million times better, it just means the capacity in which he could hurt me is even greater.

Chapter 18

Greyson

Present Day

I wait for Liz to give me permission.

After years of longing for her, I don't want to wait any longer. But I will if it's what she wants.

I'd do anything for her.

I can tell she's flustered, so I don't take another step.

The tension in the air is palpable. But I just wait.

Finally, she answers with my name. It sounds reverent coming from her lips. It's the permission I've been waiting on. So, I close the distance between us, kissing her with a wild abandon.

It's like nothing I've ever experienced before.

The sparks that have been flying between us all night are a full-blown fire right now.

I love how I can feel the flush on her face where I'm cupping her cheeks.

Her long, dark lashes graze my skin as she smiles against my mouth. Knowing her, she's taunting me, waiting for me to lose myself. Instead, I tease her right back, nipping her bottom lip gently, hoping it will be her undoing.

Sure enough, she gives into the kiss even more.

She tastes sweet. Like cinnamon with a hint of coffee.

I pull her in closer. She moves her hands up my chest until they're cupping the nape of my neck. The way she runs her fingers through my hair is tantalizing.

I kiss her more fiercely, swallowing her sounds of pleasure as she kisses me back with just as much passion.

I groan from somewhere deep in my chest when she bites my lip, as if getting revenge from earlier. She smiles against my mouth when the sound reverberates between us.

This woman.

I didn't know a kiss could feel like this.

Had I known, I would have waited my whole life for Liz. The thought makes me feel desperate to look at her. To take her in. To admire her beauty. Her emerald green eyes are captivating. The flush on her cheeks fills my chest with pride, knowing I'm the one who put it there. Satisfied with what I see, I tilt her head back and begin placing kisses down her neck.

I start behind her ear and work my way down until she whispers, "Grey."

That nickname. It's intimate. Reserved only for her.

I look at her as I whisper my nickname for her right back. When I do, I see the same desperation in her eyes that I feel in my soul. I want her. Only her. Forever.

I bring my mouth to hers again, gently, reverently this time, hoping she can feel how much I adore her. Because I do. I adore this woman. And I'll spend the rest of my life proving it to her.

What's happening between us is all-consuming. I don't want to stop. But I will if Liz gives me even the slightest inclination that she isn't comfortable.

Carefully, I place my hands on the back of her thighs, lifting her so I can set her on the countertop behind me.

Every move I make is slow. Deliberate. While I want to enjoy every part of her, I know there's no reason to rush.

She places her hands on my shoulders to steady herself. I smile against her mouth. Because she's crazy for thinking I would ever let her down.

When she's seated comfortably on the counter, I settle in between her legs. It's easy to enjoy the way she feels pressed against me. I let my hands rest on her upper thighs as our kisses become more heated.

Too soon, she pulls away from me. I immediately miss having her close, making me feel desperate. Needy. Things I'm not used to feeling.

It isn't until I take a step back when I see the look on her face. I watch as her chest rises and falls rapidly.

I wouldn't say she looks regretful. She almost looks like she's in pain.

I give her the time she needs to control her breathing.

She jumps down from the counter and starts pacing back and forth.

"Greyson, I can't."

Her words are a punch to my gut. And I know I need to tread carefully. "Was I moving too fast?"

When she stops to look at me, it's clear she's holding back tears. I admire her for keeping them suppressed, but I don't want her to hold back with me.

"No." For the first time since meeting Liz, she's choking on her words. "It's... It's not that. I thought I could do this."

My confusion grows. "Do what?"

She looks ashamed when she asks, "Can you take me home? Or if you don't want to, I can call an Uber."

She doesn't give me a chance to say anything before making a beeline for the front door.

My heart feels heavy in my chest, but I grab my truck keys and follow her, anyway.

I want to know exactly what's going on in her head. But I won't push her to find out.

We spend the first few minutes of the drive to her apartment in silence. She hasn't looked at me once. Instead, she's staring out the passenger window.

"Liz?"

"Hmm." She still won't look at me.

Honestly, I don't know what to say. I'm not used to seeing her so solemn. I'm not even sure if that's the right word.

As I continue to drive toward her apartment, I go over everything that happened tonight.

I know she enjoyed what happened between us as much as I did. It was obvious. I rack my brain for an answer, but nothing stands out. Which can only mean one thing: Liz is in her own head. And whatever has her so upset has nothing to do with me and everything to do with him.

* * *

The sound of my cell phone ringing interrupts my workout.

As much as I want to turn it off and ignore the world, I don't. On the off-chance Liz calls me, I want to be available to talk to her.

I need to be available to talk to her. For my sake.

I feel like a madman. It's been two days since our date. And it's been two days of wondering what made her avoid me.

I reached out to her on Sunday before my shift at the station. She didn't respond.

I texted her this morning asking if she's okay. She didn't text back.

The more time that passes, the more I worry about what happened in my kitchen freaked her out. Which would be a shame, considering it was the best kiss I've ever had.

I pull myself from my reverie to answer my phone.

It's Penny. She's the only other person I'm willing to keep my phone on for.

"Hey, Penny. What's up?"

Her gentle voice echoes through the speaker. "Greyson, dear. I'm afraid I need some help."

"What's going on?"

"The contractors are here, but they've made a mess of things. I can't get to my shed which houses some of the paperwork I need, and—"

I cut her off.

She doesn't have to say anymore for me to know I need to head over. I was planning on it this evening, anyway. It's Monday. Liz usually volunteers when she has the time. I'm hoping she'll be there.

"Penny, say no more. I'll be there in about forty minutes. Is that okay?"

"Oh, thank you! I'll see you soon."

When I make it to the shelter, I immediately see what Penny was talking about. It's a mess. The place will be sweet when it's finally done, though.

I find her and Margaret in the office upon making it inside. "Hey."

They look up from the computer at the same time. Each offers me a smile.

"Hi, dear." She looks at her granddaughter. "Why don't you take Greyson out to the shed? I need to finish up here."

"Are you sure, Gran? I can work on the books if you prefer."

She waves a hand dismissively. "I got it."

Margaret and I walk outside to where the contractors are working. "How are you feeling about all this?"

She chuckles. "It's a lot, but I'm proud of her for not giving up on this dream."

"Wasn't this your idea?"

She blushes, though I'm not sure why. "Not really. She's had the land for years, but did nothing with it. It was always the plan, but losing my gramps changed things. I always wanted to take over this business. I thought it was the perfect excuse to get her to actually do what she set out to do."

"She's really lucky to have you, then."

"Do you want to see the lay of the land? I can show you around?"

As much as I would like to see what the contractors have been working on, I don't want to give Margaret the wrong idea. "That's okay. I'm here enough. I'm sure I'll see it all soon."

A look of disappointment crosses over Margaret's face. I can tell she feels embarrassed. "Am I that obvious?"

This is awkward. Maybe there's a reason Penny sent her granddaughter out here instead of coming with me herself.

I chuckle to ease some of the awkward tension. "No. I just didn't want to give you the wrong idea. I'm sorry."

"Don't apologize. I should have known you're already taken. I hope you don't mind me asking, but it's Liz, isn't it?"

"How'd you know?"

She laughs. "Honestly?"

I nod my head, wondering where she's about to go with this.

"I asked her about you. A while ago. She acted a little weird. I thought maybe you guys have a history or something."

I laugh. "We definitely have history. But it isn't what you think."

"Well, you two would make a ridiculously cute couple. I mean you're..." She blushes as she lets her words trail off. "And she's gorgeous, so it makes sense."

I smile. "She is. And thank you for the compliment."

Margaret just laughs as we continue our trek toward the shed.

It doesn't take long for me to clear a path and get everything Penny needs. All the while, I can't seem to stop thinking about Liz, especially after hearing what Margaret said. I know she has feelings for me. I just wish I knew why she's so afraid of them.

* * *

Walking into the station, I find Walker and Sam hanging out in the main room. "Yo."

I get a fist bump from Sam. "What's up?"

"Not much. How has it been today?"

"Not bad. How was your date on Saturday?" Walker asks.

"Nice. I take it Liz finally gave in?"

I chuckle at Sam's question. "Surprised?" I turn my attention to Walker. "I thought the date went well."

Honestly, it was the best date of my life. Actually, it was the only date I've ever been on. But because it was with Liz, I'll always consider it the best date of my life. I just hope she lets me take her on another one.

Walker clasps my shoulder. "I'm glad it went well, man. I'm happy for you."

"Same. Kate said she had a feeling Liz would finally give in."

"Yeah, too bad she hasn't talked to me since."

"Give her time." Coming from Walker, he must know something I don't.

I'm willing to bet Liz already confided in his wife. And I'd love to know what he knows, but I don't want to come across as desperate. I've already decided if I don't hear from Liz this week, I'll show up at her apartment. I don't know what to do beyond that. But it's better than nothing.

I nod my head in Sam's direction. "When did you and Kate start talking like old friends?"

"We don't. She's stressed about some stuff. I checked in on her, and we got to talking."

I grin. "You have a thing for her."

"We're friends, man."

"For now."

He just shakes his head. I do him a favor by leaving him alone, but I know a pining man when I see one. I'm still a pining man myself.

I give Walker my attention. "What do you know about Liz that I don't?"

"Do you want to tell me why you're asking first?"

"I haven't heard from her since Saturday. I don't know what happened or what I can do about it."

He shrugs. "She talked to Maylee, and they're supposed to hang out tonight. I wouldn't worry about it."

I let out a long sigh. "I wish I wouldn't worry about it, but I don't know what to do."

"Look, if I've learned anything from being with Maylee, it's giving her space when she clearly needs it is important. She always comes around. Liz will too."

"I hope you know what you're talking about, man."

He just chuckles in response.

I don't have time to give the situation anymore thought before we get called out.

I'm thankful for the distraction.

Chapter 19

Liz

Present Day

I can't focus.

I'm never off my game at work.

It's my fault.

I haven't spoken to Greyson since our date on Saturday night. I feel terrible about it, but I don't know what to tell him.

He was a perfect gentleman. In fact, it was the best date I've ever been on. The amount of thought he put into it boggles my mind. I could cry just thinking about it. He didn't impress me by taking me to some fancy restaurant in the city. Or by taking me on some crazy adventure. He was only worried about what would make me feel most comfortable. He truly outdid himself. Which is why I'm struggling with my inability to let myself fall for him.

Or let him love me the way he's proved he can. Time and time again.

A soft knock at my office door pulls me from the thoughts that are currently distracting me. I'm a mess.

"Come in."

Steph walks through the door, warily.

Clearly, I haven't done a good job of hiding my mood.

"Your four o'clock canceled. Do you want me to move any of your other appointments?"

As much as I want to tell her to cancel the rest of them, I can't. I have a couple of clients who I need to see today to get things prepared for their court dates.

"Can you see if my five will move up her appointment by an hour?"

"I sure can." She turns for the door but stops in her tracks. "Is everything okay with you? I don't mean to pry, but you seem off."

I sigh. "I just had a long weekend. Don't worry about me. I'll be fine."

I feel guilty lying, but I don't have the energy to talk about Greyson.

Apart from Maylee, no one knows about our date. I'd like to keep it that way for the time being. At least until I figure out how to get a handle on my life.

"Okay. Let me know if you need anything."

I smile, though it doesn't reach my eyes. "Thanks, Steph."

* * *

Thankfully, the work week went by without a hitch. I spent a few late evenings at the office, but nothing too crazy.

Unfortunately, one of those evenings was Monday night. I was supposed to catch Maylee up on all things Greyson, but a last-minute case got in the way. With knots in my stomach, I knock on her door before letting myself in.

She comes out of the kitchen, laughing. "You just couldn't wait, could you? I was about to open the door."

I flip my hair over my shoulder. "You know me." I look around for any sign of Walker.

"Don't worry. He's at work all night."

I sigh in relief. "Good."

She heads to the couch, and I follow, smiling when I see two glasses of red wine already waiting for us.

"How was the date?" She doesn't miss a beat.

I fill my best friend in on my date with Greyson. I start from the moment he picked me up, filling her in on everything that happened until the moment I freaked out.

When I finish my rundown of the date's events, she takes a few minutes to gather her thoughts.

"Have you talked to him since?"

I want to cower in the corner, but I don't. Instead, I answer honestly. "No."

"Has he reached out?"

I grimace. "Yes."

"Liz!"

I point my finger at her. "No! Don't 'Liz' me! It's been over five years since I've felt all these *feelings*." I emphasize the last word of my sentence before admitting defeat. "I don't know how to handle this."

She lets out an exasperated breath. "What do you mean?" Her question must be rhetorical because she doesn't give me time to answer her. "I don't think you need to worry about how to handle anything. Just enjoy what's happening between you and Greyson. I think you deserve this. You deserve to be happy *with* someone. Don't you think so?"

I take a sip of wine. Then I take a deep breath. "I *think* I'm a twenty-seven-year-old woman who needs to get a grip. One epic, mind-blowing kiss should not make me want to run for the hills."

"Don't do that."

"Do what?"

"Don't make this about the kiss." I try to cut her off, but she talks over me. "No, let me finish." She sighs. "Liz, you're a twenty-seven-year-old woman who is *allowed* to feel things. You ran. But not because of the kiss. You ran because you're scared of your feelings."

"What exactly are you saying?"

"You're the most stubborn person I know. You're so stubborn you've somehow avoided feelings you need to feel. Please, please, listen to me. And know that what I'm about to say is coming from a place of love. Okay?"

I nod my head while keeping quiet.

Maylee takes a slow, controlled breath. I steel myself to prepare for whatever she's about to say.

"You are *allowed* to still be angry at Dylan for what he did to you five years ago. You are *allowed* to still grieve your unborn baby. *And* you are *allowed* to fall in love with a man who is crazier about you than anyone else ever has been." She sighs. "You are an expert at making sure everyone around you finds happiness and healing. But somewhere along the way, you stopped seeking those things out for yourself. That isn't fair to you. And right now, it isn't fair to Greyson, either."

I sit, stunned, with tears threatening to spill down my cheeks. And I say the first thing that comes to my mind. "I want to be so angry at you."

My best friend throws her hands up in the air. "Then be angry at me!"

"I can't be."

"Why not?"

"Because you're right! I *am* scared. I'm afraid to feel things in the capacity I did five years ago because look where that got me. What if I get hurt again?"

"What if you don't?" There's optimism in her voice. I know she's hopeful for me.

"How do you know I won't?"

I watch her get up from where she's sitting. She disappears into the bathroom for a minute, walking back with a box of tissues. As she sits back down next to me on the couch, she hands it to me.

Grabbing my free hand with one of her own, she squeezes it gently. "Liz, if I've learned anything from being with Walker after what I went through with Ethan, it's this: Love has just as much power to heal as it does to hurt. Maybe even more so. It's worth the risk."

I sniffle. "What about the rest?" My voice comes out shaky.

I don't have to tell her what I mean. She already knows.

"You get through the rest together. But to do that, he needs to know why you're so afraid."

"And if it happens again. What then?"

She sighs. "You and I both know I'm not the person you need to have this conversation with."

I think she's done, but there's something in her expression that makes me stay quiet, anticipating whatever it is she's planning to say.

"There's someone you know very well who has been through exactly what you went through."

Somehow, more tears pool at the bottom of my eyes. I don't bother fighting them.

All these years later and my parents still don't know about Dylan.

They don't know about any of it.

It's time.

* * *

Last night was tough. I still feel like I'm riding an emotional roller coaster. Not having a clue about when it will finally slow down. It certainly won't be this morning, given where I am.

Currently, I'm standing outside my childhood home. It's a big two-story house with red brick and a white picket fence. The hanging swing on the wrap-around front porch still calls out to me after all these years. But that's not why I'm here.

I take a deep, calming breath before rapping my knuckles against the mahogany front door. I hear footsteps on the other side before someone disengages the lock and the door flies open.

"Honey! What a pleasant surprise! Come in!"

I take in my mom's smiling face, along with her gorgeous red curls that match my own.

Suddenly, I feel guilty for not stopping by more often, considering my apartment isn't that far down the road.

"Hi, Mom. How are you?"

She doesn't answer at first.

Instead, she pulls me in for a hug. "Great!"

"Is dad here?"

She pulls away. "Unfortunately, not. He's out golfing with some colleagues."

Honestly, this conversation will be easier without him.

"Can we talk?"

My mom looks at me with concern on her face. "Is everything okay?"

What a question.

I don't answer her.

Instead, I move down the entryway into the massive living room.

I forgot how much I loved this house growing up. It's bright. The living room windows line the back wall, allowing the natural light in. They overlook my parents' gorgeous backyard. I smile as I recall some of my favorite memories while growing up here.

I'm pulled from my reverie by the sound of my mom's voice behind me. "Liz, honey. Is everything okay?"

With tears in my eyes, I turn around.

"What's wrong?"

My legs feel unsteady beneath me. I sit down on the couch to ease my nausea. The nerves. The guilt.

"How did you do it?"

She joins me on the couch, asking, "Do what?"

"How did you move on after each miscarriage?"

"Honey, where is this..." She stops mid-sentence. I watch as realization hits her, not bothering to wipe my eyes as my tears fall.

"Elizabeth Renée Carter. When?"

I sniffle, and then look up at the ceiling. I collect myself as much as I can before explaining everything. "About five years ago."

The look of pure shock on my mom's face is gut wrenching. I should have told my parents a long time ago. But I was too afraid of how they would've reacted.

She says nothing as I fill her in on everything. Starting with the very first moment I met Dylan Sinclair... until the very last time I ever talked to him.

When I finish, she wraps her arms around me and holds me while I cry.

I'm not sure how much time passes as I sit in my mom's embrace, wishing I would have come to her five years ago. She would have been so angry, but I know she still would have offered me what she's offering me now. Her comfort. There's nothing that comes close.

I lift my head from her chest to look her in the eye. "I'm so sorry."

She wipes my tears away. "Stop it, honey. We're long past apologies at this point."

"Thanks, Mom."

"Why now?"

Sitting up straighter, I think about how to respond.

There isn't a reason to hide anything from her. Not now. So, I decide being honest with her is my best option. I should have been honest with her a long time ago.

"I haven't dated since then. And I've been more than okay with my decision not to. But..." I let my words trail off. It's weird to be having this conversation with my mom so late in life. It should have happened much earlier.

My mom smiles at me knowingly. "You met someone."

I smile too, despite my tears. "Yes. I want to move on."

She brushes a few strands of hair out of my face, sighing as she does. "Sweetie, there is no moving on from the kind of loss we've experienced. There is only moving forward."

Choking on a fresh wave of tears, I ask, "How?"

"By doing what you've already been doing."

She must see the confusion on my face because she keeps speaking. "Liz, continue to live your life to the fullest. You are so successful. Your dad and I are so proud of you. Don't let your grief hold you back from experiencing all life has to offer." She raises a brow, smiling. "That includes falling in love with someone who will be your strength when you have none. Dylan obviously wasn't right for you if he couldn't handle you at your lowest."

"How do I know Greyson can?"

"Give him a chance to show you."

"Mom, I don't want to be let down again."

The truth is, thinking about going through this with Greyson one day is excruciating.

I don't want to believe he would do what Dylan did. There's also the emotional pain of a miscarriage to think about. Not a day goes by when I don't think about the son or daughter who should be here with me.

More tears find their way down my cheeks. "I mean, what if we go through this one day?"

"Liz, honey. If Greyson is truly right for you, then he will face these things with you instead of running away at the first sign of hardship. That's what you do for the people you love. You fight as hard as you can to move forward... *together.*"

I wipe my eyes dry before leaning in to give my mom a hug. "Thank you."

"Do you want to stay for a bit?"

"There's actually something I need to do."

"You got it." She winks. "Don't be a stranger. And I want to meet this young man."

I laugh, feeling lighter than I have in months. Maybe even years.

"You will."

It's time to go after what I want.

Who I want.

Chapter 20

Greyson

Present Day

Opening my front door to Liz's beautiful face is the last thing I expected to be doing this evening.

When I see her standing on my front porch, it takes all my effort not to pull her into a hug.

Instead, I take in the sight of her.

It isn't normal for me to see Liz dressed so casually. She has on a pair of black leggings with an oversized T-shirt. Her wild, red hair is resting on top of her head in a messy bun. From what I can tell, she isn't wearing any makeup either.

I'm not sure if her showing up like this is a good thing or a bad thing. All I know is I wouldn't mind getting to see her like this every day for the rest of my life. She's gorgeous.

Finally, she smiles at me, though the smile doesn't reach her eyes. "Will you come somewhere with me?"

Her invitation catches me off guard, but I don't have to give it a second thought. "Of course."

"Okay. I'll drive."

She's silent during the drive, but I don't mind. I give her the space she needs to work through whatever's going on in her head.

When we show up at a pocket park overlooking a small body of water in a neighborhood that has been around for a while, I'm a little confused. But I let Liz take the lead, curious about what she brought me here for.

She says nothing as we get out of her Jeep and walk toward a park bench.

When we're seated comfortably, she turns sideways on the bench to face me. We make eye contact for a second before she looks out over the water. Her cheek is resting against her knees. I'm not sure what's going through her head. But something is weighing on her. That much, I can tell.

"I owe you an apology."

My heart sinks in my chest as I think about what her apology could mean. Does she no longer want to see what we could be? I try my best to hide my doubt from her.

She sighs. "I'm sorry I've avoided you. You didn't deserve that."

"It's okay."

She brings her eyes to mine. "No, Grey. It's not."

When she calls me by the nickname that she gave me last weekend, hope fills my chest.

I have to stop myself from pulling her close to kiss her senseless. I know I need to listen to what she has to say before making any sort of move. Though I hope I get to kiss this woman again. Take care of her. Love her. It's all I've been able to think about.

She's focused on the water in front of us. But I know the wheels are spinning in her head. I can tell she's fighting an internal battle. My heart aches to reach for her. But that's not what she needs right now. I give her silence, waiting for her to find whatever it is she's searching for.

"I used to come here as a kid. When I got older, it became my favorite place to think." She lets out a deep breath. Whatever she's about to tell me must be difficult for her to talk about.

"I dated this guy. In college. We dated for about a year. Dylan. Our relationship progressed quickly. I hadn't ever dated anyone seriously before him because my parents were strict."

She looks down at her hands before returning her gaze to mine. "I was reckless in my decision making from time to time. I put our relationship on this pedestal, thinking he was my future. We both had dreams. And we made plans based on those dreams. Then life happened. After I made a reckless decision." I remain silent, letting her collect her thoughts. "I ended up pregnant at the end of our junior year."

All the air leaves my lungs. Like I've just been punched in the gut. Knocked out.

Out of all the things she could have said, I wasn't expecting her to say that. My mind races to multiple places, attempting to put together a puzzle it doesn't have all the pieces to.

"What?" My question comes out on an exhale. It probably wasn't the best thing I could have asked, but I'm a little shocked.

When Liz's eyes fill with tears, I move in closer to her. Just enough to feel her body heat despite the chilly weather.

I grip her hand firmly in mine, so she knows I'm with her. "Hey. What is it?"

She sniffles. "He or she would turn five soon. Sometimes I let myself wonder what my life would look like."

Her words shoot me in the heart. "Would?"

"I miscarried twelve weeks into my pregnancy."

Her answer isn't what I was expecting. I thought maybe she gave the baby up for adoption. Or it's with the father.

This must be one reason Liz is so passionate about what she does. Family law. I could see it being a coping mechanism for her. Fighting for families that aren't hers. Since she couldn't fight for her own.

The tears in her eyes run down her cheeks more furiously. She tries to hide her face from me, but I use my fingers to raise her chin gently, so her eyes meet mine. Tenderly, I wipe away her tears.

"Dylan and I broke up a few months later. He said being with me hurt too much."

"He said that?"

She only nods her head.

What a coward.

How could he leave her after she experienced something like that?

He's lucky I don't know where he lives. I would have no problem showing up to kick his butt for hurting such an incredible woman. A brave and beautiful woman. She's one of a kind.

"Did you two ever try again?"

She scoffs. "No. I haven't talked to him since. Besides, I don't think I would have given him a second chance had he asked for one. He changed. He started partying a lot more and was hooking up with random girls any chance he got. Maybe it was his way of coping. It didn't matter to me either way. I was angry. I'm still so angry."

"I'm sorry he did that to you."

"Don't be." She lets out a shaky breath. "The reason I freaked out after our kiss is that I'm so afraid to hurt the way I did back then. I have felt nothing like I did... *like I do*... since him. It just made me realize how much power you have over me. That, and I don't trust myself. It's terrifying."

"Liz, I would never—"

"I know."

"Are his actions the reason you hated me so much?"

"I didn't hate you. I just wasn't your biggest fan. Your lifestyle reminded me of who Dylan had become. I'm sorry for holding that against you."

"You don't owe me an apology, Liz."

And I mean it. I can understand why she wanted to stay as far away from me as possible. I would have treated her no differently than I treated any of the other women I hooked up with. Honestly, I'm glad she gave me such a hard time. We wouldn't be sitting here right now if she would have let me in right away.

"What do you need from me?"

She lets out a shaky breath. "I need you to take this slow."

"Anything you need."

"Right. Well, I need to know you're willing to face difficult things with me. I'm not planning our wedding or anything." She winks, drawing a chuckle from me. If she was planning our wedding, I don't think I'd mind. But that's a topic for a different day. "But if we find ourselves there one day, and we decide we want a family, I need you to be what he couldn't be. There's always a chance I could miscarry again. My mom did. Multiple times. After it happened, I withdrew in a lot of ways. We went for weeks without touching each other. I know that upset him more than he let me believe."

Her eyes fill with tears once more. It kills me. But what kills me more is knowing she was alone during a time when she desperately needed support.

I see difficult things in my line of work all the time. I see pain. Fear. Agony. Loss, too. But I also see family surround each other. Support one another. And love each other fiercely through it all. Liz needs that. And I want to be exactly what she needs.

I pull her into my lap.

When she's seated comfortably on my thighs, I tuck some loose strands of hair behind her ears.

"Listen to me, Liz."

She looks at me with vulnerability in her expression. "I'm listening."

I place my hands on her hips. Anchoring her to me. "I will always fight for you. I don't care what we face. But I promise we will always face it together. I will hold you up when you can't find the strength to stand on your own. Dry your tears when there are too many to count. And I will always choose to love you, even when life brings you to your lowest." With as much conviction as possible, I say, "I will *never* let you down, my beautiful Lizzy girl."

She smiles at me with a blush on her cheeks and tears streaming down her face. And this smile. This smile is my favorite because it reaches her eyes. Knowing I put it there fills me with pride.

"Promise?"

"I will do my best to prove it to you. Every day."

"Okay."

I smile. "Okay."

Liz surprises me by bringing her lips to mine in a tender kiss. It's sweet.

This moment is about her, so I let her take the lead.

Still planted on my lap, she moves as close to me as she can get, bringing her hands to either side of my neck as she deepens the kiss.

I keep my hands planted firmly on her hips, wanting her to feel secure right where she is.

I can taste the salt from her tears, but she still tastes like cinnamon and coffee. The combination doesn't surprise me. In fact, it's becoming one of my favorites.

Liz runs her fingers through my hair.

Feeling the delicate brush of her fingertips on my scalp is enough to drive me wild.

I'm not sure how long we kiss before Liz pulls back, practically panting as she does.

When her eyes find mine, she smiles bashfully. She burrows her head in my neck, but not before I notice how flushed she is. I let her stay where she is. But only because I love getting to see sides of this woman I didn't know existed.

She's always so sure of herself, always exudes so much confidence. And boldness. While I know it's because she's very much both things, I also know she's no amateur in hiding what's under the surface.

There's a lot more to her than what she lets people see. I hope, with time, she lets me see every bit of who she is. I know every piece of her is exquisite.

Finally, she finds enough composure to look at me. I can tell she feels much lighter after having the conversation we just did. It comforts me to know we can move forward from here. At her pace. Whatever she needs it to be.

I place a soft kiss on her forehead. "Can I take you on a date tonight?"

She smiles at me. "Please."

I laugh at her answer.

* * *

Liz and I are sipping on our beers at one of my favorite breweries.

She wanted nothing fancy tonight since she claims she didn't dress for it. I tried to tell her it didn't matter. She's the most beautiful woman in the room, no matter where she is.

As soon as the server delivers our appetizers to the table, she digs in.

I stare at her as she stuffs her face with the bar pretzel and cheese we ordered.

When she catches me, she asks, "What?"

I chuckle. "Nothing."

She points a finger at me. "No. It's not nothing. You were staring."

My chuckle turns into a laugh before I let it fizzle out. "You're just cute."

She smirks. I'm glad to see it after having such a heavy conversation just an hour ago.

"And I wonder where it all goes." I wink.

She scoffs at me. "Well, that was rude. I was about to tell you I think you're cute, too."

I lift my eyebrows. "Do you?"

She rolls her eyes. "Don't let it go to your head. How's your step-sister?"

Her change in subject surprises me, but I don't mind it. Honestly, it means a lot that she's asking about my family.

"Good."

"Yeah? Has she left you alone since you went to see your mom and Phil?"

"Not really."

She laughs. "You aren't one for details. Are you still on the fence about him?"

Sighing, I think about her question.

I was hoping this conversation wouldn't come up tonight. I'm not necessarily on the fence about Phil.

As a twenty-nine-year-old, it feels a little late in life to get to know a brand-new father figure along with three step-siblings who are also adults.

I contemplate whether to open up to Liz about it. I'm new to this dating thing. Sharing details about myself isn't something I'm used to doing either. But it's Liz. After everything she told me today, I know it's only fair. She may have some good advice.

"It's not that. The whole situation feels awkward to me."

"How come?"

"I just think it's a little late in life for me to get to know him and his kids."

"Can I be honest with you?"

I nod my head, remaining silent.

"If it were me, I would try. Family is family. It doesn't matter that all of you are adults with separate lives. If I found out I had a few step-siblings, I would do whatever it takes to get to know them."

I consider her words. They make sense coming from her. Liz is the glue in her relationships. She has always been good at bringing people together. She doesn't know a stranger.

"Yeah. I guess you're right."

"You guess?" She winks. I chuckle. As I do, she rolls her eyes. "Plus, I mean..."

"What?"

She lets out a deep breath. "What if any of you have kids one day? Wouldn't it be fun to have a bunch of nieces and nephews running around? And for your kids to know their cousins well?"

I know what she's getting at.

Personally, I haven't thought about things from that perspective. Not that long ago, I thought I didn't want to get married.

"Is that what you want?"

My question is bold, but I'm genuinely curious.

I notice Liz gulp before answering. "I do. But I don't want you to get to know your siblings because of me. I want you to do it for you. And for them."

"I'll think about it."

She rolls her eyes before going back to munching on our bar pretzel.

We finish our beer in companionable silence before I work up the nerve to return to a difficult subject for her.

"Mind if I ask you something?"

She nods her head as we get up from the table. Without thinking twice, I thread my fingers through hers, realizing this is the first time I've ever felt comfortable enough to do so.

"Is Dylan the reason you put off law school?"

She sighs. "Yes, and no. Everything that happened between us hurt. I think putting off law school was my way of grieving."

"It's impressive, you know." She looks at me questioningly. "The way you live life. I admire you for it. I wish I could have handled my hardship with as much grace."

There's so much more I want to say. But I won't. I want to respect Liz's wishes to take this relationship slowly. It won't be easy, but I know it will be worth it.

"Thanks." She stops us in our tracks, turning to face me on the sidewalk. "Greyson, apart from my mom and Maylee, you're the only person who knows what happened. It's why I have dated no one since him. It's also why I want to take this slow. I just want to make sure you truly are okay with that."

I bring my lips to the side of her head, giving her a quick kiss. "I told you, I'll do anything you need."

Chapter 21

Liz

Present Day

The sound of my phone ringing distracts me from the cases I've been mulling over for the last couple of hours. When I see Greyson's name flashing across my screen, sparks fly.

A few weeks have passed since he agreed to take things slow with me. I can tell it's taking some self-control on his part, but I appreciate his willingness to move at my pace.

There are things I'm still fearful of. Although I'm trying my best to trust Greyson. He hasn't given me a reason not to.

Apart from Maylee and Walker, our friends don't know we're seeing each other. He was hesitant to keep it hidden, but I explained to him I need some time to get used to being in a relationship again. I can only take so much at once.

I quickly answer my phone before he gets sent to voicemail. "Hi."

"Hey. Are you okay?"

"Yeah. Busy day."

"Are you free tonight?"

My guilt sets in as soon as he asks.

To protect myself, I've tried not to spend every waking second with him. I know myself well enough to know that when I fall; I fall hard.

I won't lie by saying I don't miss him, though. Because I do. A lot more than I expected to.

"I'm sorry, Grey. I have a girls' night with Maylee. What about tomorrow night?"

He sighs. "I have a shift tomorrow. But I'll see if one of the other guys can cover for me. I really want to see you."

"Do you?"

"Is that so hard to believe?"

"I just never pegged you as the type of man who would ever admit that to a woman."

"Only if that woman is you."

Heat pools in my belly as I picture his smug face on the other side of the phone.

"Are you sure about that?"

"How about I prove it to you?"

"I like the sound of that."

"I'm sure you do. I'll find someone to cover my shift tomorrow, so I can spend the evening proving to you that you're the only woman I'll ever need."

Even though he can't see me, I shake my head. "Careful, Greyson. You promised to take things slow."

He chuckles. "What did you think I meant?"

I smile. "Oh, nothing. I'll see you tomorrow."

"You drive me crazy, Lizzy girl. I can't wait to see you."

I smile as heat creeps up my neck.

For the first time, I'm thankful Greyson never dated seriously. He wouldn't be single if he had.

I just hope he doesn't break my heart. I don't think I can survive any more pain.

* * *

"So, what's it like being Greyson's girlfriend?"

I shove my best friend's shoulder. "I told you I'm not his girlfriend. We're dating."

She rolls her eyes as she takes a sip of her wine. "What's the difference?"

"The difference is we don't have a label."

"What are you so afraid of?"

I sigh in frustration. "I don't want to feel any pressure."

"How does Greyson feel about that?"

I set my glass of wine on the table, preparing to defend myself if necessary. "He's willing to move at my pace."

"Yeah, I get that. But don't you think he's been through enough?"

Defensively, I ask, "What's that supposed to mean?"

"What I mean is, hasn't he proved enough how he feels about you? I know he wasn't always your favorite person, but the two of you know each other so well. I don't think you need to spend months dating before making things official. Let yourself enjoy this, Liz. You deserve to be happy."

Falling into the couch cushions, I groan. "I know, okay? I just don't want to get hurt."

"He isn't Dylan."

I give my best friend a pointed look. "I know that."

"Then don't treat him like he's going to hurt you the way Dylan did. Think about what he told you after finding out. He's crazy about you. Go all in."

Her smile makes me do a double take. I wait for her to say whatever's on her mind, knowing whatever she's thinking is the reason for the smile on her face. "I have a good feeling about this."

I pick up my glass of wine, finishing it. "My instincts agree with you." I admit, albeit reluctantly.

Maylee laughs before finishing her own glass of wine.

I know she's right. And I need to trust my instincts. I need to trust Greyson, too.

Thankfully, he ended up finding someone to cover for him tomorrow. He deserves the version of me who gives all of herself, fearlessly. I plan to give him that version. To the best of my ability.

* * *

Sparks fly as soon as I open the door of my apartment and see Greyson standing there, waiting for me.

Instead of saying anything, I wrap my arms around his neck, pulling him into a hug.

I lean back far enough to see the confusion on his face.

Before he says anything, I press my lips to his in a kiss I meant to make soft. While our kisses may start that way, they always turn into something more. The chemistry between us is indescribable. I can't believe it took me so long to realize it.

Greyson slides his hands down, resting them on the small of my back and pulling me closer once they reach their destination. He smiles against my mouth.

He tastes like honey and mint. The combination is addictive. Or maybe it's just him.

The sensations I feel are relentless as I revel in how natural things feel between us. Overwhelmingly so.

When I pull back to look at Greyson, his hair is in disarray from where I ran my fingers through it. I laugh, patting it down as I do.

He smiles. "What was that for?"

I smirk. "You're gorgeous, and I wanted to do something about it."

He lets out a laugh before winking at me. "You're welcome to do that anytime you want." Grabbing my hand, he pulls me out of my apartment. "Come on."

"What's the rush?"

He looks back at me with heat in his eyes, and I know exactly what he's thinking.

* * *

I know where we are as soon as Greyson puts his truck into park.

Hyde Park is one of my favorite places in Chicago. The views are breathtaking.

Curiously, I look over at the man who continues to surprise me.

He just winks. "Wait there."

He comes around to the passenger side of his truck to open my door, helping me out after he does.

Taking my hand in his, he leads me to a picnic area near a gazebo overlooking Lake Michigan. My eyes zero in on the picnic blanket and basket already set up for us.

I drop his hand as I turn to face him. "Did you do this?"

He nods. "I did."

"You just keep surprising me."

"Good. That was the goal."

He leads me to the picnic area. Tingles dance along my skin from where he places his hand on my back. Every touch from him creates sparks. It isn't a feeling I'm used to. But I love it.

Once we're seated, he removes each item from the picnic basket.

I study the spread. "This looks amazing. I didn't know you liked to cook."

He shrugs. "Honestly, I didn't either. I think having someone to cook for makes it more fun, though."

He eyes me warily, waiting for my reaction to his admission.

"That's sweet. Food is the way to my heart, so you can never go wrong cooking for me."

He throws his head back in laughter. I watch his Adam's apple bob as he does.

It's no secret that Greyson is one of the most attractive men I've ever laid eyes on. I've always known it. But now, I truly get to enjoy it. I'm glad I finally gave in.

He returns his eyes to mine, and I take in the features of his face.

His eyes are a deep brown. Up close, I get to admire the gold flecks surrounding his irises. Although in some lighting, they resemble the color of honey.

His cheekbones and jawline are prominent, making his face look chiseled.

I'm not sure how long I admire him before he clears his throat, getting my attention. I drop my head to hide the blush on my cheeks.

"So, I've learned. I had a little help with dessert, though." My eyes widen and my mouth waters as he pulls out what looks like a cinnamon roll cheesecake. "I hope you don't mind, but I asked Maylee if she could provide dessert for our date."

I raise an eyebrow. "Was the cinnamon roll cheesecake her idea or yours?" Before he has time to answer, I add, "There *is* a correct answer, by the way."

"Technically, it was her idea. My only request was to make sure it included cinnamon."

"I guess that's good enough." I wink.

We dig into our food, chatting about casual topics. Greyson spends some time telling me all about what it was like growing up with his mom. The more I get to know him, the more I see him for the momma's boy he is. Who would've thought?

I recall the conversation I had with her months ago while we were cleaning up her kitchen after dinner. Like any mother, she had nothing but wonderful things to say about her son. There's one thing she said that stuck out to me, though.

Greyson has had a rough go of things. I fault his father's absence in his life for that. But he has a heart of gold. As soon as he learns how to deal with his pain healthily, he will make someone very happy one day. I hope he doesn't wait too long.

I smiled kindly at her, thinking through her words. Truthfully, they softened my heart enough to give Greyson a real chance. Any boy with a mother like Jenny is bound to become a wonderful man. And while it's still surreal to think about, I know he'll be a wonderful husband, too.

It's crazy, but I hope I get to be a part of his future. The thought reminds me of a question I've been meaning to ask.

I let Greyson finish his bite of food.

"What made you change your perspective on relationships, and why me?"

Once he's done wiping his mouth, he fidgets with his napkin a few times. Then he sits up from where he's resting on his arm, giving me his full attention.

"I knew that if I wanted a chance with you, I needed to change."

I nod, but say nothing in response, waiting for him to give me a little more than that.

He sighs. "I know that doesn't sound like the best reason. I'm not proud of my past choices, but they are in the past, Liz."

"I know."

He takes my hand in his and then kisses my fingers. "I've always admired you." He smiles briefly before his face goes serious. "I knew you were too good for me. You still are. That's why I tried so hard to win you over. I enjoyed the challenge, but it got old. Especially when I realized a woman like you deserves so much more than I was offering."

"I like that answer."

"I'm not done." He smirks. "You're gorgeous, kind, smart, funny, and you live life to the fullest without a care in the world. You have this way of making the people around you feel valued. I didn't deserve your friendship, but you gave it to me, anyway. I can't thank you enough for that."

I stare at him for a few seconds, still taking in his words.

He smiles at me, which causes heat to creep up my neck until my face flushes.

I glance down at the blanket beneath me. It does no good.

Either Greyson saw the flush on my cheeks. Or he's very aware of the effect he has on me. Gently, he places his fingers under my chin to return my focus back to his face. "I enjoy watching your body react to my words." He moves his hand from under my chin to cup my cheek, rubbing his thumb back and forth. "And my touch."

I'm can't hide my face as I feel it turn an even darker shade of red.

Butterflies flutter wildly in my stomach. And it takes more energy than it should to control my breathing.

Slowly, he leans in.

I wait in anticipation for another mind-blowing kiss.

When his lips are only centimeters from mine, I wait with bated breath, trying to ignore what he does to me. How flustered he makes me feel.

At the last second, right before his lips meet mine, he brings his mouth to my ear and whispers, "How about dessert?"

As he pulls away, he winks.

I'm too flustered to say anything, so I let him cut us each a slice of cheesecake instead.

As he does, he looks at me like he didn't just cause my whole body to break out into goosebumps. I know he's very aware of it.

All the while, I'm left wondering how on earth Greyson scaled every single wall surrounding my heart.

Chapter 22

Greyson

Present Day

"How are things going with Liz?"

I look around the break room, making sure none of our friends are within earshot.

Walker chuckles when he catches me. "Chill, man. I wouldn't have asked if anyone else was in here."

I dip my chin. "Things are great."

"That's good." He raises his brow. "I take it she still isn't ready for everyone to know?"

"Honestly, we haven't talked about it in a few weeks."

The more time that passes, the more I want to make things official with Liz. I don't want to pressure her, though. I've been waiting for her to approach me about it instead.

"Is she letting you call her your girlfriend yet?"

"No, she isn't. And what's with the twenty questions this morning?"

He raises his hands in mock surrender. "My bad, man. I'm just checking in." He clasps a hand on my shoulder. "I'm proud of you."

I take a sip of my coffee before acknowledging his words. "As much as I appreciate the sentiment, cut it out. Marriage has turned you into a softie."

He barks out a laugh. "Are you planning on bringing anyone to family day?"

His question comes out of left field, but I'm thankful for the subject change. "Not sure. You know I usually don't. Is Maylee coming?"

"She is. You should invite your mom. I haven't seen her in a while."

"I'll think about it."

"Bring Liz, too. I bet she'll come if you ask her."

"Why would I do that?"

My best friend looks at me knowingly.

I prepare myself for whatever he's about to say, knowing there's a very specific reason he brought this up.

"Why wouldn't you?"

"She isn't family."

"Not yet."

The coffee in my mouth goes down the wrong pipe, causing me to break into a coughing fit.

I didn't prepare myself for two simple words to catch me so off guard. Especially a comment like that. I don't know what's with Walker today, but he needs to cut this out. Not that what he said is wrong.

"Seriously, what is with you this morning?"

"I'm just waiting for you to admit that you're in love with my wife's best friend."

"I'm not talking about this with you, man. We aren't teenage girls."

He stares at me. The silence is almost too much. I know he's waiting on me to get over my pride. Reluctantly, I do. "How did you know?"

He shrugs. "You've been different."

"No." Running a hand through my hair, I let out a frustrated sigh.

This topic makes me uncomfortable. It's unfamiliar. I'm not sure how to navigate it. "How did you know Maylee was the one?"

He gets this look in his eyes that I can only describe as love. Maylee's good for him. Marriage suits him. And honestly? I envy him for it. But then again, maybe it isn't too late for me. Just because my father completely failed at it doesn't mean that I will. I'm not him and I have my mom to thank for that.

"From the moment I met her, she made me want to be the best version of myself." He shrugs. "Her happiness was all that mattered to me. It still is."

What he said sounds familiar.

After mulling over his words, I realize they sound a lot like Phil's from dinner months ago.

I nod in understanding. Because I *do* understand. I feel the same way about Liz.

***

Surprisingly, Liz beat me to the shelter today. I don't mind though. I've been watching her interact with the dogs in the outdoor play area.

There's one she seems to have bonded with. Big time. He's a German Shepherd mix. I think his name is Milo. I'm currently watching as he follows Liz everywhere she goes. Occasionally, she crouches down, talking to him like he can understand every word she's saying. Honestly, he gives her enough attention to make me think he can.

I think I'm being discreet until I hear what Liz says to Milo next. "Hey, boy! I think we're being watched. What should we do?"

Milo barks in response, making me laugh.

She spins to face me, placing her hands on her hips. "What exactly are you doing over there?"

Raising an eyebrow, she waits for my excuse.

I walk closer to her until I'm standing only a few feet away. "I can't help it. You're a natural with them. This one seems to have taken a liking to you. Not that I blame him." I wink, hoping to make Liz blush.

It doesn't work, but I'll gladly take the smile she's aiming at me. "You are the biggest flirt if I ever knew one."

"You know you love it."

If it's possible, her smile gets even bigger. "I do."

Closing the distance between us, I stride toward her. Pulling her close, I place a quick kiss on her lips. She doesn't resist.

"Are you almost done?"

She places her hands on my chest, looking up at my face. "I was planning on taking Milo for a walk. Why?"

"I was going to see if you wanted to sneak away for a few minutes before I help Penny complete some things with the contractors. Mind if I join you instead?"

"I'd love that."

I kiss her lips once more.

Once we get the dogs back into their kennels, Liz grabs a leash for Milo. I offered to get him situated, but she refused.

We start our walk on the trail behind where the contractors are finishing up the training facility. I take her hand in mine, thankful for the extra alone time I have with her. Our schedules keep both of us busy. But I'm glad Liz still volunteers when she can. It's been a while since she has made it.

After we pass the construction zone, she asks, "Do you know what Penny is having them do? I haven't been around enough to ask."

I had been wondering if Penny broke her retirement news to Liz yet. I guess I have my answer.

It isn't my responsibility to fill her in, even though I want to. She deserves to hear it from Penny. I just hope she finds out sooner rather than later. I don't like feeling like I'm lying to her.

"She's having them build a training facility."

"Oh, that's cool. Is it just for the shelter dogs or will it be open to the public?"

"I'm not sure. She hasn't given me many details."

"I hope she plans on hiring more staff members."

"I'm sure she will. Volunteers can't run a training facility alone." I hesitate before changing the subject. "How come you haven't adopted Milo? You seem to like him as much as he likes you."

She looks at the dog, smiling. "Believe me, I've thought about it. But I live in an apartment, and he deserves a yard. Plus, I work

208

long hours sometimes. I'd feel bad leaving him by himself all day."

"That makes sense."

We walk along the trail with Milo, hand in hand. What we're doing, it feels natural. I would spend every afternoon doing this with Liz if I could.

It isn't until we turn around to head back to the shelter that I get an idea.

Once the training facilities are open, I want to train Milo as a gift to Liz. I know she isn't crazy about the idea of owning him while she's in an apartment. But I know she won't be there forever. Not if I have anything to do with it. I'm more than willing to adopt Milo and keep him at my place until she lives there with me.

The sound of Liz's voice pulls me from my train of thought. "What are you thinking about over there?"

I suppress my smile and squeeze her hand gently. "How crazy I am about you."

Her face turns a shade of pink. "You are not."

"Seriously. I was thinking about you."

"Well, I'm right here. You can talk to me. It's even better."

"You aren't wrong."

In typical Liz fashion, she throws a smirk my way. "I know."

"Can I ask you a favor?"

"Of course."

I clear my throat. The action doesn't go unnoticed by Liz. She grabs my arm, stopping us in our tracks. "Greyson Wright, are you nervous right now?"

I smile at her sheepishly. "No?"

She laughs at my answer. The answer that was supposed to come out more confident than it did.

"I might need some moral support next weekend."

At first, she looks confused, but I see it on her face the moment she realizes what I'm asking. Her eyes grow wide.

"You're getting to know more of your step-siblings! That's exciting. Of course, I'll be your moral support." She bumps her shoulder against mine playfully. "Even though you don't need me."

"No, I *do* need you." I step closer to her. "I'll always need you."

She smiles down at her feet before looking back up at my face. She's never looked at me like this before. With complete vulnerability. Admiration. Maybe even love.

"How do you do that?"

"Do what?"

"Make me feel all giddy. Literally every time I'm with you."

"It must be a gift."

She rolls her eyes. "Yeah. Okay."

I chuckle as we continue our walk back toward the shelter, though I don't want it to end.

When I'm with Liz, I forget about the things that usually weigh me down. This is what I've been missing my entire life. I never want to go without it again. Without her.

Had my father felt this way about my mom, I doubt he ever would have cheated. There's no way. Liz has become the most important person in my life. I could never do anything to hurt her.

"Are you sure it's okay if I come? I don't want to intrude."

"Actually, my mom and Phil invited you. I don't know how you did it, but you won my mom over without even trying."

"I'm not sure why you're surprised. Jenny and I are practically best friends."

I laugh, secretly loving that my mom is already a big fan of Liz. She has ulterior motives with inviting Liz to our family barbecue. Little does she know I'm already a few steps ahead of her. I just hope Liz will let me tell my family about us.

When we make it back inside, I leave Liz at the kennels while I go search for Penny, reminding her to come find me before heading out.

As I approach the front office, I make a mental note to remind Penny to fill Liz in on every update before leaving for the day. I don't feel comfortable keeping the news from her, knowing how much she adores Penny and values her time here.

"Hey. What do you need from me to get everything completed?"

Penny jumps, placing a hand on her chest as she does. "Goodness. You scared me, dear."

I hold back my chuckle. "Sorry about that."

From behind the computer, Margaret says, "Don't be sorry. It's not your fault she's easily spooked."

Penny clears her throat. "Anyway, I wanted to get your thoughts on something before finalizing it. Come over here." She gestures toward the computer. I walk over to where she's standing behind Margaret.

What I see on the screen catches my eye. There's a virtual replica of the training facility. It's painted in black. Above the door is a charcoal sign with lettering that reads: "Burt Training Facility".

"That looks awesome. Is this the design you're going with?"

Penny nods. "I think so. I wanted your thoughts."

"I appreciate that. But I think it's up to you and Margaret. Although, there's one more person I think you should ask."

My eyes flick to Margaret as she looks over her shoulder at me knowingly.

Penny sighs beside me. "I know. Is she still here?"

"She is. You should go find her."

Without another word, she strides out of the office.

I let out a deep breath, feeling relieved Liz will finally be in on this.

Casually, I say, "It's about time she finds out."

From just outside the door, I hear Liz's voice. "Find out what?"

What terrible timing.

Penny must have just missed her.

"Did you see Penny on your way up here?"

She shakes her head.

Margaret looks at me with wide eyes. I don't acknowledge her, instead I make eye contact with Liz again. She looks between Margaret and me.

"What don't I know that you do?"

"Liz—"

She cuts me off. "Is there..."—She gestures between the two of us—"Has there ever..." She lets her words trail off. Though, I think I know what she's assuming.

Before I have time to respond, Margaret mouths, "I'll tell her", before getting up from the desk.

Meanwhile, I'm left in the office, reeling over what Liz could have possibly thought we were keeping from her.

I wanted to respect Penny's wishes since she made it clear she was planning on telling Liz. But now, I'm questioning whether I made the right choice. She'll be upset either way.

Curious, I walk over to the door, hoping to hear the conversation happening in the hall.

I catch a few words of what Margaret is saying, but nothing more. It isn't until Penny approaches, offering Liz a hug, that I see the tears in her eyes.

I leave them to talk, while I busy myself with whatever is left to do this evening.

Chapter 23

Liz

Present Day

Volunteering at the shelter has been a part of my routine for as long as I can remember. My parents never let me have pets growing up, so I spent as much free time here as I could.

Now, getting to spend time here with Greyson has become my favorite part of it all. That thought has me smiling as I work.

It's so crazy to think about where my life has taken me.

After Dylan, I never thought I would allow myself to feel the things I feel when I'm with Grey. I love the side of myself he brings out.

Even though he hasn't been gone for long, I miss him. So, I hurry through a few things before giving up, wanting to see if there's anything I can help him with instead.

When I can't find him anywhere, I head toward Penny's office, hoping that's where he'll be.

I stop in my tracks when I see him, confused by what he's doing, standing closely behind Margaret while she's looking at the computer screen.

To no one in particular, Greyson says, "It's about time she finds out."

He sounds relieved, which confuses me. He has to be talking about me. I don't know who else he would mean.

Before I think things through, my curiosity gets the best of me. "Find out what?" The question slips out before I can stop it.

Greyson ignores my question, asking one of his own instead. "Did you see Penny on your way up here?"

I shake my head, looking between Margaret and Greyson. They both seem to know something I don't. Not that it would be strange if that's the case. I know I've barely been around since starting as a lawyer.

"What don't I know that you do?"

"Liz–"

I hold up a hand, cutting Greyson off.

I let my doubt get the best of me. "Is there..." Choking on my words, I continue. "Has there ever..." I realize how ridiculous I sound the moment the words come out of my mouth, so I don't finish.

I trust Greyson. I just wish someone would tell me what's going on.

As if she can read my thoughts, Margaret motions for me to follow her down the hall.

Once we've made it a suitable distance from Penny's office, she turns around to face me. "Don't be upset with Greyson."

I furrow my brow. "Why would I be upset with him?"

"My grandmother wanted to tell you this. She went searching for you. Greyson insisted."

Her words make little sense. If anything, they confuse me even more. "Okay, what does this have to do with him?"

She takes a deep breath. "She's retiring after the training facility is up and running."

"What?" As soon as the word comes out of my mouth, I feel a dainty hand grab my shoulder. I spin around before pulling Penny into a hug. "I can't believe you're leaving."

She rubs my back soothingly. "I know, but it's time."

My eyes well with tears. "I'm sorry I haven't been around much."

She pulls back, grabbing my shoulders. "Oh, don't be silly. I'm so proud of all your hard work. Your job comes first."

"Thank you, Penny."

"Of course, my dear."

She looks over at her granddaughter. "Now, let's go fill her in."

Margaret chuckles. "Whatever you say, Gran."

The plans for this place are amazing. I love that the last thing Penny is doing with this place is to honor her late husband.

The training facility is going to be amazing, and Margaret is going to do a great job running the place. She's passionate about it. I'm thankful she's the one stepping in. This place wouldn't be the same without a part of Penny.

After poring over the designs for half an hour, I'm attempting to track down Greyson.

I have a bone to pick with him.

While the lawyer side of me understands why he chose not to tell me he knew about this, the girlfriend (not that I'm his girlfriend) side of me is kind of mad at him for not telling me. He knows how busy I am most of the time. Which keeps me from spending as much time here as I would like.

Finally, I find him cleaning up a few things before closing time.

With my arms crossed, I lean my hip against the doorframe of the storage area. I don't make my presence known right away.

"How long have you known?"

He stops what he's doing to run a hand through his hair nervously. I can't ignore the way his bicep flexes as he does.

"A while."

I nod, keeping my facial expression neutral. "Why didn't you tell me?"

He sighs. "Penny told me she planned to. I wanted to respect that."

I can tell he thinks I'm upset with him, but I keep my features schooled.

When I say nothing, he speaks up again.

"I'm sorry if you thought I was purposely keeping something from you. I wouldn't do that, Liz."

It's the doubt in his voice that has me closing the distance between us, leaving only a little space.

I smile. "You know I'm not mad at you, right?"

He breathes out a sigh of relief. "You're not?"

I step closer to him. Close enough that I have to crane my neck to meet his eyes.

Honestly, I love our height difference. He has a good six inches on me, possibly more.

"No. I understand why you didn't." To clear up his doubt, I choose my next words carefully. Admitting what I'm about to is a gigantic step for me.

"I trust you, Grey."

His entire body relaxes as soon as the words leave my lips. "Are you sure?"

I lift my hand, placing it on his cheek. "Of course. I'm so sorry I made you doubt that."

He shakes his head, moving the hand I placed on his cheek far enough away to kiss the inside of my palm. The gesture is simple, but has enough power to cause the dormant butterflies in my stomach to take flight. These days, they never leave. Always ready to be triggered by the man standing before me.

"Don't apologize." The gentleness and sincerity in his tone are undeniable. So is the look in his eyes. It's a look filled with adoration. Desire. Maybe love, too.

Three little words are on the tip of my tongue, but I hold myself back. I'm not quite ready to say them, though, I know I feel them.

I'll remember this moment—at an animal shelter of all places—as the moment I realized I am completely and irrevocably in love with Greyson Wright.

When I smile up at him, he places his hands on my hips to pull me closer.

When there's no room left between us, I let my head rest against his chest before pulling back to look into his beautiful, deep brown eyes.

"Thank you for being you."

"Why are you thanking me?"

I shrug. "I'm just thankful for you. Is that okay?"

He kisses me softly. "Of course. I'm thankful for you, too. Are you up for a night out?"

"What do you have in mind?"

"I think our friends want to get together. There will be some live music on Division Street tonight."

"Are you asking me if we can show up together?"

He gives me a soft smile. I can see the uncertainty in it, as if he's expecting me to be opposed to the idea. "We don't have to tell them yet if you're not ready."

"Are you sure?"

"I promised to take this at your pace. I'll do whatever you need me to."

"Okay. Thank you."

He hides his disappointment well.

I smile, slyly.

Confused, he looks at me. "What's that look for?"

Messing with him is too much fun.

"Why haven't you asked me to be your girlfriend yet?"

"Are you serious?"

I wink and wait.

He takes both of my hands in his. "Lizzy girl, will you please be my girlfriend?"

I blush. Which feels foolish, considering an almost thirty-year-old man asked me, a twenty-seven-year-old woman, to be his girlfriend. But I kind of love that he did.

Finding my composure, I answer nonchalantly. "Okay."

The smile he throws my way could move mountains. "Is that a yes?"

I smile back. "Yes."

He takes my face in his hands. "It's about time." And then kisses me senseless.

* * *

It has been far too long since I've gone all out for a night out. Something feels different now that I'll be clinging to Greyson's arm all night. In front of our friends.

After spending over five years thinking I would never be in another relationship, this feels monumental. What surprises me most is, I'm not even freaking out in the slightest.

I finish applying my makeup before doing a once over in the mirror.

I have on a pair of ripped black jeans, with thigh high black boots, and a forest green top. My black leather jacket completes the look. I won't lie. I look great. And I know I'm about to drive my boyfriend crazy the entire night. The thought has me smirking at myself in the mirror before there's a knock at my front door.

I open the door to reveal Greyson in gray jeans paired with a black long sleeve shirt. It clings to every dip and curve of his muscles, unapologetically.

When my eyes meet his, there's an intensity in his gaze. It's filled with more heat than usual. I can't help but wonder what's going through his mind.

He shakes his head. "Wow. You look..." He lets his words trail off, leaving me to fill in the blank. Which is fine by me, considering I've rendered him speechless.

I smirk. "Are you okay out there?"

He reaches for me, grabbing my waist to pull me to him. "You are stunning."

"So are you." He chuckles. "Seriously, you're incredibly handsome."

He smiles down at me. "That's quite the compliment coming from you."

He brings his lips to mine in a quick kiss. Although, it doesn't end up being quick.

When he pulls away, I'm left breathless.

"Are you ready?"

I'm too flustered by him to form a response, so I stand still. He laughs while grabbing my hand and pulling me out of my apartment.

The drive to the bar is quick, filled with lots of laughter.

We walk into the bar hand in hand.

It isn't until we spot our friends that I cling to Greyson's arm. They're seated in a booth at the very back of the space. He kisses my temple before heading in their direction.

Steph spots us first, surprise all over her face. She fans herself, saying, "Wow. Does it feel warm in here?"

I laugh, throwing her a wink. "It must be you."

"No. It's definitely the two of you. You two make quite the couple."

Maylee smiles. "Does this mean it's official?"

"You knew?"

She focuses on Steph and shrugs. "Maybe."

Greyson nods in their direction. "Where is everyone else?"

"Sarah wasn't up for a night out, so Matt's with her. But the guys are at the bar ordering drinks."

He turns his attention from Maylee to me. "Do you want me to grab you a drink?"

I look at him and nod. I want to go with him, but I know my girlfriends are about to ask me for all the details. He kisses the crown of my head before joining his friends at the bar.

My attention shifts to Maylee and Steph as I slide into the booth. "Where's Kate?"

"Bathroom. Now spill."

I laugh at Steph. "Spill what?"

"When? How? Where? Give me something!"

Just as I'm about to respond, Kate returns from the bathroom. "You look gorgeous, Liz." She eyes each of us, and then asks suspiciously, "What are we talking about?"

"The woman on Greyson's arm tonight."

She looks over at the bar, trying to figure out who Steph is referring to. "I don't see..." I see it the minute she puts the pieces together. Turning to Steph, she says, "You had me for a second."

Steph smiles, slyly.

"Anyway, we've been seeing each other for some time now. I wasn't ready to say anything until tonight."

My best friend chimes in. "I'm glad everything worked out for you, Liz."

Kate adds, "I am too."

Steph rolls her eyes. "You two are boring. I need more details than that, Liz!"

"There aren't that many. We've been hanging out, and now he gets to call me his girlfriend. The end."

Kate gives me a knowing look. "I'm sure that's a big win for him."

I smirk. "I'm sure it is."

Steph places her elbow on the table, resting her chin in her hand. "What's he like when it's just the two of you?"

I can't hide the blush that forms on my cheeks, thinking about all my interactions with Greyson. "He's incredibly sweet. Honestly, I didn't know he had it in him."

She counters with, "Are you glad you finally gave him a chance?"

With a smile on my face, I roll my eyes. "Will you quit asking questions if I say yes?"

She only laughs. "Not a chance. I can't wait to hear more details at a later date."

A few seconds later, the guys return to the table with our drinks. All of us spend some time catching up before hitting the dance floor. I miss getting to do this as often as I once did, so I'm glad I agreed to come out tonight. Despite a long work week.

Well into the night, the band announces a slow song *for all the lovebirds out there*. Normally, when this happens, I order a drink and sip it in solitude. But tonight, I stay on the dance floor at Greyson's request.

The lead singer is doing a cover of Ed Sheeran's "First Times".

Greyson takes my right hand in his left. Placing his free hand on my hip, he pulls me to him until my chest is against his. Not able to resist, I melt into him.

As we dance, I feel more in love than I did just hours ago at the shelter.

When the song ends, Greyson spins me around one more time before kissing me right in the middle of the bar. For everyone to see.

I smile against his mouth, enjoying how right it feels to be in this moment with him. Even though the bar is full of people, it feels like we're the only ones here right now.

I'm not sure how much time passes before he breaks the kiss to look at me. As he does, he takes my face in his hands. "I'm crazy about you, Lizzy girl."

"I'm crazy about you too, Grey."

And it's true.

I'm crazier about this man than I ever thought I would be.

The more time I spend with him, the more I believe what Maylee said is true.

While love can hurt, it also wields just as much power to heal. Maybe even more.

Chapter 24

Greyson

Present Day

"Brie. What are you doing here?"

Instead of answering the question, my stepsister strides into my house like she owns the place. "Why? Were you expecting anyone?" She waggles her eyebrows at me while I consider telling her the truth.

There must be evidence of it on my face because she exclaims, "You were! It's the redhead, isn't it?" She stands still, staring at me expectantly.

I sigh. "Yes."

She squeals, clapping her hands together as she does. "Is she coming to the barbecue?"

"Yes. Which brings me back to my initial question. What are you doing here?"

The barbecue isn't for a few more hours. If Brie wants to hang out, she could have waited until this afternoon when we'll all be at my mom's.

And I am waiting for Liz. She's coming over early so the two of us can spend some time together before her work schedule picks up again. A few big cases will keep her preoccupied in the weeks to come.

"I came to hang out with my new big brother."

I shake my head.

Brie is a handful. But parts of her remind me a lot of the Liz I met years ago. She doesn't know a stranger. As soon as my mom started dating her dad, she reached out to me, ready for me to embrace her with open arms.

"Don't you have two other older brothers you can go harass?"

She rolls her eyes, scoffing. "I mean, yeah. But Chris is married with a kid, and Brett can be boring. Besides, you have more time on your hands than either of them." She plants herself on my couch before continuing her monologue. "Now. Tell me about the redhead."

"The redhead has a name."

Brie looks at me with curious eyes while I roll mine, giving in. "Liz and I have been seeing each other for a few months."

"Why didn't you tell me that last time I was over?"

"You mean when you scared her off?"

"I did not scare her off!"

I chuckle. "You kind of did."

She rolls her eyes. "Whatever."

As she's about to say something else, there's a soft knock at the front door. My heart soars at the sound, knowing who's on the other side.

I leave Brie in the living room to let my girlfriend in.

When I open the door, she winks at me before wrapping her arms around my neck. "Hey."

"Hey, beautiful. Brie's here. I didn't know she was planning on stopping by."

She pulls away, giving me the opportunity to take in the sight of her.

She's dressed casually in jeans and an off the shoulder band tee. Her hair is resting over her shoulders in wavy curls. All I can think about is how lucky I am. Liz is the most beautiful woman I've ever seen.

"That's okay. I'd love to meet her. Officially."

From behind me, Brie says, "Well, aren't you two adorable. Hi, Liz. I'm Brie. It's nice to meet you."

Instead of offering my sister a hand, Liz pulls her into a hug. I'm not surprised by the action at all. "It's nice to meet you. Sorry for running out on you the other day."

Brie laughs. "Don't worry about it."

"Are you planning to hang out for a bit?"

"I was. But I'm going to head over to Jenny's instead. My dad is already over there. And I want to give you two some privacy."

Brie has the audacity to wink at me. Which doesn't go unnoticed by Liz. But it doesn't throw her off in the slightest.

Instead, she sputters a laugh. "Are you sure? I don't mind if you hang out."

"Yes. I'll see you guys later."

With Brie finally out the door, I close the distance between Liz and me, desperate to take whatever she's willing to give since we don't have much time before the barbecue.

She lets out a sound resembling a scream since I took her by surprise. I laugh as my lips meet hers, lifting her off the ground.

When I set her back down, she has a dazed look in her eyes. "What was that for?"

I shrug. "I've wanted to do that since I saw you last. And I doubt we'll be alone much around my entire family."

Liz places a kiss to my cheek before we make ourselves comfortable.

We spend the time leading up to the barbecue, hanging out on my back porch, talking, and laughing. Everything about it feels natural. I'm not surprised. My girlfriend is the best company to keep. I can't wait to watch her interact with my mom and Phil again. Both love her. And I know the rest of my family will, too.

* * *

"You made it! And you brought Liz!" My mom pulls Liz into a hug, and then leads us into the house to greet everyone else.

Phil takes the time to introduce his sons, Brett and Chris, Chris's wife Michelle, and their four-year-old son Cason.

When introductions are over, I put my arm around Liz's waist and introduce her to my family. "It's nice to meet you guys. This is my girlfriend, Liz."

My mom's eyes go wide. "What? Oh, my goodness. I didn't know you two were together! This is great, honey! Phil, isn't this great?"

My stepdad gives my mom a knowing look, clarifying that we've been a topic of conversation between the two of them.

"It sure is. Welcome to the family, Liz."

"Thank you. I appreciate that. And thanks for inviting me."

Phil gets the grill started. The rest of us hang out in the backyard.

Liz and I are sitting on some patio furniture with Chris and Michelle while Brie and Brett are hanging out with their nephew.

Michelle is the first to speak. "How long have you two been together?"

I let Liz answer. "A few months. What about you guys?"

"Six years."

"Cason is adorable. Are you planning on having any more kids?"

My heart aches for my girlfriend at the mention of kids. She's passionate about the topic. And talking about them must be difficult for her after going through what she did. Yet she handles it with a resilience I admire.

I strike up a conversation with my stepbrother, letting the women talk amongst themselves since Brie came to join them.

I enjoy the stories that Chris shares with me about what it was like growing up as the oldest sibling.

I realize how much I missed out on because of my father. I know my mom didn't bother trying to have more kids because of his unfaithfulness to her. It makes me wonder how much different my life would look now had I grown up with a large family.

A couple of hours pass before I realize Liz is no longer sitting with us.

My eyes glimpse her red waves being tossed around by the wind as she plays with Cason.

She's on her hands and knees in the grass, while he rides around on her back. My heart constricts at the sight. It surprises me. But it isn't unwelcome.

I never think much about my future. But in this moment, watching Liz interact with my family, I let myself think about what a future with her could look like. I know there's so much she'll bring to the table. She already has. I wouldn't respect Phil for who he is to my mom or be sitting here with my step-siblings, if not for her.

Honestly, Liz is the reason for most of the good things in my life. She's the light at the end of a dark tunnel. The joy at the end of a hard day. She's the love of my life. And she may not know it, but I fell in love with her long before she finally gave me a chance.

I'm pulled from my thoughts by the sound of my mom's quiet voice beside me. "She's amazing, Greyson."

Smiling, I agree. "She is."

My mom squeezes my leg. "I'm so proud of you, honey."

"Thanks, Mom."

She nods toward the grill. "Phil is almost done. Why don't you help him with the food?"

I get up to do as she suggests, knowing there's a reason for it.

"Hey, Phil. Do you need any help?"

"Hey, son. I'm glad you came." He lets his eyes wander to where Liz is in the yard with his grandson. "I see things worked out for you."

I don't bother hiding my smile. "They did." I return my attention back to him. "You didn't need help, did you?"

He chuckles, ignoring my question. "I guess she knocked you down a few pegs, then?"

I bark out a laugh. "A long time ago. I just had to get my head screwed on straight."

"So, she'll be around?"

There it is. The reason my mom insisted I come over here. I'm not sure why she didn't ask me herself, but I'm thankful for the opportunity to talk to my stepdad about this. While he doesn't know me that well, it's obvious he wants a healthy relationship with me. Plus, I appreciate his words of wisdom.

"Yeah. Yeah, she will be. Any advice?"

"Based on what I saw between you two the last time she was here, and then again today, I don't think you need any. But give her all the respect and love you can. The rest will fall into place."

"Will do."

"Let's get the table set."

The evening goes by in the blink of an eye. The food was great, and the company was even better.

Liz was right when she said family is family. I'm lucky to have a second chance at building a relationship with mine.

Liz and I are the last to leave. She insisted on staying to help my mom and Phil get everything cleaned up.

Once we're in the car, I say, "Thank you for today."

She turns to me from the passenger seat in my truck. "What are you thanking me for?"

I reach for her hand, interlacing our fingers. "For being you." She smiles but says nothing. "Seriously, Liz. Today wouldn't have happened if not for you."

With a furrowed brow, she looks at me, clearly confused. "What are you talking about?"

Suddenly, I'm nervous about admitting this to her. But she deserves to know how incredible she is.

I clear my throat. Sensing my nerves, she squeezes my hand, urging me to answer. "I reached out to my mom and Phil about getting together after our conversation at the beer garden."

In the softest voice I've ever heard her use, she asks, "You did?"

I nod.

She leans over to kiss me on the cheek. "I'm proud of you, Grey."

Both.

I made both the women I love proud today.

It means more than either of them will ever know.

* * *

A couple of weeks have passed since the barbecue, which means it has also been a couple of weeks since I've seen my girlfriend.

Liz has been spending a lot of late nights at her office because of a few cases she's working on.

Last night I asked her if I could bring her dinner today, but she said she'd be stuck in a client meeting until seven.

I invited the guys over instead. We haven't hung out in a while. Though, I'm not fooling myself. I'm in desperate need of a distraction. Liz is all I can think about.

I worry about whether she's eaten, knowing she probably hasn't. About her getting home safely when she doesn't leave her office until close to midnight. I worry when I don't hear from her after I text or call. She's more than capable of taking care of herself, but that doesn't mean she should have to.

Finally, I hear the latch on my gate. I spin around on the deck to see Walker and Matt walking up. "Hey. Glad you guys made it."

I have the firepit going by the time Sam and Charlie show up.

We're all sitting around the fire, beers in hand, when Sam asks, "How are things with Liz?"

"Great. How's Kate?"

He shrugs but says nothing.

Charlie changes the subject to sports. All of us go back and forth for a while. We're knee deep in conversation when my phone vibrates in my pocket.

I pull it out to see a text from Liz. I almost forgot I had called her earlier to see if I could steal her away for a few hours tomorrow.

Lizzy: I don't think so. I'm sorry. Things will calm down soon.
Lizzy: I miss you, Grey. <3

I get up to dispose of my now empty beer, responding to Liz as well.

Me: I miss you more, Lizzy girl. ;)

The sound of a beer bottle being tossed into the trash can startles me. A couple of seconds later, Walker moves into my line of sight.

He nods toward the phone in my hand. "Is that your girl?"
"Yeah."
"Maylee mentioned she hasn't heard from her much."
I sigh. "Yeah. She's got a lot going on at work right now. I haven't seen her since my family's barbecue."
"Dude, that was weeks ago. Go see her."
"I've been trying. I can't get her away from her office."
"I'm sure you'll figure out a way." He claps me on the back before returning to his seat in front of the fire.
I think about what he said before deciding what to do.

Chapter 25

Liz

Present Day

Steph strides into my office with our lunch in tow. "Spill." She sits down in the chair opposite from me.

Rolling my eyes, I reach for my sandwich, but she slides it away. "I don't think so."

"Come on, Steph. I'm starving."

"Exactly. I'll give you your food as soon as you promise to give me all the dirty details about you and your gorgeous boyfriend."

The only time I'll ever concede is for food. And my boyfriend, apparently. "Fine."

Grey has so much more power over me than he knows. And I intend to keep it that way. I smirk to myself at the thought, forgetting all about Steph.

Even when he isn't around, he's distracting. Which is why I keep turning down his offers to come visit me at work. If Greyson were to stop by, there's no way I'd ever be able to get everything done. But I miss him. I miss him like crazy.

I'm pulled from my thoughts at the sound of Steph clearing her throat.

When I look at her, she's smiling like the Cheshire cat, making me laugh. "What?"

She narrows her eyes at me. "You're thinking about him. Aren't you?"

I want to deny it, but when I feel my cheeks go warm, I know she has her answer.

I'm not one to give up easily, though. "I can neither confirm nor deny."

She points a finger at my face. "Is that why you're blushing?"

She's infuriating. I hide my face in my hands. "Maybe."

"Don't hide it, Liz. I love this side of you."

She claps her hands together. "Now, tell me what it's like dating Greyson Wright." She points at me with her pointer finger. "And leave nothing out."

"I didn't know we were in a high school cafeteria."

"What's wrong with two grown women talking about men?" Her question is rhetorical. "Quit avoiding this conversation. I want details."

I take a bite of my sandwich before washing it down with some water.

Steph and I have gotten close since I started working here, but she doesn't know much about my dating life. All she knows is that it's nonexistent. I've shared nothing about my past with her. I prefer that part of my life to stay where it belongs. In the past.

"What do you want to know?"

She shrugs. "What's he like? Does he treat you right? Is he a good kisser? You know, the usual."

I smile. "He's incredibly thoughtful. He treats me very well. And the man can kiss."

"When did all this happen?"

"It's been months. I asked him to take things slow. It's why I didn't tell you about it."

"Does his past scare you?"

"Honestly? No. He's a lot different from how he used to be. His actions prove that. I was hesitant at first—for personal reasons—but he's earned my trust. He deserves it."

What I don't tell her is how much I don't trust myself. I don't want to make the same mistakes as I have in the past.

"That's great, Liz."

It's clear she's contemplating what to ask next, so I keep eating my lunch.

Eventually, her expression transforms into one I haven't seen before. "I bet he knows how to do a lot more than kiss."

Her words cause me to choke on my food, sending me into a coughing fit.

When I finally gain control of myself, I look at her wide-eyed. "I'm sorry. What did you just say?"

She laughs, loudly. "I'm sure a man as gorgeous as him knows how to do a lot more than kiss." From across the table, she winks at me.

"Not that it's any of your business, but I wouldn't know."

"Why not?"

"You're ridiculous. Did you know that? Like I said, I told him I want to take things slow."

I'm about to give her some more context when my phone vibrates on my desk.

"Is that him?"

"Yes."

"What does he want?"

"Nosey much?"

Steph only laughs at my sass while I look down to read Greyson's text.

Grey: Can I steal you away from the office for a few hours tomorrow?

My heart deflates in my chest as I read his message. I feel terrible about how crazy work has been. But it'll calm down in just a few days.

I slip my phone into my purse, deciding to respond later.

The action doesn't go unnoticed by Steph. "You aren't going to text him back?"

"I will later. He's been wanting to take me out, but I've been so busy with case preparation."

"Liz, let that man take you out. Or let him come here. If you get too busy, I'll keep him company."

I chuckle. "I'm sure you would. And as much as I would love that, he's too much of a distraction. It's hard to concentrate when he's around."

"Well, maybe it's because of all that tension between the two of you."

I look up at my office assistant with my mouth wide open and throw a rolled-up napkin at her. "You're incorrigible."

She loses herself in a fit of laughter.

Meanwhile, I can't stop thinking about how right she is.

* * *

Pouring over cases for hours on end is exhausting. Steph left the office hours ago, offering to come back with dinner, but I declined. I was hoping I could sneak away to surprise Greyson at his house, but I lost track of time.

Hours have passed since I last heard from him. I know he had the guys over tonight, so I don't blame him. Truthfully, I'm glad he has the distraction that I know he needs. My schedule only gets like this every few weeks, but I still feel bad about it.

I return to my work. There's a little more research I want to do before calling it a night.

As I'm pulling up a web browser on my computer, I'm startled by the ding of the elevator. Quickly, I get up from my desk to see who's here.

The door to my office opens before I make it there, revealing my boyfriend.

"Grey. What are you doing here?"

He smiles brightly at me. "I came to surprise you."

There's a part of me that wants to be mad at him for showing up unannounced. He knows how important to me these cases are. But his gestures are just so sweet. All the time.

Steeling myself, I place my hands on my hips. "Well, I'm busy right now. You should have called first."

Greyson stalks toward me, slowly.

Each step is deliberate.

"Oh, really? Should I have scheduled time with you via Steph?"

I back up, attempting to avoid his pursuit, until the back of my legs hit my desk. "Mhm."

He chuckles. "You okay, Liz? You look a little flustered."

I gulp. Audibly. I know for a fact he heard it based on the smirk plastered across his face. Plus, he has that look in his eyes. The look that says he knows he has already won.

"I'm fine." My voice comes out a little higher pitched than I intended it to.

"I don't believe you." In one quick movement, he closes the distance between us.

His lips meet mine in a passionate kiss, and I practically melt into him. He smiles against my mouth when I do.

He doesn't waste time before deepening the kiss, drawing a sound of appreciation out of me.

I love the way he tastes. Like honey and mint.

He kisses me with a desperation that has only grown since we started dating. It makes me feel wanted. Loved even.

Honestly, kissing this man is like nothing I've ever experienced before.

It's electric.

It feels like I'm right where I belong.

In his arms.

As we kiss, I'm overcome with relief.

I'm so thankful for his persistence. He never gave up on me. I'll never be able to explain what that means to me.

For a moment, I forget where we are. Instead, I focus on this feeling. It's heady.

Tonight, there's nothing soft or sweet about the way we're kissing each other.

Without hesitating, he lifts me up and plants me on my desk.

I can't think straight as I let my hands roam over the muscles in his chest, enjoying every dip and curve. Finally, I let them rest on his biceps as he holds my face in his hands.

I wrap my legs around his waist to pull him closer.

Steph's right.

The tension and chemistry between us are indescribable. I know he feels it, too. But I know his respect for me is stronger. He'll wait.

He breaks our kiss, resting his forehead on mine. "I'll never get enough of you." He places a soft kiss on my forehead. "You drive me crazy."

I giggle. Yes, I literally giggle like a schoolgirl. He just smiles.

"I'm serious. Everything about you drives me crazy." He kisses my lips softly. "Your lips." Kiss. "Your passion for life." Kiss. "Your stubbornness." Kiss. "Your larger-than-life personality." Kiss. "Your beauty." He pulls back to look at me, running a hand through my hair as he does.

I place my hand on his cheek. "Grey."

To my surprise, a lone tear travels down my face. He's the only man who has the power to bring me to tears with his words alone. Happy tears, of course.

He gently wipes them away. "Will you come over tonight?"

My heart stutters in my chest at his question. I don't want to think too hard about it because if I do, the answer will be no. And that's the last thing I want to tell him. "Yes."

His smile lights up my office. "Okay. Text me when you leave."

He gives me one more kiss before leaving my office, taking my heart with him.

I love this feeling. This security. To be with someone who I know will never let me down. He has proven that. Time and time again.

I wonder if he knows I love him. I hope he does. Because for the life of me, I can't bring myself to say the words.

I don't even return to what I was doing before Greyson interrupted me.

I pack up my things, heading home so I can spend the rest of the night with my boyfriend.

* * *

My head is resting on Greyson's chest while we sit on his back porch enjoying the cool air and a fire.

He brought a projector and a large screen outside, so we could watch a movie in the most amazing backyard I've ever been in. It's almost more amazing than he is.

"I love it back here. It's so peaceful."

He kisses the crown of my head. "I'm glad."

"What made you do all this?"

Greyson's backyard is one of my favorite things about his house. The back porch is spacious and covered. Which allows for a decent amount of people to hang out all at once. The fire pit is hand built. By Greyson himself. There's a beautiful tree in the far-right corner. It's the kind of tree a treehouse could go in. If I let myself picture it, I can see a bunch of kids running around. Maybe his nieces and nephews. Or maybe they're ours. My heart swells with the anticipation of a future where I get to be the mother of Greyson's children. There's no denying how much I want that. Though I try not to get ahead of myself.

"I wanted a space suitable for friends to hang out." He hesitates, briefly. I can tell he's nervous to say whatever else is on his mind. "And my family."

"Your family?"

He nods. "Yeah. Whether it's my mom and Phil, my siblings, Cason, or you..." He lets his words trail off, though I know he has more to say.

I trace circles on the exposed skin of his stomach, just above the hem of his sweatpants. "Me?"

He nods. "Maybe kids of my own, too."

His words make me smile. I know what he's getting at.

"You want kids?"

"I didn't know I did until recently."

I breathe out the word, "Oh", while wondering at what moment he discovered his desire for a family. But instead of trying to guess, I just ask. "When did you figure it out?"

"Honestly? At the barbecue when I was watching you play with Cason."

I lift my head from where it's resting to meet his eyes. "Really?"

He nods.

"I want that, too." My voice comes out shaky, but not because I'm nervous.

It's because I'm afraid.

Terrified, really.

The future is so uncertain. I want to believe I can have everything Greyson is talking about. But after suffering the way I did; I refuse to let go of the possibility that it may not happen.

The worry must be clear on my face because he reaches up to my forehead, smoothing out the worry lines there with his fingers. "Hey, where'd you go?"

I shake my head as I let out a sigh. "I still carry around the pain of it, wondering what it would be like if things were different."

It's the first time I've admitted this out loud before. But if I truly want to move forward with this man, then he needs to know where I stand.

He pulls me onto his lap, so my legs are stretched out across the patio couch. Just like he did on the park bench when I finally told him about my past. Sitting like this with him... it brings me comfort.

He whispers, "Lizzy girl." The now familiar nickname makes me smile. "I can't imagine what that's like. But if you're willing to try again one day, then I'll be ready."

Not having any desire to spend the night in tears, I lighten the mood by asking, "You really want me to have your babies?"

Greyson throws his head back in laughter. The sound of it is enthralling. It's music to my ears. Truly.

"Liz Carter, I most definitely want you to have my babies."

"When did you change your mind about all of this? Relationships, marriage, kids, family..."

"I don't think there's a definitive moment. All I can tell you is I didn't know I wanted any of those things until you." He kisses me softly, and then we go back to enjoying the cool evening air.

I'm not sure how much time passes before I fall asleep lying on Greyson's chest.

I vaguely remember hearing him whisper the words, "I love you", before placing a soft kiss on my forehead and shaking me awake.

"Lizzy girl, do you want to stay here tonight?"

I blink the sleepiness out of my eyes before looking at him. "No, I should get home."

"Are you sure you're okay to drive?"

I sit up to give him a gentle kiss. "I'll be fine. I promise."

He nods. "Let me walk you out."

Never Let You Down

We say our goodbyes before I make the drive home. All I can think about is what I think Greyson whispered to me.

I wish I had the courage to tell him I love him, too.

Chapter 26

Greyson

Present Day

I told Liz I love her.

Not that she heard it.

But I still said it. I want to say it again. But I also don't want to scare her away.

After talking about the future with her last night, I couldn't hold in those three words any longer. And seeing her asleep on my chest only confirmed what I already know.

I want to spend the rest of my life with her.

But I'll start with this morning.

I slip out of bed to get ready to show up at Liz's apartment unannounced. Hopefully, she won't mind.

After letting her drive home so late last night, I'm worried about her. She needs all the rest she can get, considering the big week she has ahead of her. So, I'm hoping she'll let me take care of her today. The last couple of weeks without her have been torture. I want to make up for the lost time. Especially before her schedule gets crazy again.

Before heading toward her place, I stop at the grocery store to pick up everything I need to make her breakfast. Hopefully, pancakes will suffice.

About half an hour later, I'm standing in front of her apartment with a few grocery bags hanging from my hands.

As soon as she opens the door, I take in the sight of her.

Yesterday's curls have fallen, making her hair look the way I can only imagine it would after a long day at work. Or running around with our future children. She's wearing an oversized T-shirt. It practically swallows her whole. Her pajama shorts are barely visible underneath it. She looks adorable.

As she eyes the grocery bags in my hands, she smiles. "What are you doing here?"

I lift the bags slightly, feeling a little shy suddenly. Which is completely foreign to me. I've done nothing like this before. "I know you're exhausted, so I want to make sure you're taken care of today."

She crosses her arms over her chest. "I see." Then she raises a brow. "What makes you think I can't take care of myself?"

"I know you can. But you shouldn't have to." I lift the bags again. "Are you going to let me in so I can make us some breakfast?"

"Did you bring coffee?"

"Of course. It's in my truck."

Liz opens the door wider before moving out of my way to let me in. She follows me into the kitchen. "You didn't have to go through this trouble, Grey."

After getting everything situated, I walk toward her. "I know." I kiss her temple. "But I wanted to. Let me go get our coffees."

As I walk away, she reaches for my arm. "Wait."

"What?"

She closes what little distance is between us, lifts herself onto her toes, and kisses me so tenderly.

My heart stutters in my chest.

I'm surprised such a simple gesture has such an intense effect on me. It's how I know Liz is it. She's everything to me.

When she pulls back, her smile grows even wider. "There. Now you can go get our coffee."

"You're incredible."

She laughs lightly before sitting down on a barstool. "Noted."

Shaking my head, I laugh.

She's more pleasant in the morning than most people, but I don't miss the way her face lights up when I return with her favorite coffee in my hand.

I walk it over to where she's sitting. As I set it down in front of her, I lean in for a kiss. It's quick. Nothing more than a peck. But when I pull away, she's smiling brightly.

"How did you sleep last night?"

While she takes her time to answer me, I start on our breakfast.

It doesn't take long for me to feel comfortable in her kitchen.

She takes a sip of her latte. "Mmm. Great."

I chuckle. "You slept great, or the coffee is great?"

"Both."

I smile as I whisk the pancake batter. "Do you have any plans today?"

She sighs. "I don't know. Someone interrupted me at work last night before I could think about what I needed to do today."

When I look up from what I'm doing, she's got a teasing glint in her eyes.

I wink at her, motioning for her to follow me to her living room so we can eat on the couch. "I know what you need to do today."

"Oh yeah, what's that?"

"Let your boyfriend take care of you."

She quirks an eyebrow. "What does that entail?"

"Whatever you want."

"I'll think about it."

We spend a few minutes eating our breakfast in companionable silence.

Every few bites, Liz lets out a quiet sound of approval.

It isn't until she bites into a pancake that she groans. "Did you put cinnamon in these?"

I nod. "I added some to the batter."

"It tastes amazing. I usually add it to eggs when I make French toast."

"It sounds like we'll have to have breakfast together again. Your way next time."

"I'd love that, Grey. Thank you for doing this."

"I'd do anything for you."

Saying nothing, she looks down at her plate, but not before I notice the blush on her cheeks.

After finishing her pancakes, she clears her throat. "My mom wants to meet you."

"Your parents know about me?"

She nods her head. "There's a lot she didn't know about college. I talked to her about it when I realized I was falling for you." She shrugs. "She read between the lines."

"Well, just let me know when. That reminds me... there's something I want to ask you. But don't feel you have to say yes."

"Okay." She sounds so diplomatic, like she's prepared to give either answer. It must be the lawyer in her. I won't lie and say it doesn't make her even more attractive.

"The station does this... family day thing. I'm planning on inviting my mom, but I want to know if you would come, too?"

Honestly, I want her to say yes more than anything, but I'll understand if she doesn't. And while it isn't for a few more months, I wanted her to know about it ahead of time. I'm hoping by the time it comes around, she'll be more than my girlfriend. Hopefully, she doesn't put the pieces together.

Without giving away anything in her expression, she meets my gaze. "You want me to go to that?"

I nod.

She moves her plate onto the coffee table and then interlaces her fingers with mine. "I'll go. I'd love to go."

I didn't realize I was holding my breath until after she agrees. She chuckles at my obvious nervousness, but says nothing more.

We finish our breakfast, and clean up my mess in the kitchen together, laughing the entire time.

It isn't until we're almost done, and loading the dishwasher, that I get an idea.

When she stands up from starting the wash cycle, I spray her using the faucet head.

She squeals and swats at me with a towel. "Greyson!"

"Ow! That hurts!"

Laughing, she yells, "Good!" before she retreats from the kitchen.

Her short legs don't take her very far before I catch her from behind in the living room and toss her onto the couch.

I plant myself directly over her before the tickling ensues.

"Greyson! Stop!"

I can hardly understand what she's saying because of how hard she's laughing as she yells each word. "Stop, Greyson!"

Finally, I give up, looking down at her with what I know is the dorkiest smile in the world.

When I do, something moves across her expression. It's gone as quickly as it was there.

Unexpectedly, she pulls my head down until my lips are against hers, kissing me with an urgency that's never been present before.

I let her take the lead.

She deserves to have control. Especially after everything I know about her previous relationship.

I'll do things her way. Whatever that looks like.

She stops kissing me long enough to catch her breath. But what she does next surprises me even more than the way she just kissed me.

From where she's lying underneath me, she smiles before kissing my forehead, my cheeks, then my lips once more.

It's so gentle. Tender. Such a simple thing for her to do, yet it feels reverent.

I almost tell her how I feel about her.

Instead, I bring my mouth down to hers in an electrifying kiss.

After another few minutes, we sit back up.

I pull Liz into my side before kissing her cheek. "What else can I do for you today?"

"I have some errands to run. Care to join me?"

"That sounds like fun."

She laughs. "Does it?" It sounds like she doesn't believe me.

I move so I can look her in the eyes. "It's not about what we do." I sigh, trying to find the right words. "I spent a lot of time wishing I could hang out with you, Liz. So, anything I get to do with you is enough for me."

I watch her blush as she mulls over my words. Then she smirks. "Good to know."

I laugh, kissing the crown of her head. "I don't even want to know what's going on in that gorgeous head of yours."

She joins in my laughter before retreating to her bedroom to get ready for the day.

I can't say I've ever had so much fun running errands in my entire life.

If this is what it feels like to love someone, then count me in.

* * *

This weekend with Liz couldn't have gone any better than it did.

On Saturday evening, she convinced me to meet her parents on a whim. I wasn't nervous until I found out I'm the only boyfriend she has ever brought home.

They were extremely welcoming. I think it had more to do with Liz finally sharing a part of her life with them than it did with me.

Who she is makes complete sense after meeting her parents. She gets her intensity and grit from her dad. Which makes her a brilliant lawyer. But she gets her compassion and intense love for life from her mom. Which makes her an all-around great person.

She's truly one of a kind.

I'm thankful for the time I got with her because this week is big for her. She's finishing preparation for two big cases she's been working through.

I miss her. But the timing works out for me. It gives me some extra time to get Milo trained for her.

I didn't know Margaret was a professional dog trainer until I talked to her about my plan to adopt Milo for Liz. He's currently in the completed training facility with her while I'm cleaning up after the contractors. They did a great job with the new facility, but they left the place a mess.

"Hey, man."

Turning around, I find Walker standing behind me with his hands in the pockets of his jeans.

"Hey. What's up?"

"Penny mentioned you might need some help back here."

"Yeah. That would be great. I'm just cleaning up all the debris."

"Cool."

We get to work cleaning up the mess.

The shelter has come a long way since we started volunteering. I'm looking forward to seeing what kind of impact the training facility has on the business. Though I don't have an animal of my own, I hate thinking about what happens to the animals who never get adopted. Hopefully, the addition of the training center will help.

We work in silence for a while.

"How are things going with Liz?"

I look up from what I'm doing. Usually, I'm not one to share details. But with Walker, I will.

"Great."

"That's good to hear. Maylee mentioned she met your family."

"Yeah. I actually just met her parents this weekend."

He looks surprised but hides it well. "It sounds like you two are getting serious."

I chuckle. He has no idea. I want to tell him more, but I never know how much of what I say gets back to Maylee. Since she's best friends with my girlfriend, I always wonder how much of what I say makes it back to Liz, too.

He must see something in my expression he can't place because he asks, "What's that look for?"

"What look?"

He chuckles. "Come on. You know the look. The one that tells me you're hopelessly in love."

"Shut up, man." I hesitate before admitting, "I bought a ring."

His eyes go wide. "No way." I stand in silence, waiting to see if he has anything to add. "You're serious?"

"Of course, I'm serious."

Nodding his head, he crosses his arms over his chest. "I'm surprised. It hasn't been that long."

Scratching the back of my neck, I shrug. "I thought the same thing. But then I realized that I've always had feelings for Liz. Being with her has only made them grow. Nothing will change that."

Walker nods his head again. But I say nothing, figuring he's thinking through everything I said. Or still surprised by it. "I'm happy for you, man. I'm assuming Liz doesn't know?"

"No. So please keep this to yourself. And that includes your wife."

He raises his hands in mock surrender. "Hey, I won't say anything. But Maylee wouldn't tell her if I did."

"Thanks."

"Do you know when you're going to do it?"

"I haven't figured that part out yet. Hopefully, I'll know when she's ready. I'll keep you posted on details because I know she'll want her friends there. I may need help to plan things."

"That's great, man. I'm sure you'll figure it out."

We return to our clean-up efforts.

I'm left thinking about how I want to propose to Liz. So far, I have a few ideas up my sleeve, but nothing set in stone. It may be some time before I do it. The most important thing is that I wait until the moment she's ready.

After Walker and I finish cleaning up the mess out back, I go in search of Margaret and Milo.

I find them in the training facility where Milo's running the agility course. "Hey. How's it going?"

Margaret looks over at me, surprised. "You scared me!" Laughing, she adds, "It's going great. He's a pro. We're just having some fun now."

"Good. I really appreciate your help with this. I know it's a lot to take on."

"Don't worry about it. It's sweet what you're doing for Liz. After everything she's done for my grandmother, it's the least I can do."

"Thanks. Do you need anything before I head out?"

"I don't think so. Have a good night."

After watching Milo for a few more minutes, I head out for the evening to pick up dinner for Liz. I promised I would drop something off for her since she has another late night.

Even though I just saw her yesterday, I can't wait to see her again.

Walker's right.

Mariah Wallace

I'm hopelessly in love.

Chapter 27

Liz

Present Day

I can finally take a deep breath.

This week has been much slower than last week.

Despite the long week I had, Greyson tried to see me as much as possible. By bringing me dinner. FaceTiming me. And delivering loads of coffee. He's a phenomenal boyfriend.

This week, his schedule is all over the place. Which is fine. I don't mind finding something to do that doesn't revolve around him. I miss him like crazy, though.

Since he can't make it to the shelter this evening, I asked Maylee if she'd be willing to come. So, just like old times, we're both here.

Honestly, we have done little other than chit chat. It's safe to say, I miss seeing my best friend all the time. But I'm glad she's happily married. Maybe I will be too, someday.

We're currently walking Milo and Macy on my favorite trail, enjoying the beautiful weather. Maylee's been trying—and failing—to teach Macy how to heel.

I chuckle as I remember what transpired the day I tried walking her and Milo together. Which only reminds me of Greyson attending to my injuries in the bathroom and the way the slightest touch of his fingers affected me. The memory causes a warm sensation to settle over me. Even when he isn't around, he's affecting me in some physical way. The thought has me smiling to myself.

I'm pulled from my reverie when Maylee bumps my shoulder with hers. "What are you smiling about over there?"

I school my features. "Nothing. I'm just glad you could make it today. Thanks for coming."

Instead of saying anything, she laughs.

When I look at her, she's shaking her head.

"What?"

"It's okay to express emotions, Liz. And talk about your feelings. It's normal. It makes you human."

I look at my best friend, rolling my eyes. "I don't know what you're talking about."

She stops mid-step, turning to face me. "How are you and Greyson? There. Is that better? Now you don't have to figure out how to bring it up, since I asked instead."

Well. She got me there. "Fine. We're great."

"Mhm. And what were you really smiling about a few minutes ago?"

Maylee looks at me with a mischievous glint in her eyes. And just like that, the smile is back on my face. What's the point in hiding it from her?

"I was thinking about the encounter I had with him when he attended to my injuries after that little rascal,"—I point toward Macy—"made me fall and hurt myself. There was so much tension and chemistry between us. It was obvious. But I still denied it."

She smiles. It's so big and bright that it makes me stop in my tracks. "I'm happy for you."

I hesitate briefly, thinking through my next words. "I think he told me he loves me."

As soon as the sentence is out of my mouth, I take a deep, cleansing breath. It feels good to get it out there after holding it in for so long. I haven't felt brave enough to question Greyson about that night at his house. There's always a chance I didn't hear him correctly.

"You think?"

"Yeah. He thought I was asleep. And I was halfway there, but alert enough to hear him say *I love you.*"

"Wow. How do you feel?"

"Oh. I'm totally in love with him."

"But you haven't told him?"

"No."

"He hasn't said it again?"

"No."

"He's probably waiting on you. You should tell him."

Ever since that day at the animal shelter, there have been many moments when I wanted to tell Greyson how I feel. I've been in a constant battle with myself over it. Maylee knows me well enough to know that. She isn't a pusher, though, so she changes the subject. Which I'm grateful for. I can only handle so much talk about my feelings before it becomes too much.

"So, you've been spending a lot of time together?"

"Yep."

"And how's it going?"

"Fine." I look at Maylee to find her eyeing me suspiciously. This feels so much like college. "Okay, fine. It's amazing. It's hard not to worry about when it will end."

"What do you mean?"

I shrug. "Things between us are eerily like my relationship with Dylan. Don't get me wrong. Greyson is a million times better. But I'm still scared that things will blow up at the first sign of hardship."

She stops our walk to face me. "Don't let your mind go there. Your relationship with Greyson is so much different because of the experience you have. Trust yourself. Trust that you've learned from your mistakes."

I look at the ground, avoiding her gaze. We haven't ever talked about this in much detail.

Eventually, I find the courage to meet her eyes. "I know that. I'm just hard on myself, you know? It's why I told Greyson I want to move slowly. Why I want to wait. Do things differently this time."

"And how did he take that?"

"He said he'd do anything I need. He never pushes me. The night I fell asleep at his house, he let me go home. I felt bad because I expected him to beg me to stay."

"See? He's better for you than Dylan ever was."

"He is."

We continue to stroll leisurely before turning around to head back in the shelter's direction.

As the shelter comes into view, Maylee's phone rings.

She pulls it from her back pocket. When she sees who it is, her expression shifts into one of confusion. "That's weird."

"What?"

"Walker never calls me while he's on a shift."

"Well, answer it and make sure everything's okay."

She nods before answering the call. "Hey, babe."

While I can't make out what Walker is saying, I can tell it probably isn't anything good when I notice Maylee's entire demeanor change.

She's listening intently while shaking her head at whatever he's saying. But in a matter of a few seconds, her expression shifts from relaxed to worried to terrified. I see the fear in her eyes before her face goes pale and she hangs up the phone.

"MayMay, what is it?"

"We need to go. Now."

The intensity in her voice is undeniable. I try not to panic at the sound of it.

Before I can question her further, she quickens her pace as we walk back to the shelter.

I follow, trying to keep up with her long strides. "What's going on?"

"Just wait until we get the dogs put up. Okay?"

I rush after her, unable to figure out what has her so spooked. It makes little sense.

Once we have Milo and Macy put away, we get into Maylee's car.

From the driver's seat, she looks over at me with a look that I can only describe as one of terror.

There are only a few things in the world that could spook her this much. It's freaking me out.

"Maylee. What?"

"The ambulance Greyson was riding in on the way to a call got struck. Everyone that was dispatched to the call is on their way to the hospital..." I tune out her words as she gives me the only details she has.

There aren't very many of them.

Not near enough.

A tear slides down my cheek. "Is he okay?"

She won't offer me reassurance. She's been through this before, so she knows better than anyone that there's always a chance Greyson isn't okay.

All I know is I need to get to him.

As if she can read my thoughts, she shifts her car into drive, turning out of the parking lot and speeding toward the hospital.

The drive feels endless.

So endless that I have time to do some research.

I tried to stop myself from looking anything up. But I couldn't help it. The lawyer in me—as well as the practical side of me—needs the facts.

Over six-thousand ambulances get hit per year. That means at least sixteen get hit every single day of the year. A little less than half of those accidents result in injuries.

Or fatalities.

Of course, the information I found doesn't make me feel any better than I did before looking it up. Which I knew it wouldn't.

While Greyson's chances of survival are good, I still fear the worst. I can't lose him. He's the love of my life. I need him to be okay.

My mind races with varying possibilities—some good—most not so good.

After what feels like an eternity, we finally pull into the parking lot of the hospital.

Maylee drops me off at the front entrance of the emergency room.

I race inside.

Breathing heavily, I sprint to the front desk. Because I need to catch my breath, I'm unable to say anything right away.

The receptionist smiles at me. "Hi, how may I help you?"

My words come out in a rush. "Hi. I'm here to see Greyson Wright. He was in an accident."

"Let me find out which room he's in and if he's allowed visitors. Give me just a moment."

As I wait on the woman, I try to stay calm.

With my arms crossed over my chest, I tap my foot against the floor. I focus on my surroundings, taking them in. It doesn't look any different from what I'd expect. Everything is white, and it smells like cleaning supplies.

Finally, she looks up from the computer. "I have his information right here. The doctor hasn't seen him yet, but you're welcome to join him in his room. It's room one-zero-one."

I relax, knowing he's alive and well.

Hopefully, his injuries are minimal. I thank the receptionist before speed walking to his room.

Like the car ride, the walk feels endless.

Eventually, I find his room number, stopping in front of the door when I do.

I take a deep breath before stepping inside.

When I see Greyson is okay with my own two eyes, I let out a deep, cleansing breath, feeling relieved. "Grey." After I mutter his name, a tear trails down my cheek. It isn't long before more follow.

He smiles at me from where he's sitting on the hospital bed, still in his uniform. I can't help but notice how incredibly handsome he looks. "Hey, Lizzy girl. It's good to see you."

Slowly, I walk toward him. "Never do that to me again. Why didn't you call me to let me know what happened? I didn't know what I would find when I got here."

He pats the space next to him. "I'm sorry. Everything happened so fast. I couldn't find my phone either."

At his words, my tears fall even faster. I don't know why. I think I'm just relieved to see him.

Nothing compares to the unknown. Especially when it involves a situation like this. I don't know what I would have done if it would have been worse.

He winces when I take a seat on the bed next to him.

"Are you okay?"

"I think so. I got thrown around a bit. There's a good chance I have some cracked ribs. Probably a concussion, too."

I stroke his hair, gently. Then I place a tender kiss on his temple.

He puts his arm around me, pulling me close. I don't take the gesture for granted.

"What happened?"

"We were on our way to a call and got hit at an intersection. I was in the back."

I rest my head on his shoulder. "I'm so glad you're okay. I was so scared I was going to lose you, Grey. I still..." I can't finish my sentence as I'm too choked up at the thought of a life without this man.

He brings his fingers to my chin, lifting my head so I'll meet his eyes. "Hey. I'm right here. I'm not going anywhere."

"I know. I'm sorry."

Instead of saying anything, he brings his lips to mine in a soft kiss. It's sweet at first. But I can't help myself as I deepen it just a little, running my fingers through his hair when I do. I need this. The contact. The intimacy. Especially after freaking myself out the way I did.

For a moment, it feels like we're the only ones in this entire hospital.

I want to pull away, so I can tell him I love him, but before I do, a throat clears from somewhere in the room.

When we untangle ourselves from each other, I look at the door to see our two best friends.

Maylee has a cheeky smile on her face. "Sorry. We just wanted to come make sure you're okay. I thought Liz would text me. I can see why she didn't."

Greyson chuckles next to me at her words.

Walker's lips tip up slightly. "Glad to see you're okay, man. When the boss called, we were worried."

"All good. Thanks."

He nods. "We'll leave you two alone. Call if you need anything."

I smile, waiting until they make it down the hallway before giving Greyson my full attention. "Do you know when the doctor will be in?"

"I'm not sure. It should be soon, though."

"Are you feeling okay?"

He gives me a smirk. "Now that you're here, I am."

It's now or never.

After today's events, I need to tell him how I feel.

I know we're not in the most romantic place ever. Not that he'd care. He'll just be happy to hear the words.

"Can I tell you something?"

He brushes a strand of hair away from my face, tucking it behind my ear. "Anything."

I take a deep breath. "Grey, I—"

A knock at the door cuts my words off.

Greyson gives me a quick peck. "That's probably the doctor. Tell me later. Okay?"

While I'm disappointed that I didn't get to tell him how I feel, it's probably for the best. Maybe now I'll get to tell him when he isn't sitting in a hospital bed.

Shaking off my disappointment over the poor timing, I turn my attention to the doctor who just walked in.

He's focused on the clipboard in his hand, so I can't see his face. Without looking up at us, he says, "Good evening, Mr. Wright."

That voice.

I know that voice.

At the exact moment I realize who it is, he looks up at us.

Just as I suspected.

It's the last person I ever expected to see again.

Dylan Sinclair.

Chapter 28

Liz

Present Day

Almost six years have gone by since Dylan walked out of my apartment. When he told me it hurt too much to be with me.

At the sight of him, all the air leaves my lungs. My spine goes ram rod straight. And I have to remind myself to breathe. To act unaffected.

Greyson must notice something's off because he rubs my back soothingly.

His touch is the only thing keeping me calm. "Hey, are you okay?"

His question comes out in a whisper.

I nod.

Then I take in my ex.

He looks almost exactly the same as he did when I knew him.

He's still tall and broad with muscles that look even more defined than they did back then. His dark hair is longer, curling up at the nape of his neck. His jaw is just as chiseled, but the rest of his face looks worn. His job must be as demanding as mine. Maybe more.

I say nothing as I continue to take him in.

He looks as thrown off as I feel.

"Liz." My name sounds nothing like it once did coming from his lips. And that's fine by me.

Instead of acknowledging the elephant in the room, I steel myself. "Dr. Sinclair, can you please fill us in on Greyson? Is everything okay?"

Thankfully, Grey puts the pieces together, so I don't have to tell him anything.

He knows exactly who's standing in front of us.

In this moment, I'm so thankful he knows about my past. This would have gone much differently if not. Unfortunately, I can't tell what he's thinking. But based on his body language, he's not thrilled about my ex being his ER doctor.

I'm not either.

Dylan clears his throat. "Yes, of course. Mr. Wright, you suffered a mild concussion. Your X-rays also show a cracked rib. Other than that, you're in great health. You're very lucky."

Greyson nods but says nothing.

I speak for him instead. "Is there anything we need to do or know?"

"No. He just needs to limit his activity level. The crack should heal in about six weeks." He hesitates. "It's good to see you, Liz."

I don't acknowledge his words.

Instead, I squeeze my boyfriend's hand a little tighter, silently begging him to rescue me from this situation.

I thought this day couldn't get any worse.

I was so very wrong.

Instead of leaving us alone—like he should—Dylan clears his throat.

"Liz, may I have a word with you in the hall?"

I can't get a word out because Greyson beats me to it. "No. You may not."

The intensity in his voice catches me off guard. There's a protectiveness in it I've never heard before. While I appreciate him so much for having my back, a small part of me is curious about what Dylan wants to say.

I meet Greyson's eyes. "It will just take a second." My voice is soft. Reassuring. Though it does nothing to remove the desperation in his expression. I don't know how to interpret it.

"Lizzy."

While there's still a protectiveness in his tone, I pick up on the gentleness, too. The care. I know it's all coming from the same place. A place of love. His love for me. And I love him for it. I wish he knew. If only I would have gotten to tell him before my ex—of all people—interrupted us.

There's not a single part of me that wants to give him the time of day. But I want to hear whatever it is he wants to say. I'm also afraid the only way to get him out of this room is to follow him out into the hallway.

I kiss Greyson's lips softly. "I'm okay. Just give me a second."

He nods once.

Before I get up, I squeeze his hand reassuringly.

My attention shifts to Dylan. "Let's talk."

He turns for the door.

I follow. Albeit begrudgingly.

Honestly, I want him to see the lack of respect I have for him after everything he did. His actions following our breakup were immature. Ludicrous. I should have never had to question whether he ever truly cared about me the way he claimed he did.

Crossing my arms over my chest, I ask, "What do you want, Dylan?"

He smiles down at me. "It's good to see you, Liz."

"You said that already."

"Well, I mean it."

I sigh in frustration, letting my arms fall to my sides. "Cut it out and get to the point."

"I see you're just as feisty as you were back then. And since when do you go by Lizzy?"

"I don't."

"Your boyfriend didn't get the memo."

Are you kidding me?

That's what he has to say about that?

I scoff. "You don't get to say things like that. If you don't tell me why you brought me out here, then I will turn around right now, and you'll never see me again."

He searches my eyes for a second, then leans against the wall behind him.

Sighing, he runs his fingers through his hair. "I don't know. It was the only thing I could think of. You were the last person I expected to see tonight."

"Ditto."

He doesn't seem to notice my clipped tone. "You look great. How have you been?"

"I don't have time for this. Can we pretend this never happened? Great." As soon as the words leave my lips, I turn around to walk back into the room. But Dylan reaches for my arm, stopping me in my tracks.

"Wait. Can we go out for a cup of coffee sometime? Catch up?"

"No. Goodbye, Dylan."

He grunts in frustration. "Wait. I have some things to say to you."

I raise my voice and throw my arms up in exasperation. "Then say them!"

"Not here. Please. I just want to talk."

"I'll think about it. Now, can I please get back to my boyfriend?"

"Do you still have my number?"

"No."

"Is yours the same?"

I shrug.

"I'll text you tomorrow to set something up."

"I said I'd think about it."

"I know."

Without giving him a chance to say anything else, I spin around. Except I don't head for Greyson's room. Instead, I walk toward the lobby in desperate need of some air. Hopefully, he'll be fine without me for a few more minutes.

As I'm walking through the front doors of the hospital, I catch sight of Maylee.

She hurries to catch up to me. "Liz?"

I don't blame her for sounding confused simply because I don't know what to think right now, either. Not that she has a clue about what just transpired.

When I make it outside, my breathing is haggard. I turn my back away from the hospital, placing my hands on top of my head. It's the only thing I can do to find composure.

Footsteps sound from behind me, but I don't turn around. I already know it's my best friend coming to check on me.

"Liz, is everything okay?"

Before I say anything, I take a few deep breaths.

There's no need to beat around the bush, so I cut right to the chase. "Did you know Dylan is the ER doctor here? Because I sure didn't."

"What?"

Because I still haven't turned around, Maylee comes to stand in front of me. She looks shocked. Almost as shocked as I feel.

Meanwhile, I want to laugh at the absurdity of this situation. Things like this don't happen in real life.

"I didn't even know he was back in Chicago. I thought he would have stayed in Boston."

"Can you please explain to me what just happened?"

I let out an unamused laugh. "Just as I was about to tell Greyson I love him, the ER doctor walked in. He was looking at the clipboard in his hand, so I had no clue who it was until he spoke. Dylan is the ER doctor, Maylee!"

"Oh."

"Yeah."

"What did he say to you?"

I roll my eyes, thinking about our conversation in the hall. "He wants to go out for coffee. To talk."

"You're kidding."

I shake my head.

"What did you tell him?"

Letting out an exaggerated sigh, I cross my arms over my chest. "I told him I'd think about it."

"Well, do you want to?"

"Honestly, I don't know. There's a part of me—the angry part of me—that doesn't want to give him the time of day. But there's also a part of me that wants to hear what he has to say about why he did what he did. I think it might be good to clear the air. Not that it will change anything."

"And why do you need to clear the air?"

I shrug. "I don't know. For my sake, I guess. Maybe hearing him explain himself will help me get over things. Forgive him."

I watch as Maylee nods thoughtfully. "I think you should."

"What? You do?"

"I do. I know there aren't any feelings there anymore. You moved on a long time ago. But I think it will help you move past the anger you still feel. I think it will help you let everything go."

"I have let everything go."

"No you haven't. Sure, you've opened up so much with Greyson. But you still hold back with him."

I try not to seem offended. "What do you mean?"

"How long have you known you love him?"

"That's not fair."

"Just answer the question."

"A while. I've known for a while."

"Yet you still haven't told him."

I'm about to say something to defend myself, but she holds up a hand, stopping me before the words are out of my mouth. "I think your anger at Dylan makes you afraid of being vulnerable with another man. I'm not saying you haven't changed because you have. But there's a piece of you he still has control over. Hear him out and take back the fearlessness you used to have in relationships."

Her words stun me into silence.

Maybe she's right.

There's a part of me that has always been different since my relationship with Dylan ended. I always assumed it was because of the gut-wrenching loss I faced. But maybe there's more to it.

When I think hard about it, I never confronted my feelings toward the man who played a role in the life we created. The life we lost. We were so young to face something like that.

He left me with nothing more than a few hurtful words, as if our relationship was never enough. And his actions after our breakup made me angry and bitter. So much so that, for a while, I refused to trust anyone. Especially with the most fragile parts of my heart.

I could have missed out on falling in love with Greyson because of that.

I may not feel ready to meet with Dylan to talk things out, but I know what choice I'm leaning toward. I just hope Greyson will be okay with it.

I'm not ready to give in yet, though. "Like I said, I'll think about it." Heading for the door, I add, "I should probably get back to my boyfriend."

Maylee says nothing else.

Instead, she follows me inside.

Chapter 29

Greyson

Present Day

The moment I realized who my ER doctor is, I wanted to lunge across the room to remind him how much of a jerk he is for everything he put my Lizzy girl through.

Her entire demeanor changed as soon as he spoke. At first, I was thoroughly confused. But when he said Liz's name, I pieced things together.

My blood is still boiling from when Dylan asked her if she would speak with him in the hall.

I'll do anything to keep her from getting hurt. But I also know she can handle herself. The look on her face when she told me to give her a second told me as much. But now, it's been longer than I'm comfortable with.

I'm going stir crazy.

I have this fierce desire to protect her from ever hurting like she did with him. It's a protectiveness and a possessiveness I've never felt before.

If life ever puts us through something similar, I'll stand by her side instead of walking away from her like a coward. Nothing would be worse than a life without Liz.

I don't understand why he did what he did. And while I hate how Liz got hurt the way she did, I'm glad I'm the one who gets to take care of her now.

I'll never let her down.

After what feels like a lifetime, I hear footsteps approaching the door to my room. They're coming from a little farther away than I thought she went. But I'm just glad she's back where she belongs. Hopefully that's the last time she'll ever have to speak to him again. For her sake. And mine.

As the door opens, I'm surprised to see Walker instead of my girlfriend.

Disappointment fills my chest, but I hide it as best I can.

"Hey, man." He throws his thumb over his shoulder toward the open door. "Is everything okay?"

His question gets my attention. "Why wouldn't it be?"

"Liz passed us in the lobby. She seemed..." He searches for the right word, settling on, "off."

"Is Maylee with her?"

He nods, waiting for me to give him an explanation.

I let out a deep breath, running my fingers through my hair as I do. There's an ache in my ribcage from where the fracture is, but I ignore it.

"How much do you know about Liz's past?"

"Not much."

I think about what I can tell him without giving too much away. There's a reason Liz doesn't share this with anyone other than the people closest to her.

Knowing Maylee, she wouldn't have even told her husband because of her loyalty to Liz.

"She has this jerk of an ex from college. It's a long story."

"Okay. I'm not following. What made that come up?"

I laugh, though there isn't any humor in it. This situation is ludicrous.

"She hasn't spoken to him since their breakup. He hurt her almost beyond repair. Anyway, he's the ER doctor."

Walker's eyes go wide. Then he blows out a puff of air. "No kidding."

"He asked to speak with her. I don't know what he said, but she obviously didn't come back into the room after her conversation with him. It makes me mad."

"Please tell me she isn't the one you're mad at."

"No, man. Of course not. I'm mad at him and the situation. I mean, what are the odds?"

"Yeah. That's..." He lets his words trail off, shaking his head. "Where is he now?"

"Hopefully, getting discharge papers together. I'm ready to go."

* * *

Walker dropped me and Liz off at the station to pick up my truck before we headed to my house. Other than her asking how I'm feeling, she said nothing on the way home. That was over an hour ago.

Even now, as we're sitting on my couch watching TV, she's unusually quiet.

I didn't push her on the way over here, thinking she would eventually tell me about the conversation she had with Dylan. But now I'm getting a little impatient. Her silence is deafening. It isn't like her at all.

I don't want to bring it up if all it's going to do is upset her. So, I try another tactic. "Hey."

I wait until I have her attention. She lifts her head from where it's resting on my chest to meet my eyes. "What were you going to tell me before we got interrupted?"

At first, she looks confused. Then I see it on her face once she realizes what I'm talking about. "Oh. Nothing. It can wait."

"Are you sure?"

"Mhm. How's your rib doing?"

"It's fine. The painkillers are helping. Are you okay, Lizzy girl?"

"I'm fine, Grey."

"You've been quiet."

She sighs before sitting up. "I know... I'm sorry. I just have a lot on my mind."

"Does any of it have to do with your ex?"

"Unfortunately." Without waiting for me to respond, she gets up and walks to the kitchen. She grabs two bottles of water from the fridge, handing me one when she makes it back into the living room. I watch as she takes a few sips before I do the same.

Instead of returning to where she was sitting on the couch, she leans against the wall closest to the kitchen.

I remain seated, not sure what's going on in her head. "How did it go?"

She shrugs. "Fine, I guess. He asked if we could meet somewhere to catch up."

I scoff. "You're kidding, right?"

"No. He said he has some things he wants to tell me."

Getting up from the couch, I walk into the kitchen to lean against the counter opposite of where Liz is standing.

Casually crossing my arms over my chest, I ask, "What did you tell him?"

"I'd think about it."

I nod. "And what did you decide?"

After my question comes out, I hold my breath as I wait for her answer.

"I think it's best that I do."

"You can't be serious."

"I think it'll be good for me. I'm still so angry. A conversation with him—hearing him out—will help me let it go."

"You have every right to be angry, Liz. He deserves your anger."

"Maybe. But *I* don't deserve my anger. It's been chipping away at me for almost six years. It's time to hear him out. Put the past behind me."

"Haven't you already done that?"

"Not really."

I sigh, trying to stop myself from lashing out at her. "I don't think it's a good idea. In fact, I'd prefer if you didn't speak to him."

"Greyson, I value your opinion. But I didn't ask for it. I need you to understand where I'm coming from on this. It's been almost six years and I still haven't let it all go."

"So, you decided this behind my back instead? You could have talked to me first."

She walks into the kitchen and stands on the other side of the island, across from me. "It isn't like that, Grey, and you know it."

"He doesn't deserve your time."

"You don't think I know that? Greyson, this isn't about *him*. This is about *me*. What's best for *me*."

Her voice is pleading. Like she's desperate for me to understand. And there's a part of me that gets what she's saying. But isn't it possible for her to let go without letting him explain himself?

I stop myself from thinking about it further. Instead, I try my best to remain calm even though I don't agree with her decision.

It has nothing to do with jealousy, and everything to do with wanting to protect her from anymore heartache.

There's nothing he can say to her that will change what happened between them. The thought makes me angry. Angry at him for what he did. For showing back up in her life years later and acting like he's in her good graces. Asking to chat with her in front of me? Yeah. None of that sits well with me.

The more I think about all of it, the angrier I become. Which is why I don't think before I spit a question at Liz. "If you know that, then why are you giving him more of your time?"

She sighs. "I'm tired of holding on to all this anger and hurt. I never got to lay anything out. Instead, he said his piece and left me to question our entire relationship."

I hear the intensity in her voice, but it does nothing to stop me from pushing the topic more. "Why does that matter now?"

Raising her voice, she says, "It matters now because my anger at him still holds power over me! There are things about myself, I question. Things in our,"—she gestures between the two of us— "relationship that still scare me. Because of what *he* did. What are you not understanding about what I'm saying? This is not about him. It's about me, Grey."

"What are you talking about, Liz?"

She shakes her head. "Nothing."

"I don't think it's a good idea."

"Noted. But I'm still going."

"Do I get any say? Do you not trust me?"

Liz lets out an unamused laugh. It's clear she's getting impatient with me. But just like she's asking me to see her side of things, I need her to see my side of things, too.

"This isn't about you. This is about me. It's about what's best for me. What don't you get about that? And how many times am I going to repeat myself until you get it? Do you not trust *me*, Grey?"

Her question is like a punch to the gut. How could she think that? "Of course, I trust you. It's him I don't trust. And I don't agree with your decision either."

"I didn't ask for your approval. And I don't need it either."

Her words stun me. I wasn't expecting them to be so harsh.

Before I can fire any ammunition back, she gathers her things and heads for the door. I panic knowing I drove her to walk out of my house.

I rush after her, grabbing her arm before she makes it outside. "Liz! Liz, wait!"

She pulls away from my grasp rather aggressively. "No. I'm leaving. We can talk about this later."

"Or we can talk about it now."

She blows out an aggravated breath. "Okay. Fine. I didn't want to argue about this. Especially after the way you got when he asked to speak with me at the hospital." I open my mouth to defend myself, but she doesn't let me get a word out. "No. All I needed from you was some patience and understanding. I knew you wouldn't like my decision, but I expected you to understand it, Greyson. Instead, you got all offended and defensive because of it. I expect you to have my back. I'm confident in my decision. And I know it's what's best."

"Liz—"

"No. I don't want to talk to you right now."

I nod. My jaw is tense as I do. But I know better than to argue with her any more than I already have. If she doesn't want to see this from my point of view, then I can't make her.

While a part of me feels like I should fight to keep her here for the rest of the evening, I don't.

She needs the space.

Maybe I do too.

* * *

The doorbell rings incessantly as I'm laying in my bed staring up at the ceiling.

I haven't seen Liz since our fight yesterday. I checked in on her this morning to see when she's meeting with Dylan.

It was the wrong choice. Her text back was short. All it said was "today".

As I continue to replay our conversation in my mind, the doorbell continues to ring.

Beyond frustrated with everything, I finally get up to answer it, hoping it isn't any of my family members. My mom has been freaking out since she found out what happened. It wouldn't surprise me if it's her on the other side of my front door. Or if she sent someone over here to check on me.

When I get to the door, to my dismay, I find Brie.

Honestly, I'm surprised my mom didn't show up herself. I let out a grunt in frustration before letting her in.

"Hey, bro!"

"What are you doing here?"

"Your mom wanted me to check on you."

"She couldn't come herself?"

"Well, you're in a mood. She and dad have plans. I told her not to cancel. She said she called."

Brie's right. She *did* call. I've been so distracted by the situation with Liz, I forgot to call her back.

Instead of responding, I open the door wider, gesturing for my little sister to come in.

"So, how are you feeling?"

"I'm fine. There's no need for the visit."

She pats me on the chest. "I know. But I promised Jenny."

I roll my eyes, gesturing to the couch. "Right. Well then, make yourself comfortable, I guess."

"I most definitely will!"

I leave Brie in the living room to fix myself something to eat for breakfast.

When I'm about halfway done, she takes a seat at the kitchen table. "What are we having?"

"Were you this way with your other brothers growing up?"

She smiles slyly. Which is all I need to know the answer. I shake my head, returning my attention to the pancakes I'm working on. When everything is ready, I make both of us a plate before joining Brie at the table.

"Why so broody today, big bro?"

"What are you talking about?"

She chuckles. I watch as she makes herself look like she's deep in thought. She cocks her head to the side, looks up at the ceiling, and taps her chin with her forefinger. "Hm. Let's see. You are most definitely in a mood. You seem more annoyed than usual that I'm here. Oh, and let's not forget about the way you slammed around dishes while making this incredibly delicious breakfast." She sets down her fork, crossing her arms on the table after she does. "So. What gives?" She holds up her hand to stop me from answering. "Wait! Let me guess. It's the girlfriend, isn't it?"

With confusion I ask, "How did you—"

"Growing up, I watched my brothers act this way when something went wrong with a girl. How can I help?"

"You can't."

"Okay. Well, at least tell me what happened."

"It's a long story."

"I got time."

Clearly, Brie won't give up.

"Fine. But I'm only giving you the condensed version."

She nods, urging me to fill her in.

"Liz has this ex who we ran into yesterday. He asked if they could catch up. She agreed. I told her I don't think it's a good idea."

"Do you know why he wants to catch up?"

"She said he told her he has some things to say."

"What's wrong with that?"

"I just don't think he's worth her time."

"He probably isn't, but maybe she needs closure or something. Do you know what happened between them?"

"I do."

"And?"

I let out a frustrated sigh. "I don't want to get into details with you, Brie. He hurt her after some stuff they went through. I don't want her to get hurt again."

My sister nods thoughtfully. "That makes sense. But why did you take your feelings about him out on her?"

"That's not what I did."

"Okay. Well, do you trust her?"

"Of course."

"Then why are you mad at her?"

"I'm not mad at her. I just don't agree with her decision to go hear him out."

"You're an idiot."

"What the—"

Brie cuts me off. "Greyson, she probably came to you hoping you would support her by trusting her judgment. I don't know what happened between them. What I *do* know is women handle breakups much differently than men. I'm telling you; she probably needs closure. To give him a piece of her mind. There's nothing wrong with that."

I consider her words, realizing she's right.

I should have trusted Liz's decision. Instead, I made her feel like I wasn't willing to see her side of things. She clearly knows how to take care of herself.

If talking through things with Dylan is the only way for her to let go of her anger and bitterness, then that's what I want her to do.

After what I went through with my father, I know how harmful those emotions can be. I silently curse myself for not looking at her situation in the same light. She deserves better from me.

Truthfully, I don't know how she's so kind and compassionate after carrying around the weight she has been for so long. But the last thing I want is for her to feel weighed down by a relationship that has been over for six years.

If hearing Dylan out enables her to move forward with a clean slate, then I want that for her more than anything.

I know everything that happened with him is why she has taken things so slowly with me. She doesn't want to get hurt again. I can understand that.

I can also understand why she was so mad at me for how I handled our conversation yesterday.

She deserves my support, and I failed to give it to her. It's a mistake I won't make again.

Chapter 30

Liz

Present Day

Work was draining today. Not that I mind. It helped me forget about the argument Greyson and I had.

I feel bad for walking out of his house, but I knew things would have escalated.

There were moments in my relationship with Dylan when he'd try to walk all over me, and I let him because I was blissfully in love. And naïve. I'm not saying Greyson would ever do the same thing. I know he wouldn't. But I already had my defenses locked and loaded. I will always stand up for myself. It's something I should have done in college. It's something I see myself doing today while Dylan says whatever it is he needs to say.

Contrary to what my boyfriend believes, I don't want to give Dylan any of my time. But there were a lot of things left unsaid between us during our senior year. He hurt me. Badly. That's what stopped me from communicating my feelings with him after he broke what remained of my already broken heart. I'm not doing this for him. I'm doing this for myself. For my relationship with Greyson. Whether he understands that.

When I pull up to the coffee shop Dylan and I are meeting at, I take a deep breath, letting go of my expectations for how this is going to go.

Stepping into the café, I spot him right away.

I didn't think he could get any taller than he was in school, but it looks like he grew another inch or two. Since he's facing the counter to order, he doesn't know I'm here. I take the time to truly look at him—well, the back of him—while memories of our time together come flooding back.

We shared a lot of enjoyable moments together, and I'd be lying to myself if I said I couldn't picture my life with him now. If things had worked out then, I truly believe we would still be together today. But what's done is done.

Instead of ordering anything, I find a seat close to the door. As I wait for Dylan to spot me, I take in my surroundings.

I haven't been to this coffee shop before. It's on the opposite side of the city from where I frequent. The bright blues and soft grays in the space are comforting. If that's even possible.

A few minutes after I sit down, I hear, "Liz", from above me.

The way he says my name—like we're old friends—is unpleasant. I don't feel a shred of camaraderie with this man.

I give him a tight-lipped smile before saying his name curtly. "Dylan."

He takes a seat across from me. "So, that's how this is gonna be."

It wasn't a question, but I answer anyway. "I'm not sure what you expected. I'm here to listen to what you have to say. That's it."

He nods once. "Got it. How are you?"

Usually, I don't mind small talk. This is different, so ignoring his question, I ask, "What did you want to tell me?"

Taking a sip of his coffee, he takes his time before answering, seeming to gather his thoughts. "A lot. But it all comes down to... I'm sorry. I'm sorry for how I ended things between us."

I pretend to ignore his words even though I needed to hear them. I didn't think I would ever get an apology from him. Not even when he told me he wanted to catch up. But there's so much more I need him to say.

"Why'd you do it?"

He sighs heavily. "I was young. I didn't know how to handle the pain of losing something I wanted so badly. Even at that age."

I know he's referring to our child. The child I miss dearly. That I think about every day.

"You were a coward. Could you not see that I was grieving too?"

My words are harsh. But I know better than to beat around the bush. Especially with Dylan.

"I know that now. Liz, I saw your pain. But I didn't know how to help. There's nothing I could have done."

I let out a quick puff of air. "You're right. Sometimes you can't. All I needed was for you to be there—in the pain—with me. We could have gotten through it."

"I know that now. That's why I wanted to tell you how sorry I am. I've had almost six years to think about what happened between us. There isn't a day that goes by where I don't regret how things turned out."

Bringing my eyes down to the table, I nod once. "Will you tell me something, then?"

He offers me a familiar smile. "Anything for you."

The familiar words he used to say to me do nothing for me anymore. I'm relieved by that. If anything, they remind me of what Greyson tells me constantly... *Anything you need*, except Greyson's words carry so much more weight. He proves he means them. Every day.

"Why did you spend senior year partying and hooking up if you were in so much pain? How could you do that knowing the amount of pain *I* was in?"

A pained expression lingers on Dylan's face. It's genuine, I know, because of the way he avoids my eyes. He still feels guilty.

"It was the only thing that blocked out the pain. It felt good not to feel. To forget. Even if it was momentary."

"I can understand that." Although, I don't agree with it.

What I *do* understand is the need to escape the pain. It was excruciating. I would have done anything not to feel it.

Today, the pain is a reminder of what could have been. Which sometimes hurts worse. It's why I used to spend so much effort on making sure I never fell in love again. I never wanted to take another chance on love if it meant there was a possibility I could get just as hurt as I had before.

What I have with Greyson is so much stronger, though. I know it is.

Like Maylee said, love has the power to heal. She's living proof of that. And now... so am I.

With Greyson, I'm willing to face whatever life throws at us because I know we will face it together.

To have someone to experience both joy and sorrow with is a gift. It makes me grateful he didn't give up on me.

The sound of Dylan's voice pulls me from my thoughts. "I'm glad you do. I truly am sorry, Liz." He hesitates. "Do you think there will ever be a possibility for us to try again?"

"What? Is that why you wanted to talk? Is that why you're back in Chicago?"

"Yes, and no. I came back to Chicago for a clean slate."

"With me?"

"With life. Boston was great. It is great. But I didn't want to be so close to my ex-wife."

I blanch. "I'm sorry. What? You got married?"

He nods once in confirmation.

The information is shocking. It also has me feeling unsettled. I don't like that he had the audacity to ask me for a second chance only after committing to someone else previously.

Out of genuine curiosity, I ask, "What happened?"

"All that matters is she wasn't you."

Abruptly, I stand up from the table. It takes effort to control my tone of voice when I say, "No. Absolutely not. You don't get to say things like that to me. I forgive you. But you will never get a second chance from me. I moved on the moment you walked out of my apartment."

"You're telling me you don't wonder about what could have been?"

Looking around, I notice we have the attention of a few people in the coffee shop. Hastily, I walk toward the exit with Dylan on my heels.

When we make it outside, I spin around.

Taking in a deep breath, I let the words fall out of my mouth quickly. "I do. But you are never in that picture. The only person in that picture with me is our child. I don't say that to hurt you. I say that because it's the truth. *If* you would have stood by me, then I know we would still be together. But you didn't. Your choice has consequences. I spent years convincing myself I could never fall in love again. You did that to me. You don't deserve me, Dylan."

After I finish, he stands still, staring at me in silence. Too many emotions move over his face for me to pinpoint how he's feeling at this moment. Not that it matters. I know how I feel. And how I feel is all that matters.

"Do you love him?"

His question throws me off. As much as I want to tell him how much more I love Greyson than I loved him, I won't. He doesn't need to know that.

"That's none of your business."

"I never stood a chance, did I?"

Slowly, I shake my head. "Not after how you handled everything. But I'm glad we had this conversation. You're forgiven, and I wish you the best."

And I mean it. I do. I don't want to be angry anymore. There isn't any reason to be. Hearing him explain himself and apologize is enough.

"Goodbye, Dylan."

His jaw tightens before he says, "Goodbye, Liz."

The drive to Greyson's house feels long. I know it has nothing to do with what happened with Dylan, and everything to do with what I'm finally ready to get off my chest.

I'm irrevocably in love with him. I should have told him the moment I realized it, but I got scared. Scared of the future. Of the unknown. Not anymore, though. He deserves to hear it. And the thought of standing in front of the man of my dreams to tell him I love him has me feeling as giddy as ever.

I make the rest of the drive with a huge smile on my face. The best part is, I don't feel ridiculous for it.

I feel lucky. Lucky to have someone to love. Someone who loves me back. Fiercely.

When I pull into his driveway, I put my car into park, leaving my things behind as I get out to knock on his door.

As soon as Greyson opens the door, I take him in.

He's the picture of perfection. From his short, dark hair to his rough, calloused hands, to his adorable dimples, to his unbelievably big heart. I love everything about him.

I must be sporting the same dorky smile from earlier because Greyson looks at me, confused.

Here goes nothing.

"I'm sorry for leaving yesterday. I didn't want to say anything that I didn't mean."

"I'm sorry, too. I should have supported you, no matter what."

I take a step closer to him. "There's something I need to tell you."

His lips tip up in a smile. It's a smile I haven't ever seen before. Then I realize he has been waiting for me to bring this up since we were at the hospital.

He knew.

He knew what I was going to say.

I look into his deep brown eyes, spotting each gold fleck. Each one keeps me grounded. Steady on my feet.

"Grey, I love you. I love you so much. I'm sorry it took me so long to tell you that."

Once the words are out of my mouth, I feel my face flush. But I don't move. Instead, I wait on Greyson.

In one quick movement, he pulls me toward him so our chests are resting against each other. I have to strain my neck to look at his face, but I don't mind one bit.

"I love you too, Lizzy girl." As soon as the words are out of his mouth, his lips crash against mine in a kiss that feels even more electric than our first.

Without hesitating, I wrap my arms around his neck and open for him.

I revel in what it feels like to be in his arms. Had I not given him a chance, I could have missed this.

After a while, I'm no longer able to hold back my sounds of pleasure.

Greyson swallows each one as he kisses me. It's unlike anything I've ever felt before.

It feels good to give into the undeniable chemistry between us.

I let my fingers explore each dip and curve of his back before bringing them up and then around his neck.

He breaks our kiss, looking at me with so much reverence. "Not yet."

For just a second, doubt enters my mind. "You don't—"

He's quick to cut me off. "Believe me, I do. I've wanted to do this for years." He kisses me softly. "But I want us to take our time. I want to be married to you first, Liz."

While I know he's been with other women, I understand what Greyson is saying. And there isn't anything I can say that will tell him how much his words mean to me. So instead, I pull his lips to mine, kissing him passionately.

He takes his time kissing me back before trailing kisses down my neck.

Slowly, he works his way back up until his mouth is at the shell of my ear.

Never Let You Down

He whispers the words, "I love you," leaving goosebumps all over my body.

I'm barely able to whisper the words back before his mouth is on mine again.

All the while, I think about what he said to me. The look in his eyes when he said it.

He has no doubts that I'm it for him.

And I know he'll never let me down.

Chapter 31

Greyson

Present Day

Liz is bold and beautiful.

I take in every part of her.

Her long, wild, red hair. Her petite frame. The way her emerald eyes light up when she looks at me.

Everything about her is exquisite. Perfect.

She's standing at my door, professing her love for me. It's fairytale type stuff, and I'd be lying if I said I wasn't digging it.

It takes a minute for the words to sink in after she says them. Twice.

Once they do, in one fluid motion, I pull her to me, saying, "I love you too, Lizzy girl."

In the next second, my lips meet hers in an electrifying kiss. There's no teasing or taunting with each other.

Never Let You Down

We're desperate for each other, only wanting more.

She tastes like cinnamon and coffee.

My favorite combination.

Now and forever.

Dying to get to some place more comfortable, I take her in my arms, bringing her further into the house. She's light as a feather.

Our kissing never ceases.

She drives me crazy as she uses her fingers to caress every inch of my back. I didn't know something so simple could make me want her even more.

She pulls back. "You don't—"

I'm quick to stop her from giving into the doubt I see on her face. "Believe me, I do. I've wanted to do this for years." I kiss her. "But I want us to take our time. I want to be married to you first, Liz."

She's the only woman I'll ever make love to. It's why I want to do things differently with her. I want the marriage. The house with the white picket fence. A dog to call ours. Kids to take care of. She's mine. And I'm hers. Only hers. I want to experience everything with her.

If I could go back and do everything differently, I would. What I have with Liz would have been worth the wait. While I can't change my past, I can do my best to be a better man moving forward.

The longer we kiss, the more Liz relaxes. She's kissing me with even more passion than she was just a few seconds ago. Before I was honest with her about where I stand. I smile against her mouth. She doesn't know how much she means to me.

And I'm convinced that nothing has ever felt better.

* * *

I'm lying on my couch after watching a movie with Liz. Today was probably the best day of my life. I can hardly believe I'm saying that.

A year ago, my life looked much different. I never imagined wanting to spend the rest of my life with another person. Much less starting a family with that person. But, with Liz, I can see it. I want it. I want everything with her. No matter what.

She's curled up on her side, facing me with one hand resting on my chest. I watch as her chest rises and falls in a perfect rhythm. Her wavy, red hair splays out behind her. She looks peaceful. Beautiful.

As I look at her, I let my mind drift to what it felt like when she told me she loves me.

How much those words eased an ache in my chest I wasn't even aware of.

I get off the couch while trying not to disturb Liz.

It's a wasted effort though, because as I turn toward my bedroom, she grabs my wrist with her hand.

She turns her body, so she's lying on her back. "Where are you going?"

I lean down to kiss her temple. "I was going to take a quick shower. Why?"

"I'm kind of hungry." As if on cue, her stomach grumbles.

The sound makes me laugh. "Of course you are."

With a smile on her face, she rolls her eyes. "Do you have anything sweet?"

"I'm looking at her."

It's hard to look away from the blush that forms on her cheeks. "I'm not sure I'll ever get used to your charm."

I chuckle. "I hope not." Unable to help myself, I kiss her temple again. "I'll go see what I've got in the kitchen. Wait here."

As I turn around to walk away, she says, "Grey."

"Yeah?"

"I love you."

My heart leaps in my chest at those three words.

I've known for a while how I feel about her. And while I had an inclination that she felt the same, I didn't want to pressure her into telling me.

Hearing her say the words now is better than I imagined it would be.

This woman is my world.

"I love *you*, Lizzy girl."

She smiles.

I press a soft kiss to her lips before leaving the living room to make my girl something sweet.

It isn't long before Liz joins me in the kitchen. She takes a seat at the table, her eyes watching my every move.

I walk over to her with a bowl of ice cream. "Something sweet for my Lizzy girl."

A gorgeous smile lights up her face, along with a pink blush. "Thank you."

I dip my chin toward the bowl. "Aren't you going to try it?"

She raises a brow while picking up her spoon. "Have you never seen someone eat ice cream before?"

Her question makes me laugh. "Oh, I have. It was quite the experience." I wink, so she knows what I'm referring to.

She doesn't make me wait much longer before taking a bite of her ice cream.

As soon as it hits her tongue, her eyes widen before she rolls them up toward the ceiling. "Oh, my goodness. You didn't? Where did you get this?"

It turns out I truly will do anything for Liz. "I got it from the same ice cream place we went to a while ago. If you call to place a special order, they'll sell you a pint of whatever flavor you want."

Spoon in hand, she uses it to point at the bowl. "You know you're going to have to keep your freezer stocked with this now, right?"

I laugh. "I figured. It's why I ordered a few pints. I'll order more when it gets low."

Her smile stretches across her entire face. "You're the best."

After scooping myself some cinnamon ice cream and joining her at the table, I go out on a limb by casually asking, "How did things go earlier?"

She finishes her bite of ice cream, regarding me.

There's a thoughtful expression on her face. "I'll tell you, but then we never bring him up again."

"Was it that bad?" Uneasiness forms in the pit of my stomach. I do my best to ignore it while waiting on her response.

"Let's just say I think he walked into that chit chat hoping for an outcome where he and I end up together."

My eyes widen. "Are you serious?"

She chuckles. "Yeah. He apologized too, though. Which I appreciated."

I think about what I want to ask about next.

While I don't believe that Dylan deserves her at all, I can't help but wonder if things would be different if I weren't in the picture.

Liz must recognize something in my expression because she says, "Spit it out, Grey."

"How could you tell?"

She chuckles. "You get this look on your face. I don't know how to explain it, but I can tell when you're thinking extra hard about something. Maybe it's because you were never one to think before he speaks." She winks.

I shake my head. "Touché." I hesitate briefly. "Would things be different if I weren't in your life?"

"No."

I breathe out a sigh of relief at how quickly she answers my question.

I'm glad she didn't have to think about it. Lifting the corners of my lips just a little, I add, "Care to expand on that answer?"

She rolls her eyes playfully. "Someone just wants to be flattered."

I hold my hands up in mock surrender. "Not at all. I'm genuinely curious to know why."

"I know. I'm teasing." She sighs. "I think I forgave him a long time ago for what he did. But anytime I picture what could have been, the picture is crystal clear. It has only ever been me and my child. I'm not saying I wouldn't have wanted our child not to know him well." She shrugs again. "I guess I just know what I want in life. After the way he handled things between us, I knew I didn't want him. It sounds harsh, but it's the truth."

"Do you think you still would have given me a chance?"

"Grey, I don't want to talk about what ifs." She reaches across the table for my hand. "You are everything I need and all I want. That's all that matters."

"I know. I want you to know I'm all in. Whatever that looks like."

I hope she picks up on what I truly mean.

It doesn't matter what we face. I want to stand by her. Even in the pain. I'll be whatever she needs me to be.

We return to our ice cream, clearing out our bowls in a companionable silence before Liz tells me she needs to head home for the night.

Before she goes, I remind her about family day coming up in a few weeks, hoping she's still up for it. I may have a few things planned for her before then. The best part is she doesn't suspect a thing.

* * *

"Yo." Greeting everyone, I stroll into Walker's house.

Sam looks at me first. "Hey, man. How have you been?"

"Pretty good. It's good to see you guys."

It has been a while since I've seen everyone. My concussion and cracked rib have kept me from work. But the doctor should give me clearance soon.

After grabbing a beer from the fridge, I join them on the couch.

Sam turns to me. "How's the girlfriend?"

"Great. Anything happen between you and Kate yet?"

He rolls his neck out. "Not in the way you mean."

I nod but refrain from asking for details. They hang out frequently. But knowing Sam, there's probably something going on with Kate. If she's in need, I'm not surprised he stepped up to the plate. He's one of the most stand-up guys I know.

Steering the conversation in a different direction, I ask Matt, "How's Sarah doing?"

He lets out a long sigh. "Impatient." All of us chuckle before he adds, "The baby should be here any day now."

Walker chimes in. "Keep us posted."

I look at him curiously. "When are you and Maylee planning to expand your family?"

He shrugs. "Not sure. We're open to it, but have set nothing in stone." He hesitates before raising a brow at me. "Have you and Liz talked about the future?"

I look around at my friends, recalling each conversation I've had with Liz.

"We have."

All four of my friends look at me curiously.

Giving in, I say, "I'm going to ask her to marry me."

Sam's face breaks out in a huge grin. "I knew it." Tipping his beer bottle toward me, he adds, "I knew you'd end up a married man soon."

I chuckle while Charlie and Matt offer me their congratulations.

Truthfully, I wasn't planning on telling anyone until after it happens, but these guys are family to me.

Plus, I know it will mean a lot to Liz that I talked about it with them. Our group is close. I bet it won't be long until all of us are happily married.

All I know is I can't wait until I am.

Chapter 32

Liz

Present Day

Closing the door to my office, I say bye to Steph as I make my way toward the elevator.

It's hard to believe I'm leaving before she is on a Friday night. I worked overtime this week to make sure I could make it out of here at a decent hour. Which has been happening a lot more recently.

I'd be lying if I said it wasn't because of Greyson. It totally is. When he has weekends off, I spend little time at my place. Tonight is no different. We're inseparable.

Steph gives me a smirk. "I can't believe all it takes to get you out of here is a booty call."

Eyes widening, I laugh. "Steph! It isn't a booty call!"

I hear her laugh as I step into the elevator, making the long descent to my car.

As soon as I slip inside, shutting the passenger door, my phone rings.

I smile when I see Greyson's picture lighting up my screen.

"Hey, Grey."

"Lizzy girl... change of plans."

My smile falters. "Oh no. What happened?"

We were supposed to meet at his place, but maybe he got called into work.

"Nothing bad. Can you meet me at the shelter? I'm helping Penny with something, and I'm not sure how long it will take."

"Is everything okay?"

He chuckles. "Yes. I promise. Just might be awhile and I want to see you."

There's an ache in my cheeks from smiling so hard. It happens a lot these days. "Aw, do you miss me that much?"

"Always. Now get that gorgeous behind of yours over here."

Laughing, I back out of my parking spot. "I'm on my way."

On my way to the shelter, I stop to pick up some sweet treats. Greyson said he had dinner covered tonight, which I love. Food is the way to my heart, and he knows that well. However, I'm sure we won't be eating anytime soon now that he's got stuff to do for Penny. It must be important, considering she called him on a Friday night.

When I pull up to the shelter, the lights are off. Looking around, I spot a faint glow of lights coming from behind the building near the training facility. It strikes me as odd, but I don't question it. Instead, I head toward the front doors, hoping they're unlocked. My phone's flashlight should be enough to see where I'm going once I get inside.

The first thing I see when I get to the building is a handwritten note taped to the front door.

I peel it off, using my flashlight to read what it says: *Lizzy girl, I'm out back. -Grey*

What is he up to?

Pushing my curiosity aside, I walk around the side of the building, up the familiar walkway to the back.

Following the path, my stomach churns with anticipation at what I'll find. I have a feeling Greyson has something up his sleeve tonight.

When the brand-new training facility comes into view, tea lights lining the gravel path to the front doors catch my eye.

Upon further inspection, I notice arrows formed out of red rose petals that lead to the giant front doors of the facility. There's a sliver of light peeking through where the door is slightly ajar.

Stepping inside, I scan the dimly lit arena. I freeze when I see my boyfriend standing with Milo. He's wearing a black suit, sporting a confident smile.

I'm sure my face shows just how confused I am. "What's going on?" As soon as the question comes out of my mouth, the gorgeous smile on Greyson's face gets bigger, but he says nothing.

As I walk toward him, I fire off a few more questions. "What are we doing in here? And why are you so dressed up? And why is Milo with you?"

He chuckles. "You look gorgeous today." He walks to where I'm standing, closing the little distance left between us. Milo is quick to follow.

Grabbing my hand, Greyson pulls me to him until we're chest to chest. "I was starting to wonder if you stayed at the office."

"No. I wasn't sure how long this would take, so I stopped for some snacks." Pulling back just a little, I ask, "Are you planning on answering my questions? Is this another one of your epic date nights?"

He laughs, not realizing I'm seriously curious. Truly dying to know what's going on.

Since our relationship has picked up speed, Greyson can't resist spoiling me senseless. Our dates are always full of lots of unexpected surprises. Most of our dates *are* the unexpected surprises.

Last weekend, he took me to the zoo. It was completely out of the blue. The other day, he convinced Steph to move all my appointments so we could go on a day trip to Starved Rock State Park. He has proved to be the most thoughtful man I have ever known. I hit the jackpot.

Finally, he answers me. "Sort of." I look at him, confused. He just keeps smiling. "I adopted Milo."

My eyes widen. "You what?"

He chuckles. "Penny and Margaret agreed to let me use the training facility to get him trained up for you. I know how much you've bonded with him." Greyson looks at my favorite furry friend. "You ready to show her, boy?" Pointing at a blue cot, he says, "Place."

Ignoring the commands being given to Milo, I meet Greyson's eyes.

My words are barely above a whisper when I ask, "He's mine?"

Greyson takes my hands in his. "I was hoping he could be ours."

He doesn't give me a chance to respond before turning around to face the agility course, keeping a firm grip on my left hand.

With a single nod of his head, a whistle blows, though I don't know who else is in here with us. Not that it matters. I'm too distracted as I watch Milo take off. I laugh with utter joy as he weaves through obstacles, jumps through hoops, and runs through tunnels. It's fun to witness.

After completing the course perfectly, he trots back over to us. Only now, he's wearing a purple ribbon around his neck.

Upon closer inspection, a glint of sparkle hanging from it catches my eye.

Before I have time to process anything, Greyson drops to a knee in front of me. And now I know exactly what's going on.

Looking up at me from where he's kneeling, he smiles proudly. The lights above us illuminate my favorite gold flecks. And there's so much emotion in his beautiful brown eyes. It's overwhelming.

He takes my hands. "Lizzy girl, it's difficult to put into words just how much you mean to me. You've changed my life. Since the day I met you here at this shelter, all I've wanted is to be around you. I think I fell for you long before I realized it. You are the only woman I have ever loved. And you are the only woman I want to spend the rest of my life loving. Will you marry me?"

Overcome with emotion, I nod before finding enough composure to answer him. "Of course, I'll marry you."

Taking the ring from around Milo's neck, Greyson jumps up to place it on my finger. It's a stunning princess cut diamond ring with diamonds around the band.

When I return my gaze to Greyson's, there's a sheepish expression on his face. "Do you like it?"

"Are you kidding? I love it. And I love you, Grey."

Bringing his face inches from mine, he whispers, "I love you, too," before picking me up and spinning me around.

I laugh as butterflies flutter wildly in my stomach.

This is the last thing I expected tonight.

Greyson kisses me passionately before setting me back down. "Are you ready to celebrate?"

I smirk. "What do you have in mind?"

Saying nothing, he takes me by the hand and leads me back outside. As soon as the windy Chicago air greets us, he raises our joined hands up and yells, "She said yes!"

Suddenly, the outdoor lights come on and I'm greeted by the smiling faces of our friends. All of which erupt into hoots and hollers.

As everyone moves toward us, I take in the décor.

They must have set everything up while we were inside the training facility.

A handmade sign reads "Congratulations" in Steph's cursive handwriting. Under it, my favorite food and drinks cover a picnic table. In the center of it is an elegant two-tiered cake.

Greyson pulls me toward our friends, where we meet them in the middle of the expansive outdoor area between the shelter and the training facility.

Maylee is the first to wrap her arms around me. "Congratulations. I'm so happy for you."

I squeeze her tightly. "Thank you."

Before I can recover from one hug, I'm being pulled into another. This time by Steph and Kate simultaneously.

They laugh as they wrap me in a Liz sandwich. "I'm glad you got over yourself and gave that hunk a chance."

Laughing, I pinch the back of Steph's arm, causing her to squeal and jump away from me.

Kate laughs as she takes her place, hugging me again. "I'm so excited for you." She pulls away. "Let us see the ring!"

The girls gather around as I hold out my hand, moving my fingers so the diamond sparkles under the lights.

Steph claps her hands together with a giant smile on her face. "It's gorgeous!" Looking over my shoulder, she finds my fiancé. "You killed it, Greyson."

He steps around his friends to place an arm around my shoulders. "I know I did."

I can't stop the smile that spreads across my face at his words, knowing he isn't talking about the ring at all.

As we chat with our friends, Penny and Margaret find us. I step away from everyone to greet them both.

Hugging Penny, I say, "Thank you for this."

She pulls me in as close as she can. "Of course, my dear." She releases me from our embrace to place her hands on my shoulders. "But if there's anyone to thank, it's my granddaughter. She helped to make this night happen."

My eyes move from Penny to Margaret. The woman who has become such a sweet friend to me.

"Thank you so much. Greyson mentioned you helped him get Milo trained. I guess it was you who had a hand in making sure he made it through the course with a ring around his neck."

She laughs. "Of course. When he told me what he had in mind, I couldn't say no."

"Thank you. This place means so much to me. As do the two of you."

Penny reaches for my hand. Her grip is gentle. "You as well. We appreciate your help around here. Greyson's too. This was a wonderful way for me to enter retirement."

I laugh as I pull her into another hug.

A few minutes later, Greyson joins us.

As he chats animatedly with Penny, I watch in awe, feeling extremely thankful for him.

I'm also extremely thankful for this night. It was incredibly thoughtful of him to organize this. Being with my favorite people at my favorite place is the best way to end the best day of my life... so far.

Besides, Greyson and I have the rest of our lives to spend quality time with one another.

I can't wait to be his wife and the mother of his children.

For now, I'll enjoy celebrating our engagement at the place it all started.

* * *

"Is your mom coming with us?"

I'm making a cup of coffee in Greyson's kitchen. We're about to leave for family day at the station.

About a week after we got engaged, I asked him if he invited me to go, knowing he was going to propose. It was then that I found out he bought the ring a few days before he asked me to go, waiting until he knew I was ready for him to pop the question.

I can't believe I despised this man not even a year ago. But I will always be incredibly thankful for his persistence. It's what got us here.

It's also what allowed me to let my guard down. I feel more like myself than I have in a long time. And while we got engaged quickly, deep down, I know it's right.

While I haven't moved in yet, I spend most of my time at his house. I enjoy having someone to come home to after a long day. At least, until I go back to my apartment in the evening.

Greyson places his hand on the small of my back, kissing my temple. "She and Phil are meeting us there."

Turning to him, I ask, "You invited Phil?"

"Yeah."

I smile before giving him a quick peck. "I'm proud of you, Grey."

"For what?"

Wrapping my arms around his waist, I look up at my fiancé. "For embracing your family. Watching you with them. It makes me like you even more. Makes you more attractive, too."

He raises a brow. "Is that so?"

I smirk. But Greyson doesn't give me a chance to respond. Instead, his lips meet mine in a tantalizing kiss.

Running his hands through my hair, he deepens our kiss.

I pull back before we get carried away. "We need to go."

"Yes. We do. But I get you all to myself later."

"We'll see." I wink before walking out the front door.

We pull up to the station at the same time as Jenny and Phil.

The look of pure joy on Jenny's face is contagious. "Lizzy! How's my future daughter-in-law?"

Yes. Greyson's mom calls me Lizzy.

After hearing him refer to me as 'Lizzy girl' as often as he does, the rest of his family picked up on it. Just the Lizzy part, anyway. Truthfully, I don't mind. It's endearing, if nothing else.

Laughing, I wrap my arms around her neck. "Amazing. How are you?"

I give Phil a hug too as I wait for Jenny's answer.

"Wonderful!"

Greyson hugs his mom and Phil before tugging me close. "Thanks for being here. You guys ready?"

"Of course, honey."

We walk into the station to find a few rectangular tables set up. Along with a buffet table already full of food.

Getting introduced as Greyson's fiancé is still something I'm getting used to. But I wouldn't have it any other way.

When all the introductions are out of the way, we make our plates, joining Walker, his mom—Wendy, and Maylee.

It isn't long before Sam joins us with his parents and each of his sisters.

A few minutes into the meal, we fall into idle chit chat with each other.

I'm listening to what everyone is saying while also thinking about how thankful I am for these people. We're more than friends.

We're family.

Greyson leans in to whisper, "I love you" in my ear.

"I love you, too."

And I do.

The love I have for him is overwhelming.

All-consuming.

I love Greyson Wright more than I've ever loved anyone else.

And I can't wait to build our future and family.

Together.

The End.

Epilogue

Liz

Many Years Later

"Mommy!" From outside my office, I hear Carter, my 4-year-old—and the oldest—calling my name.

I stand up from where I'm sitting at my desk to meet him at the door.

When he makes it to me, I immediately hold my arms out. He never fails to jump into them with every ounce of strength he has.

I'd love to say he gets his rambunctiousness from his dad, but the energy comes from me.

What he *did* inherit from his dad are his dark features. They share the same dark brown hair and beautiful brown eyes. He's going to be quite the heartbreaker someday.

"Hey, buddy! Where's everyone else?"

I hear Brie say, "We're coming" before she walks into my office with Briana, my two-year-old, who's named after her aunt. She also takes after her dad. All dark features. She's beautiful.

She's also obsessed with her aunt Brie. I don't blame her. Brie is the sister I never had. Throughout my marriage to her stepbrother, we've grown incredibly close. I wouldn't have it any other way. She has been a tremendous support to me and Greyson.

"Hey, Brie. Where's Grey?"

"He should be up in a few minutes."

Carter turns to me, rolling his eyes. "Yeah. Grace wouldn't stop crying. Daddy said it's because she has a poopy diaper."

Grace is our youngest, and I'm proud to say that she's the spitting image of me with her green eyes and curly red hair. I can already tell she's going to be our most stubborn child. Just like her mom.

Ruffling my son's hair, I laugh. "Uh oh. We don't like those, do we?"

He makes a stink face and then shakes his head.

We're going out to dinner as a family tonight before we drop the kids off with my in-laws. My thoughtful husband surprised me by booking a weekend trip for us. It's much needed. I've had a tough time lately.

While Grace's birth brought so much joy and excitement to our lives, we weren't sure if we would get to meet her.

I miscarried twice before she came along. I was anxious through the entire pregnancy and had a few complications during the delivery.

Greyson has been my rock through it all. I don't know what I would do without him. Honestly, I don't think I would have tried for Grace without his support and encouragement.

As if on cue, he strides into my office, looking as gorgeous as he did the first day that I laid eyes on him.

I know, I know. It took me a while to admit it, but there's no denying it now. The man is incredibly attractive. Tall, dark, handsome, and totally my type.

With Grace in his arms, he kisses me. "Hey, baby."

"Hey."

"How was work? Are you ready to go?"

Grabbing my purse, I say, "It was great. I got everything done that needed to be done before Monday."

He smiles. "Good."

As we walk out the door, our six-month-old baby girl coos in his arms. She rests her head on his chest before letting her eyelids flutter closed. My heart melts at the sight of it.

Watching my husband be a dad to our children has been an incredible gift.

I fall more in love with him every day.

He has given me the life of my dreams.

* * *

Greyson

Never Let You Down

My wife and I are cuddling on the couch in the cabin I rented for the weekend, enjoying the last of our time here before we get back to the real world.

While being a dad is the most fun I've ever had, I miss spending quality time with the most amazing woman I know. I planned this weekend entirely for her. But it turned out to be just as necessary for me as well.

I kiss the crown of her head. "Tell me how you're doing, Lizzy girl."

My wife is incredibly strong. Her confidence in everything she does—especially motherhood—inspires me every single day. But I would be naïve to think that everything is as it should be in her heart. We have as many children in heaven as we do on earth. I know it weighs heavily on her.

She sighs. "I'm hanging in there."

"Talk to me."

Sitting up, she says, "I'm so thankful for Grace. But I have a hard time understanding why we didn't get to meet any of our others. I don't know if I want to try again."

With my arm around her shoulder, I stroke her hair. "Is that what's been on your mind since her birth?"

She nods as a few tears make their way down her cheeks.

I pull her into my lap. It's become our favorite way to have heavy conversations.

"Liz, I told you I will do whatever you need. If you want to be done, then we'll be done. But I'm open to growing our family even more if that's what you decide you want."

She blows out a shaky breath. "I know. It just hurts. Wondering about what we could have if I wouldn't have miscarried."

"I know, baby."

"I made a doctor's appointment to see if there's a reason. My decision will ride on what I find out. I'm not sure if I'll be able to bear another loss, Grey."

My heart breaks for my wife. I'm hurting, too. But it's even worse knowing Liz carries around the pain. And the guilt. She doesn't need to. I've told her as much. But it's difficult for her not to feel like it's her fault.

"Just promise to talk to me. You don't need to face any of this alone. I'm here."

I watch as a few more tears cascade down her face.

Placing my fingers under her chin, I say, "Hey." Kiss. "I love you, okay? We'll get through this together. I'll never let you down, Lizzy girl. I promise."

Amidst her tears, she smiles, and I'm reminded of how stunning and strong she is.

"I know. I love you, Grey."

After a while, she falls asleep on my shoulder. I hold her as I think about our life together, and the journey that brought us to this moment.

It hasn't always been easy. But it's been more than worth it.

She changed my life in so many ways.

Because of Liz, I know what it's like to be loved unconditionally... and what it means to give all of yourself to someone with complete faith. How to be a good son. Friend. Brother. Husband. And father.

Liz Carter is the best thing that ever happened to me. She always will be.

Acknowledgments

Wow! I can't believe I have two books under my belt. This is a dream. One that I get to live and enjoy for as long as the stories keep coming to me. All glory goes to my Heavenly Father. So, thank You, Lord, for this gift of creativity. I promise to cherish it and use it for YOU.

There are so many people to thank for this novel. While the book was dedicated to him, he still deserves a thank you here as well. Garrett, I couldn't do this without you. Thank you for listening to me talk about characters and plots for hours. Thank you for dealing with the tears, too. Writing and publishing books is no easy feat. I'm not sure where I'd be without you.

Mikala, thank you for reading this as I finished each chapter. The friendships in this book remind me of ours. I couldn't do this without you.

Amanda, thank you for reading this. My favorite feedback came from you. I'm so glad this book made you "feel". That was the goal! I hope others feel the same way.

Miranda, thank you for beta reading. Your feedback was helpful and appreciated. I am so thankful for your endless support.

Danny, thank you for being the best hype man.

Your enthusiasm and support mean the world to me. Thank you for beta reading as well!

Kelsey, thank you for beta reading! I appreciate the time you gave to this story even though we don't know each other. I'm thankful social media brought us together. I look forward to watching your Type 1 Diabetes warrior grow!

Kim and Megan, thank you so much for your support. I'm so thankful I get to work with both of you!

To my readers, thank you so much. You're the reason I keep writing. I appreciate your support. It means more to me than you will ever know.

To anyone who knows what Liz went through, you inspire me. This book is for you. I pray that you come out stronger. May Jesus gift you with His peace. A peace that surpasses all understanding.

About the Author

Mariah Wallace lives in Hutto, Texas with her husband and their three fur babies. She is passionate about creating heartwarming stories filled with real life scenarios and authentic relationships. When she isn't writing, you will either find her with a book in hand or outside enjoying the Texas sunshine. She also loves Jesus, fitness, red wine, ice cream, and traveling with her husband.

Follow Mariah on Instagram!
@mariah.a.wallace

Printed in Great Britain
by Amazon

40155946R00189